$ 3.00

MERLE'S BILLIARDS

EDWARD GROSEK

America Star Books

Softcover 9781632492135
PUBLISHED BY AMERICA STAR BOOKS, LLLP
www.americastarbooks.com

TABLE OF CONTENTS

MICKEY

Merle's
BILLIARDS

1978

January
SUN	MON	TUE	WED	THU	FRI	SAT
1	2	3	4	5	6	7
8	9	10	11	12	13	14
15	16	17	18	19	20	21
22	23	24	25	26	27	28
29	30	31				

February
SUN	MON	TUE	WED	THU	FRI	SAT
			1	2	3	4
5	6	7	8	9	10	11
12	13	14	15	16	17	18
19	20	21	22	23	24	25
26	27	28				

March
SUN	MON	TUE	WED	THU	FRI	SAT
			1	2	3	4
5	6	7	8	9	10	11
12	13	14	15	16	17	18
19	20	21	22	23	24	25
26	27	28	29	30	31	

April
SUN	MON	TUE	WED	THU	FRI	SAT
						1
2	3	4	5	6	7	8
9	10	11	12	13	14	15
16	17	18	19	20	21	22
23	24	25	26	27	28	29
30						

May
SUN	MON	TUE	WED	THU	FRI	SAT
	1	2	3	4	5	6
7	8	9	10	11	12	13
14	15	16	17	18	19	20
21	22	23	24	25	26	27
28	29	30	31			

June
SUN	MON	TUE	WED	THU	FRI	SAT
				1	2	3
4	5	6	7	8	9	10
11	12	13	14	15	16	17
18	19	20	21	22	23	24
25	26	27	28	29	30	

July
SUN	MON	TUE	WED	THU	FRI	SAT
						1
2	3	4	5	6	7	8
9	10	11	12	13	14	15
16	17	18	19	20	21	22
23	24	25	26	27	28	29
30	31					

August
SUN	MON	TUE	WED	THU	FRI	SAT
		1	2	3	4	5
6	7	8	9	10	11	12
13	14	15	16	17	18	19
20	21	22	23	24	25	26
27	28	29	30	31		

September
SUN	MON	TUE	WED	THU	FRI	SAT
					1	2
3	4	5	6	7	8	9
10	11	12	13	14	15	16
17	18	19	20	21	22	23
24	25	26	27	28	29	30

October
SUN	MON	TUE	WED	THU	FRI	SAT
1	2	3	4	5	6	7
8	9	10	11	12	13	14
15	16	17	18	19	20	21
22	23	24	25	26	27	28
29	30	31				

November
SUN	MON	TUE	WED	THU	FRI	SAT
			1	2	3	4
5	6	7	8	9	10	11
12	13	14	15	16	17	18
19	20	21	22	23	24	25
26	27	28	29	30		

December
SUN	MON	TUE	WED	THU	FRI	SAT
					1	2
3	4	5	6	7	8	9
10	11	12	13	14	15	16
17	18	19	20	21	22	23
24	25	26	27	28	29	30
31						

CHAPTER 1
THE BREAK-IN

Sunday after Midnight, July 9, 1978

It was after midnight in Albany, N.Y., time now to rob the pool hall. Rudy clicked on his penlight. He pushed aside the tile underneath him. Holding the penlight in his teeth, he twisted and lowered himself cautiously out of the drop ceiling of the men's room of the Cue and Cushion where he had hidden himself just before the place closed. He stepped onto the sink and then onto the floor. He was alone in the dark, trespassing; his heart was pounding, yet his hands were dry and steady.

He emerged from the men's room and stood, breathing shallowly and listening intently. He turned the corner and into the long hall. Street light through the front windows from Central Avenue, the city's main thoroughfare, gave a faint illumination to the place, and he was able to see through the dimness all the way to the rear of the hall, to the reinforced service door. He exhaled, then went along the side wall with short quick steps, over the carpet, past one after another of the nine-foot long pool tables to the door in the back wall.

This door opened inwardly, and it was barred on the inside with two thick wood planks that rested in clamps welded to the door's casing. It was closed only with a spring lock but fully obstructed from opening when the wooden bars were in place.

Without hesitating, Rudy stepped to the door. He lifted the upper of the two planks from its clamps and leaned it against the wall, then lifted the other plank and set it next to the first. He gripped the door's handle tightly and squeezed it down until he heard a click. Using both hands, he drew the door open. Sonny, with the suitcase, loomed in the doorway and just as quickly slipped inside. A third young man, Mickey, laggardly followed him. Sonny took him by the arm and pulled him forward, and Rudy noiselessly reclosed the door. Sonny handed the suitcase to Rudy, picked up the planks one at a time, and replaced them in their clamps. Rudy motioned with his head, and the three intruders filed back along the side wall, past the pool tables and toward the front.

The Cue and Cushion Billiard Lounge was silent, its cue sticks and colored balls and Brunswick tables dormant, waiting for the next day, when the lights would be turned on and everything would come to life again. Rudy, the youngest of the three, led the way, his back straight, his eyes scouring the room and its shadows, his cheeks concave with tension. Rudy Merle had burglarized once before. He knew that just as important as the property to be made off with was the need to control the trepidation of executing such a crime in the night.

Trailing Rudy was Mickey Gonzag, twenty-three years old, his eyes lit with curiosity, his gait and carriage casual, as if he were walking into a restaurant. Mickey was the type who appreciated his cohorts and who coveted what he observed them doing and owning. He worked nights at the Columbiana Hotel on Wolf Road: he vacuumed carpets, ran deliveries and errands, loaded and unloaded guests' luggage, put up signboards, laundered sheets and towels, made minor repairs, and so on. He had, once a long time ago, peered into the front windows of the Cue and Cushion but had never come inside.

Last came Sonny, who walked purposefully, as a foreman in a factory might walk. Sonny Peggaluso was in his mid-twenties and a custodian on the night shift at Albany University. Six years ago he had married and thenafter been divorced. He liked cars and watching basketball games, he swam at the YMCA in Schenectady, and he played for small amounts of money at pool and cards. Occasionally, Sonny would imagine himself in precarious situations, thinking or fighting his way out of danger. But he would not need to fight tonight; he and Rudy had planned out everything too well for that.

The three rounded the corner formed by the protruding rest rooms. Here was the Cue and Cushion's waiting area. Saying nothing, Rudy knelt in front of the first of the two cigarette vending machines. He set his suitcase softly on the floor, unsnapped the case's catches, and lifted the top. Inside were Sonny's pry-bar and two rings of small cylinder-style keys, one of which, Rudy was hoping, would fit into the round lock-slots of the two vending machines and open them.

He took the pry-bar and handed it up to Sonny. The keys caught Mickey's attention. "Hey, do you think those keys –"

Sonny gripped Mickey's shoulder and moved him in the direction of the stairs that descended to the basement. His voice was fraternal but firm. "Mickey, never mind Rudy. Your job's in the cellar. If the money's down there, you'll find it. You're lucky." His eyes were wide open and looked commandingly into Mickey's. At the head of the stairs, he patted Mickey's shoulder and told him, "Shine your light down the stairs, do *not* shine it upward. Understand me?"

"What's in the cellar?"

"I heard there's a small kitchen down there."

"What should I look for?"

"I figure the money'll be in a cloth bag or in an ordinary grocery bag. It'll probably be among other bags or in a drawer or... at the back of a shelf." He nodded to Mickey. "We don't have much time. Get started."

Mickey smiled. Going down the stairs, he switched on his flashlight and thought, "I am lucky."

Sonny was pleased with the way he was handling and steering Mickey. And he was confident that this break-in and robbery would proceed and succeed exactly as he and Rudy had planned it. He turned and began searching in the spots where it seemed to him likely that Paul Curto, the owner of the Cue and Cushion, would have had his houseman hide the receipts for the weekend.

Cigarette and candy vending machines had circular lock openings that admitted only specially made keys. Rudy picked up the first ring. The keys on it were small hollow barrels, each with a tiny tab to guide it into the slot of the cigarette machine's lock. Each barrel had teeth at its open end that fit into gaps in the lock's inner dial. Thus, the dial was gripped and turned and the lock opened and closed. These machines were two different models built by the National Cigarette Machine Company. Both displayed two rows of eleven columns of cigarette brands, each column for a different brand and each choice with its own plunger. Both machines were self-lit with pale white interior lights, and at the top of the front of each was the hole for its round key.

Methodically and delicately, Rudy applied each of his keys to the round lock holes of first one machine, then the other. But each time, either the key was the wrong size for the lock or it simply failed to turn the lock's inner workings. He reached behind the machines, unplugged both and tried inserting and turning the keys, one by one, but again with the same lack of effect. He sat back on his heels. He knew what this meant.

Sonny knelt close beside him. Rudy turned at the waist, and Sonny shook his head 'no.' "I checked the drawers behind the counter, the desk, the cash register in here and the one in back of the lunch counter, and the drawers there and the refrigerator too. And the vacuum cleaner closet. Nothing. There's no extra woodwork behind the counter or under the shelves. The desk has no false backing. There's nothing with a padlock on it." He looked grimly, then agitatedly at Rudy. "It's in a canvas bag or maybe in a small briefcase. –Maybe it's in the ladies' room!"

"No, the money's in one of these machines." Rudy said this as if he was admitting a difficult but inescapable conclusion.

"What?"

"None of my keys fit." He and Sonny were inches apart. "They're the keys for the machines we have at our place, the machines we used to own, two I palmed from the salesman who sold us the new ones, and two I bought in a hardware store. I thought all these were pretty much alike, but they're not." He pointed to the lock holes on Curto's cigarette machines. "These are special locks." He poked emphatically at the machine facing him. "The money's in a fat envelope that's standing up against one of the inside walls of one of these machines!"

"Are you sure -?" Sonny's voice ascended.

"There's enough room in there. Either that, or the houseman takes the money with him when he locks up and then drives right to Curto's house!"

These surmises each made sense. Sonny swiveled his head to the machines, dumbfounded; the machines looked back, inscrutable. "Yeah," he agreed. He tightened his lips. "Hell, we can't break in here twice! We'll have to tear the sides off these machines." He held up his pry-bar.

"Aaah… We'd need a large hammer and a larger crowbar!"

"We're not leaving empty-handed! We'll cover the glass with towels so it doesn't shatter all over the floor. I saw towels behind the lunch counter. We'll kick in the glass, and I'll shove my way past the cigarette packs. If the money's there, I'll pull it out!"

Rudy disliked having to resort to noise and destruction, but he liked Sonny's determination and ruthlessness. And Sonny was the boss. "O.K." He moved his suitcase out of the way. He would put as many of the cigarette packs that Sonny did not crush into it.

Sonny swore softly. He stood and turned toward the lunch counter. "I'll get the towels."

"Hey! Hey! Sonny, Rudy! Come down here. I found it!" It was Mickey, calling up from the cellar.

Sonny started for a second. He jerked his head to the cellar stairs, then to Rudy. He moved to the stairs and began down the steps, one at a time. Behind him, he heard Rudy. Mickey had found a bulb suspended from the ceiling and had pulled the chain hanging from it; and in the light from the bulb and from their flashlights Sonny saw, as he was descending, spaghetti noodles and pieces of bread and other food over the cement floor. There alongside a kitchen work-table was Mickey with a victorious smile, his forearms and palms extended toward the table, as though he were presenting a birthday surprise to children entering the room. "I found it," he repeated.

And there upon the table, inches from Mickey's indicating fingertips, were bundles of bills blocked together to form a square stack about two feet in height. The stack stood on top of newspapers in which it evidently had been neatly wrapped and Scotch-taped. Sonny halted on seeing this spectacle, then continued to the table and picked up one of the bundles. It was a rubber-banded pack of ten dollar bills, and without removing the rubber band he flipped through it.

When Rudy saw the money, his mouth fell open and his arms collapsed to his sides. He rushed to the table, took another of the bundles, and flipped through it too. The bills were real. He looked at the tower of money –there were four bundles to a layer –and bent over it and began poking and counting the layers. After counting half way up, he straightened and looked at Sonny. Up to this while, Rudy had been persuading himself to be indifferent to the risks they were taking, but now he was aghast. "These aren't the weekend receipts," he cried, "this is something bigger! Something illegal!" His mouth remained open.

"And it's all ours," laughed Mickey. His mouth was open too and his face was shining.

———

CHAPTER 2
COVERING THEIR TRACKS

July 10, 1978

Rudy looked frantically about the cellar, darting his eyes, scanning every part of it, as if he were expecting a guard or a watchdog to materialize from somewhere. But the cellar was limited and everything in it was in the open: his eyes passed over a stove, a refrigerator, a tub-sink, the table, a water heater, brooms, cardboard boxes and burlap bags, onions and garlics on strings suspended from one of the rafters and an oversize garbage can. He clenched his teeth.

"What do you think?" Sonny asked him pointedly, but without waiting for a reply, he turned to Mickey. "How did you find this money?"

"Ha! I started to look where you guys would look. Then I thought, 'I should look where no one else is gonna look.' So I dug into the garbage, past the greasy spaghetti sauce and the chicken parts, and I felt the package. I pulled it out and tore off the paper it was wrapped in." Mickey began laughing jubilantly. "And there it is!"

Rudy was shorter than Sonny. He moved to in front of him and tilted up his face. "What all do you know about Paul Curto?"

"Just what everybody knows. He has a small construction company. He builds a half dozen houses every summer in west

Albany or Colonie and sells them. He goes back to Italy every year or two and brings back two or three men who want to come to America. He sponsors them. He pays them minimum wage. They have to work for him for whatever he makes them agree to, say for two years. Then they're on their own."

"How can he run a company like that?"

"He puts a foreman on each house. The foremen earn union wages 'cause they have to know masonry and plumbing. The Italians are the laborers. They do the unskilled work." Sonny made a dismissive motion with his hand. "That's how Curto saves money. That's what I heard."

Rudy was shaking his head 'no.' "There has to be more to it than that!"

Sonny said, "I don't go here much anymore, and I was never in tight with his steady customers. That's all I know." He added, "Now that I think about it, a lot of the men I saw here were Italians and Greeks. I guess he knows a lot of them closely." He turned to Mickey. "Good work, Mickey." Mickey beamed back, delighted with himself. Neither Rudy nor Sonny could have done what he did, and he knew it.

Rudy's eyes were wide, and his voice was rigid. "O.K. We have to get out of here –with this money –now. Forget the cigarette machines!" He tried to compose himself. "Sonny, there have to be others beside Curto involved with this much money. There's more than a cubic foot of it on the table! Why was it in a garbage bin?"

Mickey laughed in triumph. He was elated with the find and the resulting excitement. "Let's take all this money and trash the cellar!" He grinned broadly and fiercely, as if the money on the table were vindicating him for everything he had ever been reprimanded for.

Sonny shook his head at him. "Mickey," he said calmly and as seriously as he could, "we shouldn't do that, and I'll tell you why not."

"Yes! Yes! Yes!" Mickey sang. "Think of the look on Curto's face when –"

"Mickey, if we wreck the cellar, Curto'll know outsiders raided his –"

"So what!" Mickey sounded as if he wanted to affront Paul Curto, whom he had never met.

"Mickey, Sonny's right. We don't dare wreck this place."

"I found the money!" He bent forward at the waist, his arms at his sides, his smile fading fast. "Let me have the say on this!"

Sonny turned to Rudy and said, "Rudy, go up and get the suitcase and fill it with this money." He pursed his lips and nodded to Rudy with a malignity in his eyes that meant, "Let me convince Mickey in private."

Rudy bounded up the steps. Sonny bared his teeth. He rushed suddenly at Mickey and with his left hand grabbed a fistful of his hair. He jerked Mickey's head back and growled softly into his face. "You gotta understand this, Mickey: we *don't* want Curto to know we ransacked his cellar. We want him to think that someone *–one* person –who hangs out here –knew precisely where and how the money was stashed and took it quickly and cleanly!"

Sonny's eyes –his orbs, the surrounding flesh, the brows, the lashes, the lids, even the upper ridge of his nose –glared furiously and unblinkingly at Mickey. Mickey grimaced. Sonny tightened his grip and with his right hand took Mickey's mouth and squeezed it angrily until Mickey gurgled, "O.K., O.K. Jeeze!" Sonny released his hands, and Mickey cried, "You didn't have to pull my hair." Tears ran down his cheeks.

"I had to get tough. You didn't understand when I told you nicely." Sonny let himself cool slightly. His face softened. "The first thing we're gonna do is wrap up something bulky and put it in the garbage can where the money was."

Rudy had come back down with his suitcase and was filling it with the bundles of money. Sonny found an empty box. He crushed it down in shape, and he and Mickey wrapped it with the newspapers and placed it in the garbage can. They wadded up more newspapers that were in the cellar and stuffed them in the can. Sonny swept the floor carefully into a dustpan and sprinkled the sweepings over the wadded newspapers. Mickey found a can of tomato sauce. They broke it open with the pry-bar and dribbled some of the sauce over the sweepings.

Then Sonny said to Mickey, "I want you to remember exactly how the cellar was –when you came down." Mickey thought for a second, then moved. He tidied up the row of boxes and potato sacks along one wall that he had disarranged and pulled a pair of worn work boots from under the table where he had kicked them.

"Good." Sonny turned to Rudy. "O.K., do you see anything we overlooked?" Rudy got on his knees and shined his light under the table and the sink and then under the staircase. He bit his lip for a moment. He took a washcloth from the sink and wiped off the table and the refrigerator door handle. He opened the refrigerator, looked inside, and closed it. Agreed that the cellar was as it had been, they put out the light and trekked back to the main floor.

In the same way that they had in the cellar, they checked the waiting area and the different spots Sonny had searched in, looking, one place at a time, for any petty disruption or evidence they might be leaving behind. Rudy opened the suitcase again to confirm that he had in it the two rings of keys plus Sonny's pry-bar. He plugged the cigarette machines back into the wall socket and re-examined the floor space where he had been kneeling. "Wait!" He re-entered the men's room and clicked on his penlight. He reached up and made sure the ceiling tile was squarely in place, and then with his handkerchief he diligently cleaned prints from his sneakers that he had left upon the sink. "That's it, I think."

Thus satisfied as much as was possible, the three trooped along the side wall and back to the rear exit. Sonny removed the planks from the door and laid them quietly on the floor against the back wall. Rudy opened the door and peeped out. He held the door for his two accomplices, he took one last look at the pool hall and its tables, slipped out himself, and pulled the door by its outer handle fraction by fraction until he heard the latch click.

———

CHAPTER 3
COUNTING THE LOOT

Monday, 2 AM, July 10, 1978

They had exited the building onto Bradford Street. Bradford was a short sidestreet that ran parallel to Central Avenue, that is, parallel to the front and back of the Cue and Cushion. All its buildings' windows were dark now, and the air there was still and humid. Sonny glanced at his watch: it was half past 1 AM. They had been more than an hour in the pool hall. "No talking," he ordered, "till we get in the car." Sonny suddenly had become blunt and cold, as if he were angry. He would stay this way until they were safely in his apartment.

They walked hurriedly and unevenly, some moments three abreast, then two in front and one behind. They turned right to North Lake Avenue, then on it past West Street to Washington Avenue where Sonny had parked his Cutlass. He unlocked the car. "Rudy –in the back. Mickey, you're in front with me. Quickly!" In seconds, the motor and lights were on, the car was in gear, and they were on their way to Sonny's apartment.

Sonny's car was a white 1970 two-door Oldsmobile Cutlass S. It had a manual transmission, bucket seats, and plastic upholstery. There was plentiful leg room in front and a rear end that sloped over an immense trunk. Rudy lay back against the cushion and sighed audibly. "I'll admit my insides were shakin' like Jello-O when I saw that mound of money –

that Mickey found," he added. He had left his cigarettes in the Cutlass before Sonny let him off hours ago. He took one and put the filter end between his lips. "Too bad we couldn't re-bar the back door." He lit the cigarette. "Well, now we don't have to rip off that old man."

"Yeah," seconded Mickey. "Forget him."

Rudy, though, was less nervous now than he was conflicted. He wanted his part of the money. He knew, simultaneously, that there will be a danger of being found out by their own friends in Merle's Billiards, his Uncle Julian's pool room, if they attract attention to themselves in incautious ways like splurging on new clothes or new cars.

Mickey had no such concerns. He looked to his left at Sonny's face for traces of a return to his usual amicableness. Sonny kept his face clean-shaven; and when he smiled, his jaw dropped and his mouth broke open like a jewel box to display his teeth and upper gums. When he was most happily aroused and when his cheeks pushed up farther, his eyes squinted and he looked like a driver getting out of his race car. But at that moment, his face was concentrated and stony. He was asking himself questions: "Will Curto call the police? Where did this fortune in the garbage can come from? Is that how money is shuttled in and out of that pool hall?"

Mickey was fussy and vain about his hair, which grew thick, almost coarse on his head. But now, because of the money in their possession, he was no longer hurt over the memory of Sonny's yanking it. He was about to be rich, and his dampened enthusiasm was rekindling. He smiled, anticipating their new-found affluence, and began patting his knees in rhythm to a melody in his head.

Rudy's forearms rested protectively on the suitcase. In his mind were the sort of questions and suppositions about its contents that an accountant would make. "Are any of the bills larger than ten dollars? How many bundles did I see on the table? Could we have in our hands fifty or maybe sixty thousand dollars!?"

In the rear view mirror Sonny saw Rudy's preoccupation, and he said, "Rudy! When we get to my place, I want you to count the money. You can count it on the kitchen table."

"That's just what I was thinking."

Mickey chimed in, "I can't wait!" He recalled what Sonny had told him and Rudy in the cellar, that Paul Curto was making himself wealthy by using foreigners to do most of the hard work in his construction company. "Curto'll never know," he thought, "how his money will make us three hard-working guys rich –three guys he's never met!" He slapped his hand on the glove compartment and guffawed aloud at his private, ironic observation. "This is not a dream!" He laughed proudly, joyously.

The Cutlass approached Sonny's apartment building, slowed, and eased into the building's parking lot. The ride had taken only about ten minutes.

–

(Believe it or not, there has existed for more than a century and a half a theory of benevolent "redistribution of wealth." Its adherents sought to redress the imbalance in society caused by men who by fortune possess skills, the possession of which constitutes an "unfair advantage." This latter advantage results in the acquisition of assets and property for these men and the impoverishment of those others who were not blessed by Mother Nature with skill or high birth, but were afflicted by Her with need. And according to the doctrines of this big-hearted philosophy, the chief purpose of money is to equalize the two population divisions, that is, to elevate the improsperous half at the expense of the other half.

Nothing therein, however, formed any part of the rationale of the three in the Cutlass. They had neither ethical nor fiendish motivations, nor did even one of them feel remorse for his part in the felony. What each wanted were the profits from his nocturnal law-breaking and, of course, the excitement therefrom, just as an athlete wants both the applause and the remuneration from the sport in which he competes.)

–

They entered the apartment, and Sonny shut and locked the door. "Fellas, it's 2 o'clock." He was looking at Mickey. "No loud talking, O.K.?"

He led them into the kitchen. Rudy placed the suitcase on the table, sat, and without saying a word, opened it. Sonny put a sheet of paper and a pen and an ashtray on the table; and Rudy handed back to him his pry-bar. Sonny opened the refrigerator and took out three cans of soda, one for each of them.

As Rudy began to remove the packets of bills from the suitcase and methodically fan through each one, hoping that there were other denominations –higher ones –than ten dollars, Sonny patted Mickey on the back and looked into his eyes. "Because of you, we were lucky tonight." Keeping his hand on Mickey's upper spine, he shepherded him out of the kitchen and toward the couch in the living room. "We'll let Rudy do his work. I want to talk about Paul Curto."

Mickey was wide awake and eager, moments away from becoming "in the money," the condition of life he had fantasized about since he was a little boy. He glanced about the living room. There was the television set he had stolen from the Columbiana Hotel last winter and given to Sonny. Businessmen from out of state had rented for three nights adjoining rooms in the hotel on its top floor. They vacated the rooms late in the third afternoon, after the cleaning women had left for the day.

When he came on his shift at 6 PM, Mickey learned of the businessmen's tardy departure. Half way through his lunch break in the hotel's kitchen, he remembered something he had seen in a movie once; and later, after midnight, he went out to his van for his pliers and a wrench. He let himself into one of the businessmen's rooms with his master key. In the dark, he unbolted the room's television set from the heavy table onto which it had been secured. He lugged the set and his tools out of the room and down one of the fire stairs and out to his van.

The next evening at work, Mickey was told by the desk clerk how the cleaning women had reported the television gone and how the day manager had concluded that one of the businessmen had carried it off, probably as a joke. The desk clerk told Mickey that the day manager at first exclaimed, "How did they get it out the front doors?" Then he said, "What am I gonna do! They're back in New Jersey by now!"

Mickey smiled at the stupidity of the day manager. Afterward, the idea that a valuable object or even a person could vanish "off the face of the earth," as the saying went, fascinated him, and he laughed. "Suppose I disappeared from Albany. A lot of people will wonder where I was!"

He had gotten away with the purloined television. However, he was unable to persuade anyone he knew to buy it from him and finished the matter by giving the set to Sonny. There it was, on a table-stand facing the couch. To one side of that table and on a throw-rug near the corner were fifteen pound dumbbells, a barbell with platter-weights on each end, and a pair of hand grips. Sonny often exercised with these while he watched sports on television.

Mickey lived in his father's house and had to pay his father a weekly rent. Someday, he knew, he would have his own apartment, a place probably just like Sonny's.

They sat on the couch, and Sonny said to him, "We left Curto one clue –the back door." He sipped his soda. "As soon as he sees the back door in a few hours, without the bars on it, he'll run down into the cellar and check the garbage can." He brought his head close to Mickey's. "We cannot go to the Cue and Cushion again –*any* of us." This stricture was important, and he scoured Mickey's eyes and face for a nod or other expression of assent and compliance.

"O.K.," agreed Mickey. "What d'ya think Curto'll do?"

"He'll get angry –killer angry. If this money's not legit, he probably can't notify the police. He'll start thinking suspiciously. He'll look closely at the men he's in cahoots with and at anyone who goes into the cellar –even the meter-reader." Sonny continued to pierce his eyes into Mickey's, looking for any sign of resistance to his simple but crucial warning. "Mickey, we cannot –"

A suppressed but firm voice from the kitchen interrupted them. "I'm done." They heard Rudy set the pen down on the table top. Mickey sprang up, ecstatic, precipitous, imminently rich. He and Sonny took their cans of soda into the kitchen and sat at the table with Rudy.

Rudy's face was egg-shaped, it sloped from his forehead to his chin, which was slightly prominent. He had a bird-beak nose and a small mouth but otherwise undistinguished features. While tallying the money, he had mussed his own hair. He looked gravely, almost worriedly at Sonny. "It's good and bad news –all at once." His lips parted cautiously before speaking. "We stole $120,000!"

Mickey's eyes and mouth widened in amazement and delight at the announcement of this gargantuan "score" of theirs. Before he could hoot or cheer, Sonny caught him by the shoulder. "No noise! I told you, Mickey."

"There're 120 packets of 100 ten dollar bills," Rudy accounted, "so each packet is $1,000." He had formed in mid-table three discrete complements of forty packets. Mickey looked at the stack nearest him of grey, white, and spinach-green bills and the brown rubber bands girdling them and separating them at the same time. He lifted his hand and began to reach, and Rudy said, again to Sonny, "We can't touch this money yet."

"What d'ya mean!" cried Mickey. His next sentence sounded both incredulous and offended. "It's our money now!"

"There's *too* much money here!"

"Good! The more, the –"

"Mickey, keep your voice down." Sonny gritted his teeth at him.

Rudy continued. "Mickey, chances are this money belongs to more people than just Curto. We -listen! –have to think before we make any move at all."

"You're right." Sonny leaned into the table. "If we do pocket the money, we're gonna be inclined to show off with it –"

"So, we don't show off with it!" Mickey retorted in a low voice.

Edward Grosek

Sarcastically, Rudy said, "Mickey, all you do is fritter away your paychecks in front of everybody in Romans –and in Merle's too!"

"That's what money's for!"

Rudy stretched out his neck. "You can't help overspending. You live from one week to the next."

"Ah, come on!" Mickey turned his face to Sonny and pressed his eyebrows together. "Let's just divide up the money and go."

Mickey Gonzag's implorations and the heedlessness implied in them struck Sonny anew. He retreated an inch or two from the table and perceived Mickey now as Rudy had warned him weeks ago. "Mickey," he began benignly, "we have to face it. If we let ourselves divide up even part of this cash, you'll splash your share around and squander it. Someone'll notice you and wonder where you got all the money."

"I'll say I inherited it." He sounded defensive.

"No one'll believe you."

"Listen," Mickey said, looking from one to the other, "why did we take the risk? For the money!"

"No," contradicted Rudy, "you came along because Sonny invited you! You thought that since Sonny was running the operation, there was *no* risk."

"That's right too. I came along, and I found the money *for you*!"

"You get the credit for that. We each get $40,000 –only not for six months!"

"I don't want to wait six months." He leaned back and crossed his arms over his chest. "And you don't either!"

"That's right. But I'm gonna wait," Rudy pointed at Mickey, "and so are you."

"Why should I?"

26

"I gave you one good reason. Here's another." Rudy leaned toward Mickey. His eyes seemed now closer than usual to the bridge of his nose. And there was odium as well as annoyance in them, but signal insults like these had no effect on Mickey. "If we get caught, Mickey –say we get caught, but we have all the cash intact, we might get off. Curto might not press charges if he gets his dough back. He probably doesn't want public notoriety."

"Ah, that's ridiculous." Mickey uncrossed his arms and waved his hand for attention. "Let's compromise. We'll each take one packet out of the pot every week."

"You want $1,000 a week? That's exactly how you'll get spotted!"

"All right," he shrugged, "$500 a week."

Again Sonny weighed in. "Mickey, you know Rudy's right. We have to protect ourselves. We don't dare get caught." He tilted his head and smiled invitingly, as a nurse might smile before administering a vaccination. "You can wait six months, can't you?"

Mickey sensed now that the two were allying against him. He would have to give in a little or suffer another rebuff from them. "What about one month?"

Sonny forced out his breath through his teeth. He got up, unhung his calendar from a nail in the wall, and brought it to the table. He flipped ahead in the calendar to October. "All right. Three months." The calendar lay flat on the table. Sonny pointed to one of the dates. "Monday, October 9th is three months exactly. And none of us have to be at work Monday mornings or afternoons. Perfect! We'll hold the money back till then."

Rudy immediately opposed this attempt to compromise. "No, no. Sonny, that's only a tentative date. If there's a police investigation or there's talk in the pool room, we gotta leave the money alone."

"No –"

"You're right. We'll begin dividing up the money only if it's absolutely safe." Sonny turned to Mickey. "We don't wanna take a chance and wind up doing time or facing Curto's friends." He looked hard into Mickey's eyes. "You can hold out until October… right?"

Mickey capitulated. "All right." He grimaced. "October 9." But a new thought came to him. "Wait a minute! Who's gonna keep hold of the money?"

That question brought silence to the kitchen.

———

CHAPTER 4
HIDING THE LOOT

Monday AM, July 10, 1978

Sonny's clock on top of the refrigerator ticked for several seconds. He spoke. "It stands to reason we can't keep it here or hide it in the pool room –or in Rudy's house or leave it in your house," he said to Mickey. "But, we gotta get the money out of sight by tomorrow."

"You mean by today. It's Monday."

"Let's wrap the money up in a tarpaulin and bury it in the ground in the woods," suggested Mickey. "We'll cover the hole with dirt and sticks."

"No good," said Rudy.

"Why not? That's the best place to hide anything –in the ground!"

"Look, we gotta stash it away so it takes all three of us to know where it is and retrieve it."

"Yeh," thought Mickey. "How're we gonna do that?"

Rudy asked, "How can we lock it up with three separate padlocks?"

Sonny's head jerked up. "We can rent one of those storage units! You know, they're like a row of garages, one after the other, all joined together. There's one of these storage places near the airport. I can't think of its name."

"Yeah," said Mickey, "people stow away furniture in them. You pull the overhead door down and put your own padlock on it!"

"Can you put three padlocks on the door?" asked Rudy.

"No."

"So we put my suitcase –wait –! How big is the garage?"

"Same size as an ordinary garage." Sonny held up his hand. "I remember: Brassey's. That's the name of the storage company. They do towing too. It's on the Troy-Schenectady Road."

"I have an idea. Listen. You know my old man's Studebaker?"

"Studebaker?" asked Mickey.

Sonny knew Rudy's father and had been to Mr. Merle's house; he had seen the Studebaker and so, knew about it. Mickey did not know Rudy this well. Rudy turned to him and recounted the story of his father's Studebaker. In 1971, Mr. Merle bought a second hand Studebaker Lark VI that then was ten years old. The Lark was a cream-white two-door sedan with a horizontal strip of chrome trim on each of its sides but with otherwise a simple, compact appearance. The car performed admirably for four years.

In 1975, its water pump wore out, which meant that while the motor was on –even idling –the water in the radiator was slowly pumped out and onto the ground. In this condition the car could not be operated for more than about fifteen minutes, after which it began to overheat and Mr. Merle had to stop driving and replenish the radiator. By 1975, unhappily, the Studebaker Company was well out of business, none of the car-parts stores or junk car lots around Albany had a water pump that fit Mr. Merle's Lark, and so, the car was as unsellable as it was undrivable.

Rudy sipped his soda. "After that, my old man bought a Ford. We parked the Studebaker behind our garage and took the battery out of it. Every now and then my old man phones the junk lots and the second hand car dealers. If he can get a water pump, we'll install it, and he'll get rid of the car."

"Why d'you take out the battery? So no one would steal it?" asked Mickey.

"The car's been sitting there for… three years. You can't leave a battery in a standing car, it'll lose its power after three or four weeks. We have a charger in the cellar. We have motor oil, Prestone Antifreeze, and spark plugs down there too, just in case."

Rudy lit a cigarette and turned back to Sonny. "Anyhow, I can charge up the battery. We'll put it in the car and fill up the radiator. I'll drive it to Brassey's and park it in one of the storage garages. We'll lock the suitcase, then lock it up in the trunk!" His face firmed and brightened.

"Wait a minute," interjected Mickey, "I gotta have a key in this too."

"That's right," said Sonny, this time siding with Mickey. He and Rudy eyed each other. "Mickey has to have one of the keys to the money." A shadow played across Rudy's face. "Rudy, we gotta give Mickey a role to play in securing the money. We all have to be in on it somehow."

"Yeah," said Mickey. "Wait –where's my key?"

"You get to keep the keys to the Studebaker."

Incredulous at hearing these words, Rudy, let his hands collapse onto the table. "That's crazy!"

"That's a good idea," said Mickey to Rudy, smiling.

"I can't give the keys to my father's car to *him*! What if he–"

"How many keys are there?"

"Only two keys. One key for the ignition and one for the doors and the trunk."

"O.K.," said Sonny. "We'll park the car in Brassey's and lock the suitcase. You keep the suitcase key. We'll lock it in the trunk. You keep the ignition key. We can leave the car doors unlocked, and Mickey gets the trunk key."

"Suppose –" Mickey began.

"Mickey, this is the best we got. Never mind 'Suppose'."

"Oh… yeah."

"What d'you say, Rudy?"

This time it was Rudy who was out-voted. He pushed himself back in his chair. "What'll I tell my old man?" He spread out his palms.

Sonny lowered his eyes in thought for a moment. He raised them back up. "Tell your father one of my friends wants to work on it. Logano!" He pointed at Rudy. "He tuned up my car once. We'll take the car after he goes to work. When he notices it's gone, tell him Tony Logano has it in his garage. Tell him Logano took the water pump out and couldn't fix it. Say he's writing to a supplier out of state to try to get a replacement, old or new. Your father hasn't driven it for three or so years. He's probably given up on it, no? Maybe he won't notice it for a while."

"What if he demands I bring the car home?"

"You'll have to stall him." Sonny exhaled. "O.K., let's say you gotta bring the car back. If you gotta, we'll chain up the suitcase and padlock the chain, and Mickey'll get the padlock key. I'll still have the storage unit key."

Rudy put his elbow on the table and rested his forehead in the palm of his hand. Sonny shook his head to Mickey, a signal for Mickey to remain quiet and let Rudy accept the deal. In a moment, a look of "Oh, all right" formed on Rudy's lips, and he said, "O.K." He looked up. "That's what we'll do. And we'll stick to it. All the way." He looked from Sonny to Mickey.

Sonny was content with the way he had kept control of himself and had gotten his partners to make concessions. He looked at them. "Fellas, we have to swear to each other that we'll keep our agreements. And we don't tell anyone."

Rudy said, "I swear," and looked at the other two. He put out his hand, and Sonny took it and swore his part. They each shook hands with Mickey, who in turn made his oath. They looked at each other solemnly.

Then Sonny said, "Rudy, put the money back in your case. Take your key rings out. We'll sleep here until 9. Rudy, you can have the easy chair, Mickey gets the couch." He looked at Mickey. "So first, take your shoes off. We'll eat breakfast at that diner on Fuller Road. By then, your father," he was looking at Rudy, "should be gone to work, no? We'll go to your house and lock the suitcase in the trunk of the Studebaker. You give Mickey the doors and trunk key, then start recharging the battery. Mickey and me'll shoot over to Brassey's and rent a garage unit."

"What're you gonna tell the guy at Brassey's?" asked Mickey.

"Good question. I'll just say I'm storing my car until I can find parts to repair it with. I'll say I can't leave it where I live any longer. That'll work." He smiled. "On the way back here, we'll stop at a hardware store, and I'll buy a heavy padlock. When we get back, we'll fill up the radiator, and you'll," he pointed at Rudy, "drive the Stude –Hey!" His cheeks fell and his eyes expanded. "Is it still registered?"

Rudy's face awoke. "Aah! It's no longer registered or insured… or inspected!" He sighed. "It has plates, though."

"Jeeze!"

"Does it have gas in it?" asked Mickey.

"Now that you mention it," said Rudy, "we have a gallon or so in the garage for the lawn mower. I should add that to the tank."

"O.K. Before we set out, we'll decide on the route. You'll have to drive ahead of us. We gotta stay under the speed limit. I think we can make it there in ten or maybe twelve minutes."

"Let's bring extra water in a pail in case we need it," suggested Mickey.

"Good idea," said Sonny. Then he said, "Everyone stop and think for a full minute. What're we forgetting?"

A minute went by. Rudy said, "I can't think of anything more. But when this is over, I'm drivin' the Studebaker back at night. There'll be less chance of a cop's seein' the old registration sticker on the windshield!"

-

The remainder of the morning issued more or less as the three malfeasants had laid their plans for it. At 11:30, Sonny pulled down the overhead door of the storage unit. At the bottom of the door at one of its sides protruded a metal buckle loop that was bolted in place; and lined up, coinciding with it, was another steel loop, this one embedded in the cement footing. Sonny knelt and hooked the shackle of the new padlock through the two loops and pressed it into the lock's hole. It clicked; he tugged the lock, stood, and pocketed the key. "Guys, we were lucky today!"

"You mean I was lucky," thought Mickey.

Rudy had disengaged the Studebaker's battery and placed it in the trunk of the Cutlass. They all got into the car. Sonny drove Rudy to Merle's Billiards, where Rudy had left his car, an old Pontiac Firebird, last night. Rudy, fatigued conspicuously by now, said, "See yas tomorrow," took the battery, and went to his car. Sonny then dropped off Mickey at his father's house. As Mickey got out the car, they said 'good-bye' to each other. Mickey waved a second "good-bye" to Sonny and turned and plodded to the back of the house. He too was tired, and yet simultaneously heady and somewhat euphoric. For last night he had played a part, shoulder to shoulder with Sonny and Rudy, in something that turned gigantic. "Because of me." Then he thought. "Was it a theft –or a heist? I'll have to look that up." He reached into his pants pocket for his key to the kitchen door and felt the Studebaker key. Which made him think, "They need me to get at that money in the trunk."

He entered the house and went upstairs to his room. He took out the Studebaker key and set it in the top drawer of his dresser, the drawer in which he kept things he wanted handy, like his comb, his wallet, his tweezers, his electric shaver. "I'll remember I put it here."

He had not slept well on Sonny's couch and now, seeing his bed, felt drained of energy. He undressed, dropped down on the bed, and slept till 5 o'clock, then got up and drove to his job at the hotel. That night, as he was ironing pillow cases in the laundry room, he thought to himself, "Three months. Three months to go."

———

CHAPTER 5
MICKEY GONZAG

Without Mickey Gonzag, this story would have no chain of events, no conflicts, no unforeseen surprises. Mickey's role in it began on the morning of April 1st, a Saturday. That morning he woke up beneath the bedcover. Mickey liked to sleep cozily, "under cover," and this one was fuzzy and padded. In fact, he could not recall this particular coverlet. But, so what? Luxuriantly, he stretched his leg muscles. Doing this, he discovered that he was naked. He wondered, "What time is it?"

He curled onto his side, his eyes still shut. The bed sheet on which he was lying felt silkier than usual, so silky that he slid his arm over the sheet –and touched someone, a girl by the soft skin of her stomach. Mickey's eyes opened. "Did somebody... come in my room with me?"

He paused, then pulled down the bedcover and saw the girl next to him. As he pushed away from her and off the bed, she awoke, saw him, and pulled the beige blanket to her throat. He grabbed one of the pillows and held it over himself. "Ah! How did you get here?" He sensed something and agitatedly looked around him: this was not his bedroom! "Where are we?"

"My room. We're in my apartment."

She said this factually but sounded timid, or dubious; and his being here, inexplicably out of place, seemed more than merely strange to Mickey. "What happened? How did I get here?"

"I drove you here last night. I met you at the bar in Romans. Remember? I brought you up here. I took a chance."

Mickey looked about the room. The venetian blind over the bedroom window was closed, but morning light filtered through its slats; and he saw the bed, the dresser, the closet, a clothes rack with blouses hanging from its hooks, and a chair with his clothes heaped upon it. He turned to her, apprehensively. "What about my van?"

"It's in the parking lot downstairs. That's how I drove you here. There are the keys." She pointed to her dresser top. "We're in an apartment building."

"Did I get drunk? What did I drink?" He shook his head.

"You were drinking gin and grapefruit juice. We got to talking. You drank several glasses and got silly –but not, you know, boorish. Gin blots your brain, you know." Her voice was waxing more assured, more genial.

"That never happened before." He looked as if he were more lost than worried.

"You had too much gin."

A thought struck him. "Who else is here?"

"No one. Just us." Her last words sounded almost sweet, as if she was glad the two of them were there.

Another thought came to him. "Did we –do it?" He looked at her through the louvered sunlight.

"Yes. Well… I did it." She smiled to him contentedly, as a cat would, one that had jumped up on its master's table and had devoured everything on his plate. She shifted onto her side and propped her head on her palm.

Mickey made a step forward and took a more careful look at her. She was good-looking, he thought. He tried to think. "Did

I really screw her?" He could not remember. "What's that on her face," he asked himself, "a birthmark –or a shadow?" He was not sure. "Ah, who are you?"

"My name is Angela."

He did remember this girl! He remembered laughing with her in Romans about something and then "drinking up." He could not recall undressing himself. He wondered whether he had actually, physically done it with her. He hoped his van was O.K.

"What's *your* name?" But Angela already knew Mickey's name and address. As she was pulling his clothes off, she found his wallet. She opened it and then on a sheet of paper copied his information from his driver's license.

"My name's Mickey. I have to go to work." He laid the pillow on the bed and began dressing himself. Angela sat up and watched, enjoying his nudity. This was too obvious to Mickey and he made a short embarrassed laugh. As he was putting on his pants, Angela pulled the bedcover with both hands, wrapping herself with it, and slipped out of bed. She had meant to envelop herself as she might with a rain cape; but as she moved off the bed, the ends of this mantle parted momentarily, and Mickey glimpsed her thighs.

In his pants pocket he felt the bulk of his wallet. He took it out and checked it. There were a few small bills in it. His driver's license and Montgomery Wards charge card were in there too, so she had not robbed him. But still, he had only a small amount of money left from last night. "How much gin and grapefruit did I drink?" He sighed. He looked at Angela and said the first thing that entered his mind. "Uh. Do you have… twenty-five dollars you can loan me?"

Angela Lubelski was born with a flaw, a birthmark, a faded ruddy-brown cloud-shaped mottle on the lower right cheek of her face. There was no palpable texture to the affected skin, but it extended to her upper lip, rendering her appearance as tainted. Through her life, Angela had trained herself to speak to and conduct herself toward others straightforwardly, eye to eye, voice to ear, as if she were marked but had nothing to be terribly conscious about. She had been on dates with fellows who tactfully looked at everything but her cheek, but then side-glanced and peeked at its defect, so that she knew that in her presence they were embarrassed.

Angela had a nose that was no longer girlishly pert, a slight squint to her eyes and faint shadows just beneath them, and an extraordinary smile in which her upper lip ran straight across and her lower lip dipped to reveal her teeth. She was, apart from the birthmark, attractive and would be, had she been born without this square inch of discoloration, as promiscuous as any other restless, feminine thirty-four year old.

It was exactly then, hearing Mickey's appeal for money, when Angela realized that last night she had indeed gotten an amount of fun and gratification that might be measured in dollars. She had used him for maybe twenty-five minutes, so that, putting the dollars and minutes together, he was now charging her about a dollar a minute! She thought, "He's not bad-looking –especially when his hair spills over his forehead. He's slow, he drinks, lacks esteem for himself, he weighs maybe 145 pounds but he has muscles… "

"Do you work, Mickey?"

"Yeah. But I don't make a lot. I work in a hotel." He looked down at his belt and buckled it.

"O.K. I'll give you the twenty-five dollars." He looked up, happy and surprised; she looked back, indulgently. With this simple agreement –and yet without articulating in words the probable effects of it –Angela acquired for herself an ascendancy over Mickey.

She ushered him into the living room, which was larger in size than her bedroom and where Mickey noticed a couch, an easy chair, a small television set, and the doorway to her kitchen. Near the apartment's door was a table stand on which Angela placed her mail when she arrived home and on which also stood a small orange-striped oblate vase. Inside the vase were her wallet and her keys. Angela held the thin bedcover upon herself with her left hand and with her right, she reached out from its folds and from the vase withdrew the wallet. From the wallet, she removed some bills.

Before giving them to Mickey, she opened the drawer of the stand and took out a three inch by two inch card on which –after finishing with him last night –she had printed "Angela" and her phone number. She handed the twenty-five dollars and the card to him. "Mickey, here, and I want you to put my phone number in your wallet. You may come over here alone, by yourself, once or twice a month for the same amount." She paused. "Understand?" She looked at him unflinchingly, as if she expected him to understand, or at least to state that he understood.

He said, "O.K.," and tucked the bills and the card into his wallet.

"You *have* to phone me first." Then, with the same hand, her right hand, she unchained the apartment door. "I'm glad I met you, Mickey."

"Ah -same here!" Mickey looked at her face. Involuntarily, his eyes moved to the birthmark on it; and perceiving this shift of his sight, Angela knew what she had to do. She took the bedcover at the waist with her right hand, threw back her head, and with her left hand reached for the doorknob. The foregoing movements, of course, allowed the ends of the bedcover to fall from her shoulders to her elbows. Mickey's look dropped onto her breasts, now exposed, and he stared at them.

Unperturbed, she said, "Sundays are my favorite days, Mickey." She turned the knob and opened the door. "Remember –Sundays." She took him by his elbow, nudged him through the doorway, and closed the door.

Mickey heard Angela set the lock and slide the door chain in its slot. He turned his head and found himself in the hallway of her apartment building. The hallway was well lit and wallpapered in green. He was disconcerted, undecided, under-satisfied, and twenty-five dollars richer than yesterday night.

–

Mickey bragged to Sonny and Rudy and to one of his co-workers at the hotel about his encounter with Angela. He termed it a "fortuity," a word he had learned from television, and laughed. He did not mention the money, for he thought that if he did, his friends, of course, would want to meet this girl. During the next three weeks he wondered about her –where she worked and whether she would really pay him another twenty-five dollars. He thought about the lemon-shaped breasts she had shown to him, how they had jiggled, and how warm they would feel in his hands. And too, there was the benefit of his having a clandestine girlfriend, one whom he could simply forget about should he tire of her.

On Sunday, April 23rd, Mickey needed money. Early that afternoon he phoned Angela, who recognized his voice as soon as he asked, "Umm, remember me?"

"Of course," she replied cheerfully. She invited him to her apartment. "I'm in number 203, second floor," she reminded him.

He arrived at her door, where she was waiting for him, freshly showered, barefoot, and in a chalk-white terry cloth robe. She drew him into the apartment, locked the door, and towed him by the hand to the couch. There she made apparent her desiderata: he must strip for her and then kiss and pet with her on the couch for five minutes. On the bed he has to caress her for another few minutes, whenafter he can do what he wants –in the ordinary fashion –for as long as he likes.

These conditions sounded easy to Mickey. He consented to them; and so, what Angela said she wanted of him is exactly what she got that afternoon. And this visit, in which this time Mickey was a conscious participant, was an unqualified success: his hands and fingers were hard and vulgar, he said nothing as he fondled and massaged her, and the closer they crushed against each other on the bed, the more sleepy and peasant-like he appeared to her. And for him, the twenty-five dollars she afterward handed over was quick, tax-free cash money.

Mickey would make seven more trips to apartment number 203. While accurate narrations of the conduct of these two individuals during these afternoon assignations are not vital to the plot of this story, there is a need –in order to better characterize them and to evince the course of their liaison – to cite the dates of the visits and to give excerpts or at least summations of some of the talk that passed between them.

By the calendar, Mickey came over on May 7th and on May 21st. On this last particular Sunday, while he was dressing, Angela remarked to him that she works in the main library at Albany University.

"What d'ya do there?"

She replied succinctly that she puts books back in order on the shelves and helps students to locate information for their term papers. "That's the best part of librarianship –for me, anyway –helping students find their information. I'm pretty good at it."

Mickey enumerated some of his night porter duties at the Columbiana Hotel. He stopped buttoning his shirt and smiled to her and told her how on one occasion he had come to work tired and had slept in one of the unoccupied rooms. "As soon as I came in, I had to help unload a furniture truck. Twenty new couches! After, I went upstairs and let myself into one of the expensive suites. They're hardly used. I locked the door, and I fell asleep there for two whole hours! No one missed me," he added happily. He buttoned his shirt and said, "I woke up at 10, in time for my lunch." Then he remembered something. "Oh, I almost forgot!" He smiled. "Do you need towels? I can get you two different sizes. Brand-new. Real cheap."

By June 4th, Angela was setting aside and keeping in the apartment five five-dollar bills. And on this Sunday, as soon as Mickey entered, she gave to him a small box lined with fluffy velvet in which lay a necklace, a gold chain holding a talisman upon which was carved a man's head. The links of the chain were ovate in shape; and the stone itself was a "tiger's eye," Angela explained, a semi-precious gem streaked with honey and black colors. The figure engraved upon it was facing out, but he had only one prodigious off-center right eye. There was no symbolism to it, she told him; the uniqueness of the head –it was otherwise bald and featureless –had just captured her fancy. Mickey smiled as he lifted it delicately from the box. He remarked, "A one-eyed man. I wonder what that would be like."

After their session, after he was done and gone, Angela wondered whether Mickey had a friend like him, that is, a friend trustworthy and willing to earn money on those weekends when he did not call on her. For Angela was, more so than in the past, stirred and aroused now and pruriently curious and desirous. She wished Mickey would take her out to a bar like Romans where they might run into his friends.

Another two weeks passed. On Sunday, June 18th, after he had arrived and come into Angela's living room and removed his shirt, she noticed that he was not wearing the necklace and asked him why not. "Oh, that," he said with a placid face. "Last week I sold it to the bartender at Romans. His name's Marky. I'm in there a lot. Sometimes he buys things." He eyed her savvily. "That's something that's good to know."

Angela's face fell. But she controlled herself and held back, for she feared that by verbalizing her resentment to Mickey she would herself become angry or moody and then unable to be satisfied by him that afternoon.

On July 2nd, Mickey made his seventh visit to Angela's apartment; and this time, it seemed to her that he avoided brushing his cheeks over her birthmark as they kissed. And as he massaged her, he exhibited less strength in his gripping and rubbing, as if his hands were tiring of this phase of their foreplay. Nonetheless, that afternoon he earned his twenty-five dollars –his allowance, as he started to refer to it –which Angela paid to him. Afterward, after she had let him out of her apartment, she sighed over their arrangement. He was a stimulus, and she was his customer.

———

CHAPTER 6
THE LIBRARIAN

Wednesday, July 5, 1978

Three days later, the day after the Fourth of July, Angela Lubelski was taking her break in the library's staff lounge. Three other librarians, all women, were also in the room. Many of those who enter librarianship choose it as their profession because they prefer working with things, actual things like typewriters and catalog records, rather than sentient, deliberative human beings, like ordinary men and women. Most librarians dread reprimands and embarrassment and prefer to restrain their thoughts rather than speak their minds and risk being adversely judged later in absentia. In their conversations, for this reason, many topics such as differing religious practices are uniformly shunned. One exception to these unwritten interdictions is that it is permissible for a librarian to champion a social cause.

The most dominant of the four in the staff lounge that morning was Dottie Nelson. Dottie was the head of the library's circulation department. She was pear-shaped and shorter than most women, and in the building she wore dark full-length dresses and padded nurses' shoes. Dottie distrusted men. Men never gave her compliments, and the more she resented the distance they maintained with her in speech and space, the less she attempted to attract their interest with either dress or behavior.

On Dottie's countenance that morning was the look of a vexed woman. "Did anyone read the *New York Times* yesterday!" she demanded.

"Yesterday was the Fourth," said one of the other librarians.

"Yeah." She made a dry stare at the three. "Well, yesterday the *Times* was published, and it said that 9,000 women were arrested in New York City last year for prostitution![1]" She let her lower lip protrude to underscore her malcontentment to her listeners for these arrests.

"That's probably an accurate number."

"But listen to this: the article said only 150 men were issued summonses by police for picking up women for sex!" Her lips tightened into a slash that implied, "Do you see what I'm saying!"

"One hundred and fifty men picked up 9,000 prostitutes?"

"No! Don't you get it?!" She flayed her arms in the air. "Most of the men got away!"

"So what?" thought Angela. She sensed herself –and the others –being caught off guard by Dottie's temper and faultfinding.

Dottie's exasperation turned into righteousness. She rapped her knuckles on the table. "It's the men who should be arrested!" The women were looking at her, not into her eyes, not deeply interested but unable to turn away, their physiognomies cautiously blank. They were reluctant to be drawn into direct conversation with her, and none of them replied. Dottie canted her head and eyed them sternly. "The 'johns' who *pay* for the sex should be arrested, not the ones

1 Selwyn Raab, "Female Officers Arrest Men Searching for Prostitutes," *New York Times* July 4, 1978, pg. 8.

earning the money!" She rolled her eyeballs up and around in disbelief. "That's why we need a feminist basis for our so-called criminal justice system!!"

A while later, Angela was back in her office. In addition to working at the reference desk and sitting on the library's Preservation Committee, Angela was responsible for monitoring the HA to HC range of books in the stacks –the section for economic statistics –and for ordering new books on that subject matter. In addition, she wrote book reviews each month for *Catholic Library World* magazine. On her desk were the two reviews she had finished yesterday. She sat and took a manila envelope from one of the desk drawers and began addressing it to the editor of *Catholic Library World*.

When Angela had heard Dottie's words of anathema for men who used prostitutes and paid them, she almost blanched at the implication. Now, several minutes later and alone, she was able to compose into sentences what her recent experiences had proved to her to be true and valid. She gazed pensively but not at any particular object, and the words came to her. "Sex for pay is just another service on the market." Moments passed. "The guy gets what he wants for an amount smaller than what he would expend on a girlfriend." She turned over the manila envelope and Scotch-Taped it closed. "Too bad. Dottie'll never know the value of promiscuity. What sort of person –what sort of thinking drives Dottie to want to deprive other people of… well, fun? Is it only because she has no fun?"

–

On July 16th, that is, on the sixth day after the three looters had sealed up their plunder in the storage unit, Mickey again showed up at Angela's apartment. This afternoon, though, he was less in a frame of mind for earning his money by performing diligently his duties to his consort than in a hasty mood to see the work ended and to collect his allowance and drive back to Merle's Billiards.

Angela let him into the apartment; and as soon as she had sat down in mid-couch, he deftly undressed, plopped himself against her right side, encircled his left arm about her shoulders, and kissed her several times to pacify her. He reached inside her robe, palmed and fondled her breasts one after the other, and undid the belt of the robe. He then reached under her knees and gripped and turned her body so that she was supine.

He shifted Angela once more to center her body upon the couch and ended, to his advantage, in a prepossessing position atop her. He began tongue-kissing her, which she expected; but then, instead of kneading and stroking her as he did ordinarily, he extended his hand to her inner thighs and with his fingertips pinched and twisted the tender and sensitive skin there. Angela tried to gasp, but each time she did, he held her mouth with his, caressed the skin he had just molested, and then resumed.

Angela could not understand why Mickey was doing this to her. Did someone convince him it was a new love technique? She felt him scratch her thigh with his nails and then take a morsel of her flesh with his thumb and forefinger and squeeze it, stinging her. She shuttered involuntarily and jerked her legs apart. Which gave him the opportunity to check her with his thumb: she was dripping and, therefore, he knew, receptive. He rose up, thrust his right arm under her legs and lifted her. She let the robe drop from her body, and he carried her into her bedroom and onto the bed.

Angela's thighs were sore and warm, and she spread them apart readily. Mickey climbed between them and plunged into her, without first massaging her. Angela said nothing; and after a short while –a much shorter while than ever in his prior times with her –she felt him finish, without pacing and delaying himself and satisfying her.

"That was quick," she said, puzzled once more at his unusual behavior.

"I couldn't help it," came his reply.

Yet again, Angela acquiesced. What more could she do than make another mental note of what, to her growing displeasure, was another lapse in Mickey's zeal for his part in their arrangement? "Why doesn't he appreciate what we're doing?" she asked herself.

He dressed, and at the table by the door she paid him the twenty-five dollars. As Mickey tucked the bills into his wallet, his eyes shuttled across Angela's living room and back. He saw the carmine carpeting, the simple furniture, the brown and burgundy curtains over the window, a framed picture of two lovers running through a forest on the wall. Suddenly he wanted a place like this for his own apartment. "I'll get my own apartment after we split the money," he decided. He left for the pool room. He would see Angela only one more time.

––––––

CHAPTER 7
HOW THE MUSIC DEPARTMENT WAS SET UP

Saturday, January 28, 1978

Rudy Merle was younger and more diminutive in stature than either Sonny or Mickey. He was five feet, six inches tall, had brown hair, a forehead that was high but not broad, and eyes that were grey and close to the bridge of his nose. His cheeks were slightly convex, and his lips were lean, straight, and reticent. Similarly nondescript was Rudy's usual dress —jeans or dark trousers, shirts that were tepidly colored, and on his feet white socks and either sneakers or low-cut construction shoes.

Rudy worked at Merle's Billiards, his Uncle Julian's pool room, Tuesday through Saturday from 9 AM to 5 PM. He opened the room at 9 o'clock and began brushing the tables, emptying the ash trays, vacuuming the carpet –cleaning up from the previous day's use until just before noon when customers started coming in. Then he stayed at the front counter or in the mezzanine, letting out tables to players and charging them after they finished playing.

Merle's Billiards was the sole occupant of the building at 1050 upper Central Avenue. Inside was a spacious carpeted floor on which were twenty-six Brunswick tables plus here and there chairs and ash tray stands. As you entered Merle's, you approached the front counter, which was part of the mezzanine, a raised viewing area with small tables and several chairs where spectators could watch the pool-playing on any of the tables. Behind the front counter was the door to Julian's office, and along the back wall of the mezzanine were lockers for private two-piece cue sticks and cigarette and soda machines. Opening off the mezzanine were the rest rooms and next to them was a store room that contained, besides what a business normally keeps in such a room, a heavy work table to which were bolted down a metal grinder at one end and at the other end a key duplicator. Both machines were unplugged and were hooded with dust covers.

Rudy was never bored here, he belonged in Merle's Billiards, this was his turf, his habitat. He was a better shooter than his uncle had been in the 1950s; and it was he, not his uncle, who fitted and glued new tips on cue sticks and who planned and ran the room's amateur straight pool tournaments. Moreover, he liked the players who hung out regularly at this room: loafers, hustlers, working class guys, two men on unemployment benefits, three men who were vacuum cleaner salesmen and who had time on their hands almost every other day, college boys, a score of teenagers who smoked cigarettes and bragged about all sorts of things, some older men who played good pool but not for money, and a number of retirees. Rudy spent much of his spare time in Merle's, playing pool in the evenings with these very fellows and, not infrequently, with players from rooms out of town.

Neither was Sonny Peggaluso a complexity. After high school, Sonny spent two years studying at Albany University. He married, dropped his studies, and found night work in a bakery on Fuller Road, a north-south arterial that ran from Central Avenue and then along part of the campus to Western Avenue. After two more years, after his wife had graduated and accepted a job teaching school out of state, Sonny admitted to himself and to her that education and a professional career, one wherein the occupant of the position is salaried and titled and spends personal time on his work, were not what he wanted. "Climbing the latter is not for everyone," he told her. He wanted a forty hour a week job.

They divorced. Sonny took civil service tests. He interviewed and was hired as a night custodian and porter at the University, the same school at which he had been a student. Each week, Sonny and the other custodians were assigned different University buildings to clean or for which they were given work orders to move furniture or equipment. At 6 PM when his shift commenced, Sonny clocked in at Central Security and signed for the keys of whatever building or garage or department he was assigned to for that week; and at 2:30, he turned in the same keys and clocked out. His work varied: he hosed down dumpsters, painted stair railings, replaced burned out fluorescent bulbs, and so on.

Two years after Sonny began janitoring at the University, Rudy graduated high school and began working at Merle's Billiards. A year went by, and he and Sonny began, in 1977, talking desultorily in afternoons before Sonny was due at work. They talked at the counter and in the mezzanine. Sonny told Rudy about the waste and sloppiness he witnessed almost daily at the University. Rudy informed him of who most recently had played pool and had won what from whom, who lived where, and who was looking for work.

Eventually –or rather, inevitably –the two confessed to each other that they wanted more money than what they were taking home each week, not outrageously more but reasonably more. Sonny wanted, for example, to buy a brand new car. Rudy would turn twenty-one in November of the following year, and he wanted, after that, to have enough money to rent his own apartment and someday, to visit some big mid-western cities like Chicago and Kansas City, where, Julian had once told him, men gambled big-time at pool and cards for $100 a game.

Then, late in January after the spring semester had begun and while he was emptying wastepaper baskets in the music building's auditorium, Sonny had a larcenous thought: he and Rudy should rob the music department of some of its marching band instruments and sell them! Over time, Sonny had filched work gloves from his own department and food from one of the cafeterias, but now it hit him that the University had on its loosely-guarded premises all sorts of re-sellable objects. This idea blossomed in his mind immediately. He knew a member of a local rock band who had told him once how expensive instruments were and how he would be willing, occasionally, to consider buying instruments or even passing them on to others for money. "Instruments in top condition," he had stressed.

Sonny scanned the auditorium, predatorily now. Along one wall were arrayed the wooden cabinets in which the department's instruments –the portable ones, like horns –were stored. He approached the cabinets and saw that they were all locked. Each was numbered and each had a label sticker, he saw, reflecting its contents: "clarinet," "cornet," "trumpet," etc. The keys to the cabinets were kept in a nearby keybox that was either screwed or nailed to the wall and whose door was fastened with a small lock. "That lock's no good, it could be jimmied open with a small-head screwdriver! Even so," Sonny considered, "those horns must be worth a lot."

He talked to Rudy about this "opportunity." Rudy listened quietly, biting his nails, liking the plan. Rudy was asking himself not whether the general idea and the attempt to get the instruments out of the music building were feasible –they were, of course –but whether he had the resolve and nerve to do his part to make Sonny's plan work. With this brief doubt, Rudy felt also an exhilaration. On the spot, he made up his mind and said to Sonny, "I can do this. At night, but while you're working somewhere else on campus."

"Why?"

"So you'll have an alibi." Their connivance expanded now all by itself. "And I'll need the key to the auditorium. I'll have to find a company that manufactures key duplicating machines and order one for the pool room. I can bolt it down on a corner of that wooden table in my work room –you know, like the grinder's bolted down. The next time you're put on the music building," he pointed at Sonny, "you'll have to shoot over here with the keys. I'll duplicate them, even the keys to the janitors' closets. We'll wait a few weeks, when you're on another building." He hesitated. "Then I'll go in." There it was, their first plan; they would make two others this fateful year.

"Where do you buy a key duplicator? In a hardware store?"

Rudy scrunched up his face, then shook his head 'no.' "Somethin' tells me we ought to get it from out of town." He looked at the floor, then back up at Sonny. "I wonder, does the public library have phone books for other cities? I'll have to find out." He took out a cigarette. "How're we gonna work the keys?"

Sonny was smiling: he had a man of action for a partner. "I'll know what building I'm gonna get for the coming week on the Friday before. So, I'll let you know Saturday or Sunday. I'll bring the keys to you Monday night on my lunch break.

You gotta be ready to copy 'em quick while I run over to Burger King."

"O.K." Rudy lit up. He took the cigarette from his lips with his second and third fingers. "First, I'll have to practice making keys. I'll need some, like, keys without any teeth on them. Monday I'll take some old books we got at home and go walk around the University and act like a college guy and scope everything out. And make sure I know where the music auditorium is." He was thinking. "You know, maybe the University has phone books for other cities." He thought some more. "Let's go over the whole business. Maybe there's a rift we gotta fill in." He jerked up his head. "Oh, yeah, I'll need one of your uniforms."

They looked at each other. This was the beginning of their alliance.

———

Edward Grosek

CHAPTER 8
THE THREE TRUMPETS

January 30 and February 24, 1978

Rudy's days off from Merle's Billiards were Sunday and Monday. On the Monday afternoon after he and Sonny had conceived and outlined their plunderous scheme, he drove to the University campus and proceeded to the main library.

The librarian at the reference desk smiled cheerfully as soon as she noticed him approaching. Smiling gratuitously did not come naturally to Rudy; he smiled less, he knew, than the average pool player. As he neared, he saw the birthmark on her face. Which prompted him to look straight into her eyes. He asked whether the library had telephone books with yellow pages for other cities and for cities outside New York State. He started to explain himself. "I have to order a small machine for where I work. I think I know what it's called. It's for grinding down –"

"Oh," she exclaimed and widened her eyes in recognition. "I bet you want the *Thomas Register!*"

She said this avidly, effortlessly, without needing to consider other references. This show of knowledge surprised Rudy. "What's the *Thomas Register?*"

She stood up. "Come, I'll show you." Obediently, he followed her into the reference stacks.

The *Thomas Register* was the equivalent, or rather the alphabetized amalgamation into more than a dozen thick volumes, of all the yellow pages in all the telephone books; and in a few minutes, Rudy was seated at a long table with the volume of the *Register* that included the Ks. Under "Keys," he found the entry for the AZ Partsmaster Corporation of Phoenix, Arizona, a company that manufactured key duplicator machines and that also sold key blanks. The duplicator came with its own dust cover and was, according to the measurements AZ Partsmaster gave for it in the entry, about the size of a shoe box.

"Nuts! I should'da known to bring some paper," he chided himself. He found a sheet in one of the wastepaper baskets; and onto it he copied the AZ Partsmaster Corporation's address and telephone number, the item number of the duplicating machine and its price, and some further information for ordering Schlage metal key blanks, including "Do Not Duplicate" blanks.

This *Thomas Register* was truly a "Gift of Fate" and a thing to be appreciated. "How the heck did the publisher get all this information together," Rudy wondered. He let himself relax on the wooden library chair and let his eyes ascend to the ceiling. He thought for a moment exactly how he would, as soon as he returned home, telephone AZ Partsmaster long distance and order a duplicator and a box of key blanks. He would state that he was the manager at Merle's "–Just 'Merle's,' I'll omit the 'Billiards'." He would say that he needed these supplies immediately, that he wanted them shipped express and sent to Merle's address in Albany, collect on delivery. This way, he hoped, he would receive them by Thursday or Friday.

He rubbed the length of his finger over his lips. This order would cost almost ninety dollars. He would have to pay the postman for it out of the cash register and leave the receipt in the bottom of the drawer. Julian would find it when he closed out at midnight and the next day he would want an explanation. Rudy began fabricating. "I'll say I want to start up a side business in keys." He thought, "I'll draw up a small sign saying 'Keys Made' and have it ready for when the duplicator comes in."

He looked back to the volume open in front of him. "This set of books must've cost a lot of money." He heard students working on homework at an adjacent table. He wanted a cigarette, and his thoughts returned to the reason for which he had come to the library. "Sonny'll like this." He closed the volume and replaced it on the reference shelf. On his way out of the area, he waved "Thank you" to the librarian, and in another minute, he was walking across the University's quadrangle.

He pushed open the door of the music building and trekked up and down the stairs and through the hallways. He was memorizing the shortest way from the building's main entrance to its auditorium.

—

It was Friday, February 24th, one month after they had made their formulations and begun to prepare themselves for this night. Sonny was cleaning the locker rooms in the main gymnasium, and Rudy was inside the music building, in the second floor hallway leading to the building's auditorium.

Rudy had on one of Sonny's custodian uniforms. He had removed Sonny's name label from the shirt by cutting out its stitching with one of his father's razor blades and had pulled up Sonny's oversize pants to his waist and belted them around him as tightly as he could. In his right hand was a push-broom he had found in a janitor's closet. In his left was a thirty-three gallon trash bag from home with five towels in it. And on his head was a wool pullover cap. The hallway was empty. Regardless, he showed indifference on his face. It was after 10 PM. "All right, so far." And so far, Rudy was feeling no agitation.

He reached the auditorium door; and without turning, without allowing himself to make any side-glance or hesitation that could jeopardize his impersonation of a real custodian, he took the key he had replicated, inserted it, and let himself into the dark chamber in which he did not belong. Excitement surged in his veins. He closed the door behind him.

Rudy stood, listening and letting his pupils adjust to the unlit room, which was a band practice hall with hardwood flooring but no seats or bleachers. There were windows; but outside, snow had begun to fall, and it was curtaining and dimming the light that ordinarily shown through the panes. A minute passed. He saw the wooden cabinets along the wall and then the metal keybox. From the trash bag he took a pliers and a screwdriver. He gripped the body of the lock with the pliers and forced the blade of the screwdriver into its keyhole. With one violent twist of his hand, he broke open the simple mechanism. He put the two tools and the broken lock in the trash bag.

Inside the box hung the keys, each on a small hook and each tagged with a number. Rudy moved to the cabinets and struck a match and checked the lettering on each door. Squinting, he found three that were labeled "Band Trumpet." From the keybox, then, he took the keys numbered for those doors. The match went dead, and he slipped it into his pants pocket.

The cabinets that Rudy opened were narrow and padded. Within each, a trumpet stood erect on its bell, beside which lay its mouthpiece. Rudy lifted out and quickly wrapped each instrument and its mouthpiece in a towel and laid each bundle in the trash bag. He closed and locked the cabinets and rehung each key on its hook in the box. He closed the box's door.

"O.K.," he whispered. He turned around in a full circle and made himself see and check each of the steps he had made for evidence he might be leaving. "What am I forgetting?" He looked out the windows and saw the snow, now falling more steadily.

"Nothing." He bent and picked up the trash bag and the push-broom. At the auditorium's door, he froze for several seconds and listened against it for voices or noises in the corridor. "Nothing," he repeated. He was surrounded within by silence –and without the door by the possibility of detection. He pulled the door open and stepped back into the hallway. At that point, something inside him trembled, for by recrossing that threshold, he had become a burglar de facto. He closed the door.

The trash bag was awkward, and Rudy held it crooked tightly in his left arm. With his right hand, he kept the broom's head pressed to the floor and walked, sweeping his way to the stairs. "So far, so good." He swept down the stairs to the main entrance, then through it and out onto the big open-air rectangle formed by the many University buildings.

Here there was snow on the wide walkways but no wind. Rudy ceased sweeping and pulled his wool cap down over his forehead. He walked as he thought a janitor would walk in the snow with a broom and a trash bag, trudging at an even tempo to his next clean-up job. He made his way along the building facades located on the south side of the quadrangle, keeping in the open so that the snow could fall upon him and, he hoped, camouflage him. There were some occasional students, but he and they passed each other without any greeting or even eye-contact.

"Looks good, looks good," he whispered to himself.

Rudy's mind was alert, yet uneasy, amused at how facilely the plan was succeeding, yet heedful that someone could somehow discern that he was in disguise or even recognize him from the pool room. Ahead he saw the southwest corner and the top of the stairs, the stairs leading down to the west lawn and afterward, the parking lots. He imagined himself telling Sonny tomorrow how he carried off the "goods" – literally –through the heart of the University itself, in plain sight of people who actually belonged there. He knew Sonny would appreciate his story.

His mind jumped to another thought. "After tonight, I'll probably never come back here again. Too bad. This is a beautiful place."

Thus, traversing the quadrangle under gently falling snow, Rudy's uniform became mottled. As he neared the southwest corner, a man came out of a doorway. This man was approximately twenty feet from Rudy; he had a trimmed beard and wore a striped necktie over a green dress shirt. He was in his forties and obviously not a student. When he caught sight of Rudy, he raised his eyebrows and lips happily and motioned with his arm, as if he wanted Rudy to come inside and maybe help carry something for him. He had spotted Rudy and, ironically, taken him for a genuine custodian.

"Oh –damn!" But Rudy did not stop. He held up the trash bag for the man to see and in a deep voice called out, "I'll be right there," as if he dutifully must first dispose of the bag. "I'll come right back up," he loudly repeated.

"No, it'll take only a minute," the man entreated politely. He walked out in the snow toward Rudy; and as he did, his eyes and lips lost their geniality. They congealed, as a man's features would tighten if he were being angered unduly by a subordinate.

But Rudy remembered seeing teachers in high school pretending to become incensed during class over their students' inattention and mistakes. This display of facial anger was no more than a device. The man extended his hand, and Rudy thought, "I might have to bash him with the trumpets."

"We had a spill." There was already a fine veneer of snow on the man's head. "I need you to clean it up. It'll take only –"

The words came spontaneously out of Rudy's mouth. "That's what's in the bag, Sir." He thrust the trash bag at the man. They heard the trumpets inside clank together softly. "Someone puked –up at the other end of the walk. That's what's in here! His puke and lots of toweling –and three brandy bottles." The man stepped back, as if he should not permit himself to be so close to the bag. "I don't dare take this inside or leave it out here!"

The ire and irritation on the man's face changed to hesitation. "Uhh… "

"I'll be right back." Rudy maneuvered around the man. He propped the push-broom against the cement column where the stairs began down and where the man could see it, as if its being left there were collateral for his return. There was snow on the steps, snow that Rudy could slip on. He descended, tramping flat-footed, holding the bag with one hand and gripping the cold hand rail with his other. "I'm almost there!" He gained the bottom. "Go, go!" Without looking back, he hurried in the snow, hunched over the trash bag and breathing now through his open mouth, across the grassy expanse into the falling whiteness, toward the parking lot and his car.

––––––

CHAPTER 9
THE FENCE

Saturday, February 25, 1978

Late the next morning, Sonny awoke and phoned Merle's Billiards. He spoke briefly with Rudy, then showered quickly, dressed, and drove to the pool room. As he entered, he saw Rudy at the counter. The door to Julian's office was closed. Rudy motioned with his head, and they went into the office. There on Julian's desk lay the trash bag containing the ill-gotten trumpets, unopened. As they carefully unrolled the toweling from around the instruments, Rudy recounted every scene and move of his adventure yesterday night, doing his best to leave out nothing. Sonny listened without interrupting.

"See, if I'd'a left the broken lock behind," and he held up the remnant of the lock, "they could figure how the box was popped open. Now they can't know." Rudy stepped to the doorway of the office. Here he could continue to speak to Sonny and also keep his eyes on the counter. He heard the chatter from the room's players. "I left everything the way I found it, except for the lock –and the trumpets." He turned his head to Sonny. "I'll go to Burger King later and throw the lock away with my garbage after I eat."

Sonny liked all that he had heard. He chuckled. "I was thinkin'… when they find out their trumpets are gone, they might guess at first that someone in the main orchestra borrowed them for a concert, or a rehearsal."

"The main orchestra?"

"Yeah. There's an orchestra, there's the band. And they got a violin group –or quartet." Then Sonny said, "I think you did everything right. Good work!"

That made Rudy feel good. "I wasn't shakin' most of the time, y'know, except when that guy tried to wave me inta his building."

Probably a professor. Most of 'em are snobs. They say 'vause' instead of vase. He forgot about the whole thing by now."

"Yeah, probably."

The three trumpets lay evenly spaced on the towels. Luckily, none of them had gotten scratched during Rudy's flight from the music building. They glinted in the overhead light –undoubtedly their players had the habit of polishing them frequently –and Sonny lifted each one and its mouthpiece and turned them over, curiously, trying to familiarize himself with them so he later could talk knowledgeably about them with his rock band friend.

One of the trumpets was a three-valve Vincent Bach, all brass except for its mouthpiece, which appeared to be made of silver. The other two were two inches longer than the Vincent Bach and had slightly larger bells. They were either made of brass or were gold-plated and were stamped "Giardinelli." They also had silver mouthpieces.

Sonny set the last piece down. "Looks like you chose good stuff, Rudy! Quality merchandise!"

"Thanks." He exhaled and smiled.

They looked down at the reposing instruments –their instruments –and spontaneously, the two burst into laughter.

This was more than relief, it was the sentiment of joy for what they had worked for and succeeded at.

They rewrapped the trumpets, swaddling them so that no metal from within the toweling was visible, then carried them in the trash bag across the mezzanine into Rudy's work room. Inside, they set them down on the bottom shelf of the big work table.

"Let me use the phone in your office. I'll call my friend. Maybe I can set up a meet for tonight –you know, after you're off the counter."

"Not for here."

"No, not here. You know where the best place is?"

"Where?"

"The parking lot at the Northway Mall. We'll have the trumpets in my trunk. There's lots of room. If he likes them, we'll switch 'em from my trunk to his."

"For cash on the barrelhead, right?" Rudy was grinning, he liked that phrase.

"Right. Cash only."

—

The three trumpets indeed were worth more than $500. Sonny's friend admitted this straightaway as he examined them and talked about them fluently, as if he knew a lot about musical instruments. But, he explained, he could not sell them for more than about half that amount. And, he pointed out, he would have to keep them hidden in his apartment until he could locate buyers he could show them to. "Buyers I know I can trust," he added blandly. Sonny's friend worked days in a novelty shop in the Mohawk Mall, the kind of shop that sold small pipes and black lights, plastic skeleton heads, comic books, posters of rock stars, fragrant candles, tee shirts, and other products like snake rings and bracelets with spikes. He had on a black pea coat with half-dollar buttons, and on the back of one of his wrists was a "home-made" tattoo of a crucifix. He was moving his head now, wobbling it side to side as if he were keeping rhythm to music he was hearing from somewhere.

Then he mustered on his face a look of ambivalence, as if he could buy these horns or not. "I can give you $120. That's all I have on me right now." He sighed and went up and down on the balls of his feet.

Rudy and Sonny looked at each other. They had not prepared themselves to negotiate an exact price with this middleman. "$120," they each thought. He would make a profit of about what they were getting –if and when he found a buyer. That did not seem unfair to them. They said, "O.K."

The fence took a small roll of money from his shirt pocket and without counting it, held it out. Sonny took it, and as he was counting it and as Rudy watched, their friend cast off his seeming preoccupation with himself and, as if by a burst of inner energy, became animated. He swiftly loaded the trumpets with the towels into his car and saying nothing further, waved and drove off.

Rudy and Sonny got back into the Cutlass and, smiling to each other, split up the $120.

On the way back to the pool room, they reminisced. "We made out O.K., you know. This job went perfectly because of the planning we put into it."

"Yeah, you're right. We thought out everything."

"All the details."

Sonny eased the Cutlass into Merle's parking lot.

"We should'da held out for a little more, you know."

"Yeah. That's what we didn't plan –how much we'd get from the fence. We should of… "

"Next time we'll… next time we'll work in a price ahead of time, you know?"

"Yeah."

–

The following week Sonny checked each article, one by one, in each issue of the *Albany Student Press*; but strangely, he saw nothing in the University's newspaper about the burgled trumpets! He told this to Rudy, then asked, "You know what this means, don't you?"

"It doesn't mean much." They were in Merle's Billiards at the counter, and half of the pool tables in the room were occupied.

"No. It means they didn't report the trumpets! They're just gonna swallow the loss."

"Better yet!" Rudy smiled wryly. "Case closed!"

"See, that's how they do things at the University!" Sonny said derisively.

———

Edward Grosek

CHAPTER 10
HOW CURTO'S POOL HALL WAS SET UP

Tuesday, June 20, 1978

Before this story proceeds further, let us see how the break-in at the Cue and Cushion was contrived. Let us see how it was Sonny Peggaluso who once again recognized the potentiality, how Rudy Merle took it on himself to execute the most stealthy of the illicit tasks, and how Mickey Gonzag became the third party to what was initially a joint depredation.

There were at this time in Albany five pool rooms. Scotty's was downtown on Pearl Street. The rest were on Central Avenue: Grant's Games and Fox's, which were hang-outs for high school boys; the Cue and Cushion, a pool hall with a front lunch counter that was habituated by construction workers, warehousemen, and two book-makers; and Merle's Billiards on upper Central Avenue. Each room drew a different clientele, though occasionally, and just for diversion, players from one establishment visited one of the others.

On June 18th, a Sunday, Sonny and two friends with whom he worked at the University played pool late in the evening at the Cue and Cushion. They were the last customers to leave; and as they paid their time at the counter and were departing, the thought came to Sonny that the houseman most probably did not take the receipts with him, that he bagged up the money from Saturday and Sunday –the two-day "take" from the lunch counter as well as from the pool tables –and hid it somewhere on the premises until Monday morning when the owner could bring it to the bank.

The more he mulled this idea over, the more he convinced himself that the weekend receipts stayed overnight in the pool hall, unprotected. He decided to ask Rudy what he thought about the likelihood of his supposition.

Rudy lived at home with his father, who worked mornings and afternoons as a mail handler in the Post Office's branch on Hudson Avenue. The next afternoon, one of Rudy's days off from work, Sonny stopped his Cutlass in front of the Merles' house, trotted to the porch and up the steps, and rang the doorbell. Rudy came out, and there on the porch, Sonny recounted to him what he had seen and inferred about the Cue and Cushion after shooting pool there last night.

Rudy's eyes widened, but then he replied, "Let's say you're right. Then Curto knows all this too. He has to. It figures –the houseman locks the cash in a desk or in a safe. Paul Curto's smart. You know, I heard he does more than own a pool hall. "

"So, you don't think… the money's where someone can get at it quickly?"

"Eh… I don't know." But the notion itself was already fantastic! Where could it lead? "I'll tell you what. I'll take a look at the place today. I'll see you tomorrow and tell you what I think."

Sonny left for work.

Rudy sauntered from the porch through the living room and into the kitchen. His father's cigarettes lay on the table; he took one of them from the pack, and sat down. Except for the purring from the refrigerator, the room was silent. Rudy lit up and reflected. He liked Sonny and he wanted to rob the Cue and Cushion with him. He remembered how he had felt goose pimples, trembling, and exhilaration as he left the music building that night in February. He wanted to prove to himself that he could project this next robbery in his mind and prepare himself and do what he has to do –just like those secret agents in the movies –when the time comes.

Rudy had wants. He wanted to run fifty balls someday in a straight pool game, he wanted an affair with a sexy girl, and he wanted to carry out another dangerous operation. Here it was! He rose, made a sandwich for himself, and began firming his mind. Anything is possible, he knew, if it is done correctly. That was how men landed on the moon and returned to earth – by seeing beforehand and scheduling every move and making no mistakes. "This should be easier than landing on the moon," Rudy reasoned to himself, "if I make a complete plan for it. First, I gotta check out the terrain."

Later in the afternoon, he drove down Central Avenue to the Cue and Cushion, asked for a table in the rear of the hall, and began practicing on it with a house cue. Paul Curto's tables were also 4 and ½ feet by 9 feet Brunswicks. The cloth on the table beds and rails was Simonis too, but grey instead of green. Over and over, Rudy lined up balls and played them into the lower corner pockets, pocketing each one and making the cue ball come off the cushion in good position for the next shot. Most pool shooters, when they practice, hit the balls about randomly. Rudy methodically practiced his stroke, his timing, and his position play.

As he stopped to pick balls from the ball return and replace them on the table and as he paused now and then to chalk his cue tip, Rudy looked beyond his immediate area to the end of the hall, to the back door. The door itself was a freight door; it was made of metal, or at least was metal-plated, and was a foot wider than a regular entrance. Three triangular hinges at the inside joined it to the wall, and so, it necessarily opened inwardly. Its handle, Rudy noticed, had no keyhole, and he assumed that this absence meant that the door was a fire exit, that it was locked only at the outside.

This rear outlet, however, was secured on the inside by two long two-inch by six-inch boards of lumber that extended horizontally across the door and that fit into clamps welded to the doorway's steel frame. When these wooded bars were in place, the back door –the postern of the Cue and Cushion –could not be opened from without. "You'd need a battering ram to get in by that door," Rudy reckoned.

He laid his cue stick down flat on the grey cloth and walked briskly into the men's room and looked at the ceiling. The ceiling in the Cue and Cushion's men's room was a "drop ceiling" similar to the ones in the rest rooms in his uncle's pool room. The white rectangular tiles that he saw above him constituted an artificial overhead held in place a foot or so beneath the actual ceiling by a grid of thin metal rails or laths. Such lowered ceilings were meant to save heat and conceal wiring. "Hmmm," thought Rudy.

He resumed his practice. From the front of the room, where the cash register and the coat rack and the cigarette machines were, he heard two men arguing emphatically back and forth about a boxing match, which neither, they both admitted after several minutes, had laid bets on. Rudy practiced for another ten minutes, then brought the balls back to the counter and paid for his time. He looked around. He recognized some of the men whom he saw there, shooting pool or talking idly or waiting for something to happen: Red Shannahan, Peppi, Gene Groat, Dino, Scotch, Johnny Ninas. Most of these fellows were construction workers –tall, beefy, unionized, brash-mouthed, and impudent. Shannahan looked at Rudy. There was visible disdain on his face, as if he thought Rudy too light-weight to be in the Cue and Cushion. Or was he trying to intimidate Rudy for some reason? Rudy was glad –very glad –that this crowd was hanging out here and not at his uncle's room.

The next morning, Tuesday, upon opening Merle's Billiards, Rudy took the step ladder from the store room and carried it into the women's rest room. He switched on the lights, and the softened illumination used in women's lavatories descended. Rudy spread apart the ladder. He mounted its steps, balanced himself, and removed the tile above him. He reached up and rapped at the framework that was holding the tiles, then grasped one of the girders and tried to shake it. The entire lattice was screwed tightly to the real ceiling, and Rudy saw that it was supporting the tiles, the fluorescent light fixtures, and the cables connecting the ballasts and the bulbs.

He tightened his lips in thought. He weighed about 130 pounds, and he decided to himself that the drop ceiling's gridwork should be able to hold his weight. He put away the ladder. At the front counter, on a sheet of paper, he began outlining the break-in, step by step.

–

Later that afternoon, Rudy pulled Sonny to one side of the mezzanine and told him, casually and softly, what he had seen at the Cue and Cushion and how he was sure he could hide himself safely inside the drop ceiling, then after midnight –the moment all pool rooms in Albany must close, slip down and unbar the back door to let Sonny in. "Do *you* think it'll work?" Rudy's face was serious and yet curious. His lips were apart, and Sonny could see his teeth. "It's more feasible than the job we talked about in May, no?"

"I *like* it!" Sonny's face flushed with excitement. He had accented the word "like" and was gritting his teeth into an avaricious smile.

"Let's go over to the counter," said Rudy, "and talk quietly."

At the front counter Sonny said, "It's risky, but that alone shouldn't stop us." He pointed at Rudy, and Rudy took out a cigarette. "Let's say Curto has to be aware his receipts are unguarded all night. Still, there's no way," he swept his hand across the space between himself and Rudy, "he can foresee being broken into like this, you know?" Sonny rubbed his jaw in thought, and Rudy lit the cigarette. "It'll work perfectly if we find the money quickly, say in ten minutes, and get out."

"We go in and out, clean."

Sonny snapped his fingers. "Right! Ten minutes! I'll bet it's kept near one of the cash registers! Or in that small desk behind the counter."

Rudy blew a stream of smoke to one side. He was imagining himself and Sonny inside the Cue and Cushion, moving in the dark, knowing just what to do. Sonny motored on, zealously. "I'll bet Curto takes five or six hundred bucks to the bank on Monday mornings! Maybe more." Another thought struck him. "You know, since we were both there in the last couple days, we oughta wait two or three weeks before we do this."

"I agree." Rudy exhaled more smoke, now through his teeth. "I'll bring the keys for our cigarette machines. They might fit Curto's machines. If they do, that means lots of coins and packs of cigarettes for us too." He tightened his lips and looked to one side. "I'll bring a suitcase I have at home."

"Good idea. I'll bring a crowbar in case I have to pry open the desk or –"

"Let's hope not," Rudy interrupted. "We don't want to damage any property." He pointed at Sonny and spoke as if he was enunciating policy. "We don't want Curto to see anything wrong until he goes for his money. See, if he sees that nothing but the money was touched, he'll suspect his regular customers or the houseman, not some marauder."

Sonny laughed at the last word. "You're right! We'll need flashlights and brand-new batteries for them." A dense look came over his face. "Maybe there's more we should think about. Like –we gotta wear all dark clothing! –What about Mickey? Let's bring him in too. He can search the cellar."

Rudy bridled at this last suggestion. He shook his head. "Jeeze, Sonny, no, not him."

Occasionally, Rudy, Sonny, and Mickey went to The Courtside, a bar in Albany with a sports décor, booths, and wall-mounted televisions that were turned up in volume when sporting events were being broadcast. Mickey always drank at least as many beers as either Sonny or Rudy and always had something amusing or ludicrous to tell them about his job at the Columbiana Hotel. Such as the time the night manager had unwarily left the door to the liquor closet ajar while he stepped to the front desk to answer the telephone. "That was my big chance," Mickey gloated to them. "I reached in the closet fast, and I grabbed a fat bottle by the neck and dropped it in the laundry cart and kept pushing it down the hall, right past the manager as if nothing happened."

Sonny and Rudy laughed. "There was a black wax seal over the cork, and the label was shaped like a shield and had French words on it. 'Dom Peri… g-nome,' something like that." They laughed again. "No one'll know it's missing till New Year's Eve. That's when they'll need it!"

"What did you do with it? D'you drink it all?"

"Oh. I sold it to the bartender at Romans for ten dollars."

Rudy remembered some things he himself had seen Mickey do, and get away with. Once, he had watched Mickey try to get his van out of a tight parking spot. Mickey went forward, turned the steering wheel all the way, then went back too hard; and Rudy heard the sound of glass crunching and falling to the pavement. Mickey's back bumper had crushed one of the headlamps of the car behind him. Mickey protruded his head from the van's window, peered about innocently, squeezed his van out of the parking spot, and drove away.

Another time, he and Mickey bought hot dogs from a street vendor near the public library, and Mickey –again by accident –brushed against a woman walking past them and smeared mustard on her sleeve.

"We need a third man to search the cellar."

"You know how sloppy he is! Sonny," Rudy pleaded, "we're not going on a lark, this is a business trip!"

"What if the money's in the cellar?"

"We'll find it –ourselves! Gonzag's as sharp as a pair of wooden scissors! He's the kind of guy who's not even amazed at his own dumb behavior!"

"Rudy, look," Sonny tilted his head, trying to show patience, "we agree the money's hidden and we have ten minutes to find it."

"What if he trips and falls down the cellar stairs?" Rudy's voice now was less plaintive and more adversarial. "Or turns on all the lights in the building somehow!"

Sonny held up his palm. "I'll answer that. Mickey has mishaps –"

"Mishaps?"

" –and he takes things. But he's *never* been caught. He's lucky." Sonny poked his index finger in the air at himself, then at Rudy. "I'm the manager. You're the technician. He's the

75

lucky guy. We can use him." A moment passed. "Besides, I owe him for the T.V."

Rudy looked at Sonny, his face incredulous, then hurt, then softened and resigned, as one's mien cascades from one feeling to another when he is forced to concede or compromise. He narrowed his eyes at Sonny's. "All right. O.K. But you're in charge of Gonzag."

"I'll watch Mickey."

"He's all yours."

And thus on that Tuesday, Rudy and Sonny hatched their second burglary. Less than two weeks later, they brought Mickey into it.

———

CHAPTER 11
CRIMINAL MINDS

Sunday, July 2, 1978

On the first Sunday in July and late in the afternoon, Sonny, Rudy, and Mickey drove to The Courtside for sandwiches and beer. They took one of the semicircular booths, Sonny on one end, Rudy inside, and Mickey –jubilant with the twenty-five dollars he had gotten earlier from Angela –opposite Sonny. The three were cronies, and they felt little inhibition when they drank here and talked with each other.

The pitcher of beer and mugs arrived. Mickey filled his mug with the carrot-colored liquid, then his mouth. He swallowed. "I love beer! It helps me drink!" He laughed at his joke. "Wait till I tell you guys what happened this week." His lips were wet and red with zest. "This great-looking woman was in the Columbiana. A broad! Real tight orange dress –I mean Florida orange!" He laughed. "And she came right up to me! I was carrying boxes from the UPS truck. They had in them the mini-tubes of shampoo, you know, that the maids put in the bathrooms. She looked at me with this smile –she had a big mouth –and said, 'Hello! What's your name?'"

"I said, 'Mickey.' You know what she said to me," and he pointed from Sonny to Rudy, looking for a guess. He took another gulp of his beer. "She said, 'Mickey, I wish I had thick black hair like yours.' Yeah! Then she said, 'Listen, I need to borrow ten dollars just until my brother gets here with the suitcases'."

"Lemme guess." Rudy was lighting up a cigarette. "Because of her orange dress, you gave her the money." He shook out the match.

"Well –yeah. She, like, sashayed up to me. I thought she was going to whisper to me. She said, 'Could you, please?' Those were her words." He raised his mug to his lips and drank. He noticed that Sonny was paying close attention to his story, and continued. "So, I took ten dollars from my wallet. Guess what she did next."

"Let me guess –she stuck out her hand and grasped the money with her fingers. And her fingers were all curved and her nails were pointed."

"That's right." Mickey beamed at Rudy. "How did you know? Anyhow, she smiled another big one and turned and flounced, you know, she, like, shifted from one hip to the other as she went into the barroom." He looked at Rudy and back to Sonny. "I thought she was going to use the phone in the bar. I brought the boxes to the room where the maids keep the towels and toiletries and came back out."

Rudy rolled his eyeballs upward and exhaled smoke.

"I looked in the bar. She was finishing a drink from a Martini glass. She set my ten dollar bill on the bar. She tapped it with her finger and nodded to the bartender. Right then she saw me."

Just then, their waitress returned, interrupting them with pleasantries and the sandwiches. She was one of the regular girls, the one who tried to talk British. She would say, "Quite so," instead of "You're right," and once referring to stormy weather, she remarked, "It's beastly outside." "These look scrumptious," she now commended, indicating the sandwiches. She raised her eyebrows and added, "Don't they just?!" As she leaned to set the tray of sandwich platters on mid-table, Mickey stretched awkwardly to take his platter and glance down her blouse. She righted herself. She said, as if promising, "I'll come back in a while to see 'ow it's going."

She turned away. Sonny picked up his sandwich and prompted Mickey, "Then –?"

"Oh, yeah. She didn't hesitate, she glided up to me. Her mouth opened, and I thought she was going to kiss me. She said, 'Wait for me,' in, like, a husky voice and went to the elevator and got in." Mickey was smiling as if he had achieved something with the woman.

"So, what? You followed her up to her room?"

Rudy had meant this remark sarcastically, but Mickey replied factually. "No. I didn't see her again."

Rudy's mouth dropped open. He turned his head to his left and made one of those short derisive laughs that a person makes with his breath.

Mickey said, "You meet all sorts of people in a hotel!" He took another swallow.

Sonny glanced at Rudy. He finished chewing what he had just bitten from his sandwich. He took some beer to clear his mouth, then turned to Mickey. "You ever been on Northbrick Street, Mickey?"

"Here we go. Here's the pitch," thought Rudy. He pinned his eyes on Mickey and kept them there.

Mickey laughed, his face artless, his eyes beer-drinking bright. "Yeah. I know where that is." He was expecting a funny follow-up remark.

"It's a dead-end street. All the houses there have big yards." Sonny leaned forward, his forearms on the edge of the table, his eyes fixed on Mickey's. "The last house on Northbrick

79

is owned by an old professor. He retired a few months ago from the University. He'd worked there for... twenty-eight years, someone said. He had a good reason for leaving the University early, before he was sixty-five."

"He got fired?"

Sonny shook his head. "A year ago, he won the New York State Lottery. That, and I heard he didn't fit in with the other professors."

"How much did he win?"

"I don't know. A lot."

"How do you know all this?"

"I work at the University, Mickey. We talk about things like this." With his tongue Sonny wet his lips. "After his first monthly checks came in, he bought himself a $13,000 Rolex watch. He showed it to everybody, and showed off the bill of sale too. After he got seven or eight more months of lottery checks, he retired. He finished the semester and retired. He's about sixty. So in two years, he goes on Social Security." He tilted his head to Mickey. "The Rolex is in the house someplace." Sonny paused for several beats. "Rudy and I think one of us can get inside the house during the night and find the watch and snatch it –and run through the woodsy area and get away."

"Woodsy area?"

"In back of the old man's yard is a dried-up creek. Then there're a couple hundred feet of trees that no one owns. After the trees is Oakwood Road."

"I know where that is. There's a Cumberland Farms store there."

"That's right –on the other side of Oakwood. We've been thinkin' about this since May." Sonny shifted forward. "A few weeks back, Rudy dropped me off at Sand Creek Road and Northbrick. I jogged up Northbrick, real close by the old man's house, and through his yard and the woods to Oakwood. Rudy drove up Wilkins Avenue to Oakwood and was in the Cumberland Farms parking lot to pick me up. From the house through the trees took me three minutes."

"Three minutes?"

"You can't run fast through the woods."

Rudy straightened himself in the booth and asked Mickey, "What do you think of our reconnaissance?" His voice sounded not hostile but estranged.

Mickey was surprised by all this. "Yeah –"

"We need a third man," said Sonny.

Sonny raised his eyebrows to Mickey, and it dawned on Mickey that they meant him! "What –"

"Here's what I saw when I was running by: all the windows had drapes or curtains over them, it looked like the back door was closed only with the screen door, and there was no dog."

"We think the windows are all draped so no one can see what's inside," said Rudy.

"You want me to go into the house –"

"No, I will," said Sonny. "You park your van on Sand Creek near Northbrick. You'll have a whistle. I'll come from Oakwood through the trees. Get it!? We think 2 o'clock in the morning will be the ideal time. If a cop car comes down Sand Creek and into Northbrick, it might mean someone spotted me and phoned the police. You blow hard once on the whistle and drive away. That's all you do." He continued his intent look at Mickey. "I'll hear it and tear back through the woods and get back to Rudy's car. But I don't think I'll be seen. I'll slice the screen door with a knife and unhook it and go in. The old man's a loner and he'll be asleep."

Mickey took another sip from his mug. "Suppose you get away with the Rolex. Who gets to keep it?"

Rudy rolled his head up to the ceiling, then down at Mickey. "No one *keeps* it! We sell it!"

"Mickey," said Sonny instructively, to make sure Mickey was understanding everything, "a Rolex is all gold and diamonds. We'll take it down to New York City. There're dozens of jewelry shops near Fifth and Sixth Avenue where we can sell it for cash money. If we're lucky, we can get $3,000 for it, that's a thousand apiece."

"Why don't we sell it for more than $3,000?"

Rudy's voice was low and contemptuous. "As soon as we show a New York jeweler a Rolex without owner's papers, he'll know it's stolen. He knows that he'll be taking a chance buying stolen goods!" He turned to Sonny. "Sonny, are you actually going to trust him to keep a look-out while you're in the guy's house prowling around?! He's not gonna pay attention! If a cop car comes down Sand Creek Road, he won't see it!"

This accusation –and its insinuation –was an unmistakable insult. It was a wound. Rudy was implying that Mickey was somehow unfit to get simple things done. Mickey disliked two things: being given orders and being faulted openly by friends with whom he worked or hung out. "I can do that. I can keep watch."

Sonny asked, "Mickey, have you ever done anything like this, broken into someone's house or store? Tell me."

"Not like this."

"It's risky."

Mickey wanted to be accepted, especially by Sonny, for this venture. Sonny and Rudy seemed to know things he did not. He swallowed. "O.K." He poked the tabletop with the tips of his fingers. "I'm in. I'll do my part. I'll pay attention and keep watch."

No one said anything. At the other end of The Courtside someone laughed loudly, and Rudy lit up another cigarette. Mickey had tried to sound earnest. He looked down at his sandwich. He took another bite from it.

"But we're gonna hold off on the old man's house for two or three weeks." Sonny stated this to Mickey as if he were postponing a routine business appointment. "We have something better lined up for next Sunday. It'll mean getting some simple equipment, but it'll be less risky."

"What is it?"

"You can come in with us, Mickey," he continued, "but you gotta have a good flashlight and new batteries for it, dark clothing on, and no beer on your breath."

"Yeah, but what is it?"

Rudy interjected. "We're not gonna tell you anything more except that it's a good deal. There's money in it. It's safe. Sonny'll tell you what you need to know just before we go in."

"Go in where?"

"If you don't have a flashlight and new batteries and dark clothing, you don't go. If you've been drinking, you don't go. When we get there, you're gonna do just what Sonny tells you to do, or else you don't get your share of the money. Those are the rules." Pushing Mickey like this, with force in his voice, felt good to Rudy. He looked at Mickey offensively, as if to say with his face, "Take it or leave it."

"What d'you say, Mickey?" asked Sonny, smiling to him encouragingly.

"You gotta agree to everything, or nothin' doin'!"

"O.K.," Mickey threw in, "I'm with you, all the way."

"Good man," said Sonny. He took the pitcher by its handle and re-filled each of the mugs, then lifted his own and said, "Here's to a night of crime, one week from today."

The three young men, more alike in their disregard of moral and social boundaries than distinguished from each other in their speech and styles of daily conduct, clinked mugs.

–

This, then, was the parley and cajoling and collusion that one week later led to the break-in at the pool hall. That next Sunday night, after 11 o'clock, Rudy entered the men's room of the Cue and Cushion, stood on the sink and pushed aside the ceiling tile, and pulled himself up and over the thin metal railings. He squirmed and squeezed his legs and his body into the overhead space and pressed himself against the wall. He slid the tile back in place and waited and prayed that the rails would hold him. After midnight, after hearing the blunt sounds of the houseman's shutting the front door and locking it, he undid the tile and twisted and lowered himself carefully out of his perch and onto the sink and then the floor.

Dressed in black, striding bravely past one after another of the pool tables, his eyes jumping from one black shadow to another, his breath shorter than normal, Rudy reached the back entrance of the Cue and Cushion.

–

The story, now entirely up to date, will proceed linearly to its climax and dénouement.

RUDY

CHAPTER 12
THE 9-BALL GAME

Sunday, July 16, 1978

Very recently, Rudy, from his position at the front counter, began secretly letching over a certain high school girl who came into Merle's Billiards to watch her boyfriend play 8-ball and rotation with his friends. This girl was sixteen years old. She had black hair that she parted in the middle and air-brushed so that it cascaded fashionably in a backward direction. Her eyebrows were also black, she had a small mouth with effusive pink lips, and her nostrils were wide but not large. When she was not smiling, for example while she was indolently watching a pool game, her face took on a slightly bewildered expression. But these attributes were not all that drew Rudy's eyes and pricked his imagination. This girl always seemed to appear at Merle's in eye-arresting, mind-arousing clothing: thin blouses or loosely weaved sweaters and snug jeans.

He noticed her in early June, after the spring semester was over and school had let out. He studied her out of the sides and tops of his eyes while she was sitting in the mezzanine or down among the pool tables, absorbing her into his memory and picturing to himself how maidenly and vulnerable she must be. Since she did not play pool and had no reason to approach the front counter, Rudy, on his part, had no excuse to converse with her. He was intrigued with this lovely figure, of whom he was, he was forced to admit, out of reach.

His furtive and prurient examinations of this schoolgirl were not going unobserved: someone among the regular pool-roomers had close reason to notice them.

But otherwise, Rudy was diligent and self-disciplined both at work in his uncle's pool room and in his father's house.

On Sunday mornings, he slept until whenever he awoke. Then he rose, showered and dressed, made breakfast, cleaned the kitchen, put the week's laundry in the washer, mowed the lawn, checked the oil and transmission fluid in his car and in his father's, and put the washed laundry in the dryer. On the way to Merle's, he filled his gas tank.

The sky on the third Sunday in July, that is, on the Sunday following the burglary, was overcast and slate-colored. The air had cooled, and rain seemed likely. By mid-afternoon, when Rudy arrived at Merle's Billiards, nine tables in the room were occupied. He parked his car in the lot in front of the building; and as he entered, he counted the number of persons inside playing pool. The room was making twenty-some dollars an hour! "Good," thought Rudy.

He passed the front counter and said 'Hi' to Lloyd. On Rudy's days off, on Sundays and Mondays, Lloyd, a retired man, opened Merle's at noon and ran the room until 5 o'clock, when Julian took over, as he did on the other days of the week.

Rudy unlocked the store room. In here he kept his cue stick, a twenty ounce Palmer he had bought from one of the old-timers who had quit playing altogether. Rudy lifted the two halves from a padded case and slowly, palpably joined and screwed them together, the butt end into the shaft. He gently tightened the joint and held the stick for a moment, enjoying its wooden heft and shape. He stood it on the floor and slowly twirled it with his left hand and with his right tapped the tip with a rasp, abrading the convex surface of the leather so that it could take chalk.

Several minutes later, with his stick and a tray of balls, Rudy was at one of the back tables, alone. He rolled the stick on the bed of the table, noting that it turned over "true," with no warp in the wood. He took the stick, curled the index finger of his left hand around the taper of the shaft, leaned onto the table, and stroked –not at a ball but into the air –to feel his stance, his balance, and coordination. He lit a cigarette and placed it so that it lay on the metal fender of the rail pointed innocuously outward. Then he put the sixteen balls on the table. The background sounds, the careless talk, the vague music over the public address system all faded. Rudy began pocketing balls, stroking through the cue ball, nursing it, driving it into one object ball after another and making it spin at clusters of other balls to push them apart. After a long while of this, he practiced bank shots, hitting object balls and making them rebound from a cushion into an opposite pocket.

He stood up from the table and smacked his lips. "Do I want another cigarette?" He chalked his cue tip and turned –to see Red Shannahan leaning with his backside against a pool table that was kitty-corner to his. Rudy shook off his concentration and looked about; there were more people in the room now and more tables with players on them.

Red had been watching him. To Red, practice and drilling oneself were a waste of time; to him, money made the player. He said, "You look like you know how to shoot pool, kid. What do you play?" Red was an Irish construction worker, his face had a fair complexion and some pockmarks but was stony and distrustful in aspect. He was better than six feet tall, his hair was full in back and in the front combed into a pompadour, and today he wore a loose sweater and light-brown khakis. Rudy estimated him to be forty years old.

"Straight pool, mostly."

Red looked at him without speaking. Rudy knew that this demurring was a pretense, a hustle, a tactic to make him think that Red was seeing his shortcomings and sizing him up. Rudy stood there, his eyes attached to Red's.

The big man pushed himself off the table. "I saw you at the Cue a couple weeks ago. Let's play 9-ball. I'll start you off at two dollars a game. Double on the run." Like poker, 9-ball must be played for money. Red looked at Rudy, his brows were raised but there was no scorn or slight on his face.

"We'll play on the head table. Pay after every game," Rudy replied succinctly.

"Let's go."

Red turned and went to the racks on the walls to look for a heavy, straight cue stick. Rudy gathered the balls and chalk into the plastic tray, took his cue stick, and walked quickly to the head table, table 15, the table most easily viewed by anyone in the mezzanine, and waited for Red to find a stick that felt right to him. When Red got to the table, Rudy racked the first nine balls, put the cue ball down, and called out to Lloyd, "Lloyd, put us on time here." People in the room looked in their direction.

Red took out a quarter. "Call it, kid. After this, winner breaks always."

He tossed the coin into the air above the table. Rudy called out, "Heads." The coin rose, arched, and dropped, bounced on the table, rolled onto its edge for a second and tottered, then tipped over on its back: heads. Rudy moved to the other end of the table. Red re-racked the balls into a tight diamond shape, and it was that moment that Rudy looked up and noticed one of the Brighelli brothers sitting in the mezzanine close to the railing, watching. "He must've come in with Shannahan from the Cue and Cushion," Rudy thought.

Most players will not break 9-ball racks with their two-piece cue sticks, but it was Rudy's opinion that well-crafted sticks like Palmers or Balabushkas, which were manufactured with hard maple wood, could not be damaged by either breaking forcefully or by playing three-cushion billiards. He leaned on the cloth, stroked twice and swung his stick into the cue ball. It sailed into the mosaic of balls, bursting them apart and in all directions. The 6-ball dropped into a corner pocket. Rudy made the 1-ball, then played safe and lit a cigarette. Red made two lucky shots, missed, and Rudy ran the last five balls.

Ostentatiously, Red laid two one-dollar bills on the table. "O.K., kid, now I'm all warmed up."

Julian entered the room and saw Rudy pick up the two bills. "Good," Julian thought. Pool room owners want money games, especially with players who make risky shots and get paid after every game. Money games beget more money games.

While Red racked the balls, Rudy chalked up and looked around. Wayne, Victor, Freddie, and Joey were in the mezzanine watching and grinning to him. He set the chalk back on the rail.

Red won the next game and the next two, which means he did most of the shooting. Red was a "stand-up" shooter, that is, he did not lean over the table as deeply as most players. And when he broke, he gripped the cue stick near the base of the butt and swung with power, as if he were shoving an iron pole into a coal furnace to break up the embers. Rudy noted all this and admitted to himself that Red, beside his indelicate physical strength, was a good competitor: he seemed indifferent to everyone watching and played long-shots with temerity.

After that third win, Red said loudly, "What d'you say, kid, I'm shootin' good and you're shootin' good. You want to move up in class –five dollars a game?"

Rudy paused, not to hesitate but to let Red think *he* was looking for a weakness in him. "All right, five dollars." He moved to the foot of the table to rack the balls. Sonny and Mickey were in the mezzanine now, had they come in together? Vinnie Vincenza was standing near them. Vinnie's mother and Sonny's mother were distant cousins.

As soon as Rudy had racked the balls, Red stroked once and smashed them apart. They scrambled about, but this time nothing went in. The cue ball and the 1-ball both lay against the bottom rail, and the 9-ball hung just outside the right side pocket. If Rudy pocketed the 1-ball, he would still be at the bottom rail and nowhere in position for the 2-ball. He decided to hit the 1-ball and drive it up-table where Red would have difficulty making it and getting position on the 2-ball. But the 1-ball, when he hit it, ran into another ball and stopped near the 9-ball, leaving Red an easy billiard, which he made.

Rudy paid Red, who said, "Kid, you just bought me my dinner at the Charcoal Pit!" He chuckled derisively and looked happily at Brighelli, as if he were defeating Merle's Billiards itself. Brighelli had been scanning the room, looking hard at each of the customers, one by one. He nodded and smirked to Red and folded his arms across his chest.

Rudy racked the balls. Red broke, made a ball and ran five more –and missed an easy shot. That miss seemed impossible, yet it happened, and Red cursed. Rudy moved to the table and ran the 7, 8, and 9 balls.

"You got lucky, kid! See what happens next game!" But Rudy won the next two games, which meant he was ahead six dollars after eight games.

"All right, kid, let's get to the serious money. You ever play for ten dollars a game?"

"No," Rudy lied.

"Is that too much for you?" Red lit a cigarette, a non-filter. Rudy nodded. "O.K., Red. Ten dollars a game. Double on the run. We put up the last game, twenty dollars each."

These words, Rudy's conditions, amused and heartened Red. They meant Rudy feared that if he won, Red might refuse to pay him, might "stiff" him in his own room. "He's afraid of me," thought Red. He smiled condescendingly. "If that's what you want, kid." He was glad that Rudy felt some trepidation. He thought to himself, "You're not gonna win anyway."

Rudy waved Julian to the table. Julian and Red nodded to each other; they had known one another since before 1963, when Julian opened Merle's Billiards. Rudy and Red handed over the stake money, twenty dollars each, which Julian conspicuously counted and tucked into his shirt pocket. Julian said nothing. He pulled a chair to about fifteen feet from table 15, sat, and folded his arms across his chest.

Red racked the balls. Rudy glanced around the room. Four fellows who looked like college students were no longer playing but were standing and watching him and Red. A motion in the mezzanine caught Rudy's attention. It was Vinnie, waving his fist high in the air, encouragingly. Rudy chalked his cue. He always had wanted to be a winner at pool. He remembered how he had read *The Hustler*[2] twice and then

---

2 Walter Tevis, *The Hustler*, New York: Dell, 1962.

Willie Mosconi's book[3]. He tried to recall some of the 9-ball games he had played over the past two years. "Well, here's your chance at that winning game," he exhorted himself. He set the chalk on the rail and checked his hands: they were steady and dry.

Rudy stroked twice and broke the balls, and the 9-ball bolted from the pack to the right corner pocket.

"That's bound to happen once in a while! That's all. You lucked out!" Red paid the ten dollars; and they looked at each other across the green felt, Red feeling pettishness and enmity for this skinny kid who should be paying him, and Rudy wondering why Red talked so much. "I can beat this guy," Rudy thought to himself.

In the next game, Rudy broke, made the 3-ball, then made the 1 and 2 balls and played a safe on the 4-ball. Red looked carefully at the purple object. He circled the table, studying the lie of the remaining balls; and Rudy saw what he was considering: banking the 4-ball up the length of the table and down into the lower left corner pocket. The shot was daring but makeable if executed perfectly. Rudy stepped well away from the table and watched Red position himself behind the cue ball, balancing his frame, his legs apart, his left hand spread on the taut green surface, and his head over the shaft of the stick. There was suspense now in the room, suspense and silence. Red stroked several times, concentrating, aiming, and shooting. The cue ball connected with the 4-ball, sending it speeding up to the short rail. It rebounded and proceeded down the long rail, decelerating, brushing it gently after passing the side pocket. At the mouth of the corner pocket, though, it bobbled without dropping in.

---

3 Willie Mosconi, *Winning Pocket Billiards*, New York: Crown Publishers, 1966.

Red's features lengthened in disbelief. Rudy's eyes shifted to the others watching the game: some smiled to him, others were blank-faced and noncommittal, as if they were complying with an unwritten pool hall law on good spectatorship. It was a heart-breaking miss, and Red thumped the base of his stick hard on the carpet.

Again it was Rudy's turn; and as he shot now, Mickey and the others in the mezzanine noticed how he held his cue stick in front of him like a lance and how the cue ball, as if it were Rudy's agent, hit faithfully with a nice porcelain sound whatever Rudy aimed it at and then spun quietly over the bright emerald cloth to within a foot or so of the next highest numbered ball. Mickey used to wonder why bowling pins did not break when struck by bowling balls. Now he asked himself the same question about pool balls.

Rudy won that game. Red opened his wallet and with his fingertips pinched out of it ten more dollars and flicked them onto the table. He squatted and began bringing up balls from the return. In back of him, in the mezzanine, Vinnie jumped up and down in glee. The pool room itself was carpeted, but the mezzanine had a hardwood finish; and both Red and Brighelli turned around at the sounds of Vinnie's sneakers thudding and squeaking on the flooring. Sonny quickly put his hands on Vinnie's shoulders to rein him in.

Red turned back to the table. "All right, kid," he showed his teeth, "don't let me get a shot, or you won't touch the cue ball again today!" His voice seemed strung and nasalized. He racked the balls quickly and threw the wooden triangle to the carpet.

Again, for a second, Rudy was glad that Red Shannahan and his buddies hung out elsewhere and not here in his uncle's room; then he saw –was sure he saw –the 1-ball settle on the spot ever so slightly, as if it was not frozen to the rest of the diamond. Rudy shifted the cue ball several inches to the left and broke with running English, not dead on the 1-ball as usual but a quarter-ball off center.

There was a crashing sound, the balls scurried apart, and the 1-ball back-skidded into the right side pocket. The rest came to a halt, well deployed: none were touching a rail nor were any lying up-table. Rudy re-chalked and surveyed the glittering spheres that lay there and the mute openings surrounding them, planning with his head and his hands how he would dispatch each of the former to the latter. Red stood by, hopeful and powerless. Rudy stretched over the table and pocketed the 2-ball, then the 3-ball.

"This is the winning game," he told himself. He was circling the table now as if it were his property, his face over the stick, his elbow and wrist movements in tempo. He pocketed the 4-ball and moved to where he knew the cue ball would stop. He chalked, stroked, and swung. The cue ball hurried to the 5-ball and met it with a dry click, the 5 rolled to the pocket and fell in, and the cue ball came off the rail and stopped near the 6, which he also played and made.

The cue ball, though, traveled too far, far enough so that Rudy could not play the 7-ball directly into the side pocket. He looked at the two balls: The 7 and the cue formed an almost perpendicular line to the rail. He leaned over the table, and he heard Red warn him, "Don't dog it, kid!"

With his words, Red had meant to taunt Rudy, to get him to make a wisecrack in response and break his concentration. But in that next instant, Rudy was glad that Red had said them, for they forced him to realize that he could bank this ball, but only if he was flawlessly careful. He straightened and examined the lay-up again –where and how hard he must hit the 7-ball. He leaned, sighted, stroked several times, and then with authority, as if he had done this many times before, shot. The cue ball hit the 7-ball and stopped. The 7 bounded softly off the long rail, then across the table and into the side pocket.

This felt good to Rudy. He chalked and then dexterously, gracefully shot the 8-ball into one corner pocket and the 9-ball into the other. The cue ball came off the short rail and rolled to the center of the table and reposed, alone, shining in all directions, the last combatant on the field.

The room was still. Rudy had won six games in a row, the last by running the table without missing a shot. He rested the butt end of his cue stick on the carpet and looked at Red, his lips lean and unwavering, his eyebrows lifted, his entire pose buoyant and incurious; he was waiting patiently for Red to pay him his twenty dollars and rack the balls again. No one dared speak. Vinnie was making zany faces at Red's back, and Sonny had his forearms about the boy's shoulders and neck, ready to restrain him.

Red stared for a moment at the empty table, the useless cue stick in his hand. He turned his head toward Brighelli and saw all the spectators in the mezzanine watching him. His eyes and cheeks darkened, not so much in hue as in temper, and his lineaments contracted, showing the shame and fury he was feeling for being beaten at his own game. There are sports like swimming and skating in which a man can lose graciously and courteously. 9-ball is not one of these. Red scowled, he cursed loudly and slammed his cue stick against the metal railing of the mezzanine. He turned in the direction of the front entrance, halted, looked back at Brighelli and jerked his head as if to say, "Let's get the hell out of here!" As he strode to the door, those in his path moved aside. He yanked open the door. Brighelli got out of his seat and followed.

"Yahoo!"

"Way to go, Rudy!" called Sonny.

"What a hustle!"

"You clobbered Big Red!" That was Vinnie's voice, Vinnie, the younger brother of the girl Rudy secretly adored. She – Veronica –was next to him and Sonny, and standing next to her was her boyfriend Donald Drake and his neighborhood pals. Vinnie began clapping, and the rest in the mezzanine joined in –Freddie, Victor, Veronica, Donald, Mickey –everyone, even several fellows who had been standing among the tables watching and whom Rudy did not know by name. This had never before happened. They were celebrating the victory of a young man –one of them, over an older man, an outsider. Flushed by this flattery, Rudy laughed in joy; he put his palm over his chest and bowed to his audience: very little in life compares to the glory felt by an individual after experiencing a physical triumph.

Julian stood. He took from his shirt pocket the forty dollars and splayed the bills on the table, letting them fan out on the green surface: the payoff. He could not have hoped for a better ending to Rudy and Red's game. Mickey saw the forty dollars and his eyes widened.

Rudy picked up the money, but before he could lean down to take the balls out of the return, Vinnie ran to the table. "I got 'em, Rudy." Vinnie filled the tray and followed Rudy to the front counter, where Rudy paid Red's half of the time.

Freddie and then Joey patted him on the back and grinned to him. And Donald and Veronica and two others said, "Nice game!"

"Thanks, guys!" Rudy replied his appreciation to all of them collectively, but his eyes lingered on Veronica, Veronica who was resplendent among them all and smiling to him as she might to an athlete who had just scored the winning point. With her two words, she had acknowledged him, and the next time she should come into Merle's Billiards, he could speak to her by name.

He turned and went to the store room. He unscrewed the Palmer and replaced it in its case, then went to the sink and washed the smudges of chalk off his hands and the sweat from his face. He was thinking that he might, with his share of the stolen money, the "profits," ask Julian whether he could buy into the business. "I have until October to –"

He heard a sound behind him and turned –it was Vinnie. "Vince, have you learned in school how to read yet? There's a sign on the door."

Vinnie was laughing with his eyes. Vinnie Vincenza had delicate teenage features: his lips were pink, his cheeks were roseate, and his eyebrows had lately darkened and thickened, signaling his recent ascent into puberty. He shuffled his feet. "You mean the sign that just says 'PRIVATE'? It doesn't say 'KEEP OUT,' you know."

Rudy was too contented, too gratified not to grin. "You like to play with words, don't you!"

"What are those?"

"Electric grinders," Rudy lied. "One of 'em stopped working. I grind the old glue off the ferrule before I glue on a new tip."

"I'm thinkin' of gettin' my own cue stick."

"I'll tell you what. If you're gonna buy a second-hand stick, make sure you show it to me before you pay for it."

"It's a deal! Hey, me and Alan are gonna play rotation with Mickey Gonzag. Alan's talkin' him into it now."

"Oh –" Rudy smiled knowingly to Vinnie. "You're not going to fleece poor Gonzag, are you?"

"Yeah. Last month Freddie and Victor took eighteen dollars off him playin' cutthroat." He tilted his head and grinned impishly. "See, life is a sport, Rudy, we're just bringin' Gonzag into the arena."

Which made Rudy laugh. "I'm going across the street for a hamburger, Vince." Rudy was two inches taller than Vinnie. He put his forearm across the boy's shoulders and guided him to the door. "You take Gonzag to the cleaners. Tell me what happened later."

Vinnie burst out laughing.

An hour and a half later, Vinnie pulled Rudy aside and showed him a wallet flush with one dollar bills. "Me and Alan," he said in an undertone, "took sixteen dollars off Gonzag." His eyes were glowing with pride. "So that's about seven dollars each after payin' time." He snapped his wallet shut. "You know, rotation's a good money game for three guys if two of 'em are workin' the third guy. Alan figured it out. We let Gonzag make balls, but as long as he didn't make more than thirty-six points, he couldn't win. Either I got the high score, or Alan got it. Then we split everything after Gonzag quit. Get it?! See how useful arithmetic is!"

"You're smarter than I thought."

"Of course!" Vinnie took out a cigarette, lit it, and pulled deeply on it. "And get this. At the counter, Gonzag wanted us to loan him back some of the money! Alan told him we're gonna need the money for clothes for school in September. But then Gonzag was able to borrow five dollars from Wayne."

They laughed. "Gonzag gets paid on Thursdays. Is he out of money already?" This caused Rudy to remember something. "Hey, you owe the house eight or ten dollars, Vince!"

"O.K. Suppose I pay three dollars tonight… and you give me a ride home about 9:30. I'll pay just before we leave, how's that? O.K.?" This proposed deal suddenly caused Vinnie to perceive how next Saturday he could wipe clean his tab at Merle's Billiards.

"Hey, you sure got nerve!"

"That's exactly what you learn in a pool room, Rudolph, my man!"

–

That night Rudy retired, thinking about Veronica. He lay there under a light sheet, imagining himself with her in this very room. That his infatuation for her was not love and that his fantasies of her would be impossible to put into effect did not matter to him. He desired to explore her. "Just once with her," he wished, "for about fifteen minutes."

———

CHAPTER 13
MICKEY, MONEY, AND SONNY

Monday through Thursday, July 17 to 20, 1978

Mickey's loss of the sixteen dollars concerned him for a while. "It was just bad luck," he later rationalized. The next night at work at the Columbiana Hotel, he learned from the other porter on his shift, Arnie, that Montgomery Wards was having a sale that week on car tires. Mickey had wanted new tires for his van since last February when it lost traction and slued over an icy strip on his own street. Only by tapping his foot on the brake pedal did Mickey stop the van. He decided to buy the tires, and the next afternoon, he drove to Montgomery Wards and parked near the overhead garage door of the service entrance.

The attendant at the service desk wore a white work shirt with a label on it stating "Wards Auto." The blue necktie around his collar was knotted loosely, and the short end of the tie was tucked into his shirt between two of the buttons. He scribbled the information for Mickey's van on a work order, then stuck out his fingers and deignfully wiggled them at Mickey for his keys. He lowered his eyelids and told Mickey that the fitter will need an hour to replace the tires and balance the wheels. "So come back in an hour," he curtly iterated and pointed to the line at the bottom of the work order where the customer was supposed to sign his name.

Here was a salesman who was earning a living from tire sales and treating his customers with overbearing dictates and gestures. Mickey looked at him askance. He scrawled his signature, turned without replying, and went through the car parts section and into the Mohawk Mall's main concourse. To bide his time, he sauntered casually about the concourse, and near its end, near the Boston Store, he bought a hot dog at a food wagon and a little later an Orange Julius at another concession stand. Nearby was an empty bench. He sat down, leaned forward, and sipped his Orange Julius, playing with the straw, idly observing other shoppers. Women trickled by, most of them carrying either nothing or only a small shopping bag. Ordinarily, Mickey liked to watch girls and women, but these were not the slender specimens one sees in the mall in the evenings, dressed tightly and colorfully. These daytime types were older and heavier, dull in appearance, the kind one had to assume had married and now preferred housework over men.

Mickey was amused and at the same time puzzled by women who let themselves become fat-waisted. "It's not just the food they put away every day," he mused, "it's all that cleaning and cooking too and going to church on Sundays. You'd think they'd know better." He chortled to himself. "They're only gonna look worse next year!"

His thoughts changed course. "Four new tires. I ought to fill up the tank and drive up... to Lake George, maybe." He wanted to drive up to Lake George with a girl. "But who?" He thought of several girls. "Too bad you can't just ask any girl you see. There's a good idea! That's the way it should be!"

He eventually finished his drink and stood up. On his way back to Montgomery Wards and the service department, he passed Waldenbooks. Through the open doorway and the front windows he saw the store's books on shelves and display tables; and those books triggered a memory from his high school days, when he had to carry around and read books for his classes. He smirked to himself. "Not any more. I don't need books where I work. A book's place is on the shelf."

Mickey's eccentric thoughts and notions drifted like this. Farther along and now inside the Montgomery Wards store, he caught sight of a sign in the bedding and bath section, telling him that king-size Sealy mattresses were on sale today for fifty-nine dollars each "while they last." He remembered seeing once a van similar to his whose interior had been remodeled to look like a bedroom. It had black lights, a small wooden pirate's chest bolted against one of the inner walls, and overhead speakers. The walls had been repainted wine-red, and there was depicted on the driver's side wall a fake window with curtains. On the bed of the van lay a king-size mattress, and covering it was a plump, gaudy quilt. The guy who owned the van told Mickey that he had done the installation work himself and that it had been easy. In that instant, Mickey wished he could own a van just like that one.

"Yes!" he now thought.

The clerk in the bedding section was young, tawny-skinned and shapely. She grinned at Mickey with rubbery lips and shark-white teeth. Her blouse was open slightly, and he could see the mounds of her breasts. Mickey liked her immediately. He told her that his van was getting new Wards tires and that he wanted a large mattress for it. She replied, accenting her words with flowery, circular hand motions, that the mattresses on sale today were perfect for vans *and* mobile homes.

She inched closer to him, looked deeply into his eyes, and told him that she would throw in a fitted mattress cover and two pillows with the mattress —no extra charge —and that she could help carry the four items to his van. And then she advised Mickey, with a confidential nod, to buy a heavy, colorful blanket, "Not yet," she flourished her index finger horizontally in front of him, "but, say November, t'give the interior o'your van a snug atmosphere. Know what I'm sayin'? Like the sleep-cabins you see in a yacht. Just picture it!"

She stopped talking. How could Mickey not smile? He looked down her blouse, and she threw back her head and laughed. She took his arm and brought him to the sales counter, where he paid for the mattress with his charge card. She pushed the pillows and the sheet into a large bag that she set on top of the mattress; and she and Mickey carried all of the above to the service department and to his van, which the fitter had just finished re-tiring. Mickey opened the back doors of the van, and they set the mattress onto the vehicle's bed. Again she grinned at him. She touched his chest with her fingertips. "I know I'll see *you* around," she said slyly. He watched her as she moved, swinging away from him.

He looked at the new tires. They were so black they glistened as if they were wet, and he smiled proprietarily at them. He paid for the tires with the charge card and drove to work.

At the hotel, Mickey bragged to Arnie about his purchases. Arnie looked back with a vacuous smile –he was easily awed with oddish stories –and Mickey summed up his afternoon with, "I got lucky today!"

On that day, Mickey possessed more worldly goods than ever before, he had no troubles with anyone he worked with, and he had memories of intimacies with a half dozen good-looking girls. That was the day his life attained its summit.

–

At the kitchen table the next day, Wednesday, Mickey dawdled with his breakfast cereal, imagining to himself what his apartment might look like, the apartment he was now determined to rent straight after he gets his share of the money. He heard the mailman on the front porch and got up from the table. He brought in the mail and looked dully at a white envelope and was about to toss it out when he recognized the name on the return address. "Oh, yeah –that's from my insurance company." The envelope was from the Prussian Mutual Insurance Company and contained the van's insurance card for 1978-1979 plus an invoice for $721. The invoice stated that the premium was due and receivable in full by August 15, 1978 or in installments beginning on or before the same date. Mickey's face fell.

Later at work, this bill for $721 began to weigh on his mind. He wanted to pay it off all at once, in full. Before going to work the next afternoon, he drove to Merle's Billiards and parked in the front parking lot. The frontage of Merle's building consisted of wide glass window panels, so that the players inside had plenty of light during the day and people passing by could see into the room. Through the windows Mickey spotted Sonny and said, "Oh, good." He moved to the front door, pushed it open and strode past Rudy, who was at the counter talking with a customer.

The two friends with whom Sonny worked and hung out were playing straight pool on one of the tables in mid-room. They were playing 100 points for time and five dollars, and Sonny and two of the retired men who often played three-cushion billiards were nearby, seated on chairs, watching and kibitzing. Mickey stepped down from the mezzanine to the carpet and went as inconspicuously as he could to Sonny's side. He leaned and whispered, "Let's go outside. I want to show you what I got in the mail."

Sonny assumed that Mickey did not want to disturb the pool game by talking near the table, so he got up and followed him. They exited to the parking lot and to the side of Mickey's van. Mickey held out the insurance papers and said, "My insurance is due next month. I got this letter yesterday."

Sonny took the papers and scanned his eyes over the columns of coverages and corresponding figures. He noted the line at the bottom. "Hey, your premium is higher than mine!" He smiled.

"Yeah, it's $721! Collision and liability and roadside service. Look, Sonny. What I'm sayin' is, I need some of the money to cover it." Sonny immediately and coldly shook his head 'no.' "Come on, Sonny, I don't make as much as you do."

"Mickey," Sonny lowered his voice but spoke steadily, "we have an agreement. We don't touch the money until mid-October. We made the agreement for our own protection."

Mickey had not formed a plan for persuading Sonny to let him have some of the money they had locked away; and his arguments now emerged, one after the other, as desultory pleas. "But I need money for gas and lunches and other stuff. Why do you think... I can't go anywhere without money!"

Sonny looked at him critically. In a polite, even manner he asked, "Well, why not get a part-time job at Burger King?"

"Forget that!" He waved his hand through the air. "One job's enough."

"What about your income tax refund?"

"Refund? Oh, I didn't fill out the tax forms this year."

"You didn't file –?"

"I'll have to take the bus to work if I can't drive!" Mickey's hands were at his sides. He emphasized the last four words by bending forward suddenly at the waist.

"We're gonna stick to our agreement, Mickey."

"I have other bills too." Mickey's face was upturned, not defiant but stolid and imploring. "Rent! I have to pay my father rent and I have a bill at Montgomery Wards. I need about a $1,000, or I'll have no money for the next month!" He puckered the skin between his brows. "They all came due at once. It's just bad luck, Sonny."

This puckering endeavor was wasted on Sonny. To him, Mickey's occasions of bad fortune and specious excuses were only proof of his long-term improvidence. Again he shook his head 'no.'

Then Mickey tried a different argument, or rather, another angle. "There was nothing about the break-in on the news, you know. And there're no rumors about it in the pool room either." He laughed and his countenance brightened. "Curto probably still doesn't know –"

"Stop it, Mickey. Curto has to know! I talked about this with Rudy. Joe Brighelli was here, lookin' the place over Sunday while Rudy was shootin' Shannahan. Remember?"

"Wait, which one was Brighelli?"

"The older guy sittin' in the mezzanine! He doesn't play play pool, he just hangs out at Curto's place. What if Brighelli was here looking for guys who were flashing too much money around? What if," his voice fell in volume, "some of that hund'ert and twenty thousand was his? His brothers are construction workers and one of 'em is a shop steward in the union."

"Yeah, so?"

"Mickey, these are rough guys." Sonny shifted his gaze to inside the large glass windows. Six tables were in play. He saw Rudy watching him and Mickey, and he thought, "Maybe Rudy was right, maybe you just can't reason with Gonzag." He said, "The answer is 'no,' Mickey. Don't beg me anymore."

Mickey turned away and stepped, then turned back. (Sonny had observed a professor do this same move to another professor with whom he was disagreeing, and Sonny wondered at the time whether it was a frustration release or just theatrics.) "Come on."

"The poorer everyone thinks we are, the less we'll attract suspicion. In fact, Mickey," he decelerated his words, "you ought to get a reputation as being stone-broke."

"What –no! Come on, don't let me down. O.K.?"

It was then, hearing that last pitiful two-syllable entreaty, that Sonny realized that his friend –and Mickey was his friend –will never have enough money. The lineaments of Sonny's face came together into an overbearing look of refusal. "Mickey... no." He rooted himself on the spot, stiffening his leg muscles and staring at Mickey, demonstrating his readiness to reject whatever rationale Mickey had left.

Mickey put on a hurt expression, as he did at times to his father, but that was always a futile effort and he knew it. He turned and opened the door of his van and without saying 'good-bye,' he climbed in. He inserted the key, twisted it to the right, and wished that Sonny were more agreeable. "Tsk," he clicked out the sound and exhaled: he was leaving with the same problem with which he had arrived. Backing out of the parking lot, he began to think of other guys he knew whom he might be able to borrow from.

Sonny turned away. He heard Mickey's van leave the parking lot; and as he entered Merle's and passed the counter, he beckoned to Rudy to follow him. Rudy came out from behind the counter, and Sonny and he walked in tandem to the table where Sonny's friends were playing. As Sonny neared, he threw back his shoulders, hardened his face, and swept his eyes to everyone in the vicinity, calling for their attention. Someone asked, "What happened?"

Sonny's voice was crisp and masculine, like a policeman's. "Gonzag's broke. His van insurance is due. He can't pay it."

That was all he said, and that was enough. His two friends shrugged and went back to their play. One of the retirees said, "Huh!" and Rudy walked back to the front counter. No one seemed to want to know anything more about Mickey Gonzag's predicament.

A while later, Sonny was slouching in his chair, watching the tail end of his friends' game; and it occurred to him that he had no urgent need on which to spend his share of all that money, no gift that he yearned to buy for himself. "Some new clothes, maybe. I'll just… squirrel it away… maybe in a safe deposit box in a bank," he thought. He trusted that Rudy would do something similar. "Mickey," he scratched his chin, "will likely spend it on something noticeable, like a Cadillac." He breathed out through his teeth. He should talk with Rudy.

The pool game ended. Sonny's friends went into the men's room to wash the chalk off their hands. Sonny again motioned with his head to Rudy, and they convened near the entrance. "Gonzag has bills he can't pay. He asked me for some of the money. I turned him down."

"Good." Rudy uttered the word contemptuously. He lowered his voice and as he spoke, he angered his tone. "Think about it! What's he gonna do in October with forty grand? He's foolish enough to go to all the bars and whip a bankroll out and buy everyone drinks!" He rotated his head to check the mezzanine, then jerked it back to Sonny. "He'll throw it around like birdseed!"

This affirmed Sonny's worries. "Yeah... you're right." He bit one of his finger knuckles.

"Yeah, he needs money. But that's got nothin' to do with us!"

Sonny looked up, and their eyes met. He knew what they had to do, and he said to Rudy, "If he brings it up one more time, we'll have to get serious with him."

Rudy nodded and showed his teeth.

Sonny's two friends came out of the men's room. It was time for the three to leave for work. "Well, I got something to think about tonight," he said to Rudy.

———

CHAPTER 14
VICTIMLESS CRIMES

Saturday, July 22, 1978

Pocket billiards, largely because of the equipment utilized in playing the various games – a cushioned table with gaping orifices, balls, wooden sticks –is an automatic allurement to boys and men. A pool room, therefore, is a natural environment for males; and those who hang out in these lairs learn by emulation to disregard the law, to hustle, talk unselfconsciously, smoke, and enter into masculine friendships.

The next Saturday afternoon, that is, the afternoon of July 22, Merle's Billiards again was busy; and Rudy had stationed himself behind the front counter on a high-backed stool, ready for his customers. On his right were the time clock and the cash register, and on his side of the counter –the backside of the counter –were shelves for the plastic trays of balls. On the wall was a chart showing the rates charged for table play, which in 1978 were $1.60 per hour per player.

On that day there were, beside the regular customers, four men who drove delivery vans for United Parcel Service and who came in once a month, some older men gathered round the five foot by ten foot billiard table, and a man with his two children on a table near the windows. Rudy knew that this would be another lucrative day for Julian.

On one of the tables along the back wall were two men playing straight pool. They were experienced players in their fifties who ran twenty and thirty balls each game, and Vinnie Vincenza spent an hour sitting near their table, watching and studying their manner of play, hoping to acquire for himself some of their skills. At 3 o'clock they quit and came to the front counter to pay. A minute later, Vinnie ambled to the counter, put his arms across it, and, hugging it like this, asked Rudy, "How 'bout a cigarette?" He wore a giddy smile and looked as if he wanted to tease or play a joke on someone.

Rudy took his pack of cigarettes from under the counter and handed it to Vinnie. "Your tab is back up to ten dollars, Vince."

Vinnie held the cigarette between his lips. "That's one of two –two matters," and he held up two fingers "–we should discuss immediately. You can trust me, Rudy. What'll it take to cancel my house tab?"

"It'll take ten dollars, Vince." Rudy restrained himself from chuckling.

"Let's consider an alternative."

"An alternative to ten dollars cash?" Rudy lowered his voice. "Ask Douglass for the money, Vince."

This took Vinnie aback. He held the match in front of the cigarette. "How do you know about Douglass?"

"I saw him drop you off here a couple times. A lot of people know about Douglass, anyway. Except maybe Donald."

Vinnie sobered himself and lit the cigarette. "Douglass doesn't pay." He put out the match. "He takes you places. Like to the drive-in an' t' wrestling."

"You can trust me, Vince," Rudy mocked.

"Well, he'll buy you a present if you stay overnight in his apartment. I got the soundtrack album to *Grease*. That's all."

"No doubt." Rudy was grinning.

Two men entered, and Vinnie stepped away from the counter. One of the men asked for table 20. Rudy handed to him a tray of balls, and as the two approached the table, he clocked them in and placed the time card in the wall slot marked '20.' The old men came off the billiard table, Rudy charged them, and they paid and went to sit in the mezzanine and talk about their game.

Rudy and Vinnie returned to their positions over the top of the counter, face close to face as if in connivance. "Tell me about the album." Rudy meant, "Tell me what happened the night you stayed at Douglass' apartment."

"Well… "

"You can tell me."

"O.K." Vinnie exhaled smoke. It drifted away and frayed apart. "See, in May, just after I'd turned fifteen, Douglass took me and Alan to ride the go-carts over in Rensselaer. It was a Friday. I was already tired from mowin' our lawn. At the go-carts, he told me he'd get me the album for my birthday if I stayed the night. I never stayed over all night at a guy's place. So I phoned my mom and said I was sleepin' over at Alan's. An' Alan was right there, and she could hear his voice. So she figured it was on the up and up."

"How old's this Douglass?"

"Forty something. Mid-forties. He smiles a lot, but it's, like, a practiced smile. He blow-dries his hair. His head bobbles sometimes when he talks." Vinnie continued. "Douglass bought us pizza, then dropped off Alan. We drove to Tower Records, picked up my album. And we went to his apartment."

Rudy leaned an inch closer and said softly, "O.K. You *can't* hold back any of the details now, Vince." He stressed the word 'can't.'

Vinnie had planned to offer Rudy something else –other information –in return for quashing his tab at Merle's Billiards. But as soon as he heard this unexpected insistence, he changed his tactics. "Tear up my tab, and I'll tell you everything!"

Rudy turned his head to the left and looked at Vinnie askew. "Is your story worth ten dollars?"

"If what I tell you isn't worth a sawbuck, don't tear it up." Then he said, "You call it, Rudy."

"O.K."

Vinnie helped himself to another of Rudy's cigarettes. "Douglass keeps his girl magazines under the cushions of his couch. He has stuff like *Club* and *Hustler*. They're full of second-rate broads with their tongues stickin' out. Anyhow, he sat me in the middle of the couch and pulled out some *Hustlers* and told me to 'check out the babes' while he got us a drink."

He blew out more smoke. "So, I flipped over the pages, one low-quality woman after another." He frowned. "Anyhow, I heard him in the kitchen. He was getting 7-Up and ice from the refrigerator. He came back with these and glasses and a big bottle of Seagram's Seven. He put them on his coffee table and sat on my right side. He's an average guy, bigger than me though. Pretty strong. He mixed two glasses. He took a sip from his glass and, I remember, he put it back on the coffee table. He told me to sit up. He picked up the glass he'd made for me and shook it to make the ice cube clink. He began pourin' it into my mouth."

"What –literally?" Rudy showed both incredulity and humorous amusement on his face.

"Yeah. He put the glass to my lips and tipped it toward me so I had to drink or let the Seven and 7 spill on my shirt. And when he got some in my mouth, he tickled me and poked my cheeks to make me swallow. Then he mixed another glass. The apartment was silent, as if it were empty. I was getting excited. He tasted the glass, I guess to make sure he'd made it stronger. He put his arm around my head and gave it to me. I listened to it go down, gulp after gulp."

Rudy was listening, his mouth open. Somehow he had missed out on this kind of carousing. He himself preferred beer to mixed drinks, but it struck him now that liquor was probably a better choice for inebriating boys.

"I remember the third glass he made for me. It was mostly Seagram's whiskey. He took my right arm and reclined on it so that his body, you know, was pinning it to the couch. He got my left hand by stretching his left arm behind my back and gripping my wrist. He smiled to me nicely, as if I were, maybe, a bug he'd just snagged in his butterfly net. Then with his other hand he fed the third glass evenly into my mouth. I tingled and quivered."

"Jeeze!" Rudy felt prickling on his scalp. He was amazed; he had had no inkling that Vinnie could have endured such a fiendish ordeal.

"My jaws were slack. My head was just limp against the couch. He whispered to me, 'Swallow. Swallow.' He let the Seagram's spill steadily over my tongue and watched it drain into my throat. I felt it trickling down to my stomach. I saw the glass emptying. I saw his giant yellow eyes over the glass, urging me on. I think he wanted me to know he had planned this drinking bout and whatever else he was gonna do."

At this point, Rudy was awestruck, his mind arrested and oblivious to the sounds around him.

"He shook the last drops into my mouth and rubbed the edge of the glass over my lips. He set it back on the coffee table. Then he massaged my cheeks to make sure I'd swallowed it all. He kept eyein' me. He played his fingers around my tongue and gums to see how I might react. All I did was smile. I don't know why. But I knew I was exactly where he wanted me."

"Wow!" Rudy lit a cigarette and inhaled deeply, bracing for what would come next in Vinnie's story.

"After this, I either dropped off to sleep or blacked out. Whooo! The next thing I knew, it was the next day, in the morning. I'd slept like a corpse for, like, almost ten hours. I woke up stiff. I was foggy-headed. He made breakfast for me –scrambled eggs, rye bread, coffee, and Tylenols. I asked him what had happened."

The man with the children came to the counter to pay. Rudy clocked them out but charged him for only one player. The man made some courteous compliments about the room and promised to bring the kids back soon. They left.

Vinnie took another cigarette. His eyelids were slightly lowered. "I asked him, 'What happened?' You know what he said?" Vinnie skewed his head to Rudy. "He said, 'I did only one thing to you, something new, but I won't tell you what.' He said, 'I want to make you frustrated every time you try to guess what it was'." He lit the cigarette.

"Vince, when you go to confession, do you tell the priest stuff like that?"

"Are you crazy?!" Vinnie threw back a look as if Rudy were not realizing the foolishness of his own question. "I don't tell the priest *anything* important!" He added, "I don't tell my mother anything either."

"Well, you got the record album anyway. Would you ever do it again?"

Vinnie thought for a moment and drew in his lips. "I might, one more time. But not with Douglass. A repeat wouldn't work. There has to be an unknown outcome. Yeah, with a different guy. But I probably won't get the right chance. You have to let stuff like this happen to you when you're about my age." Then Vinnie pulled on the cigarette and said, "You know something, Rudy, I'm glad that I – "

But just then the United Parcel Service drivers came to the counter to pay their time. They too made nice compliments and left.

Vinnie bellied back up to the counter and thrust his face at Rudy. "O.K., that was worth ten dollars, man, and you know it!"

Rudy raised his eyebrows to Vinnie. He pressed the 'NO SALE' key, and the cash register opened. He took Vinnie's tab card from beneath the money drawer and flourished it. Then he tore it in two several times, reached into the office, and sprinkled the pieces into the trash can. Vinnie's face beamed. "Good!" Instead of thanking his benefactor, though, Vinnie, with his next breath, said, "Let's get to the second matter." Rudy's face said, "Now what?" and Vinnie answered, "What do you think of my sister?"

Rudy had been raising his cigarette to his lips. At the question, his hand halted in mid-air. "What?"

"See, Donald likes Veronica. He was comin' over to the house every Wednesday last semester to do algebra homework with her. I tried to catch him puttin' a move on her –but every time I looked at them in the living room, they were doin' algebra on the dining table! I think that he, like… respects her. He's polite to my mom, too –he has dreamy eye movements and a vanilla voice, and he's passive –so she likes him."

"What're you getting at?"

"You can see Veronica's a Venus. She's got round legs and plump arms, but no fat. When we go to the lake, she can swim as fast as I can." Vinnie pointed what was left of his cigarette at Rudy. "Here's more. The last time I went through her dresser drawers –"

"The *last* time?"

"I search her stuff sometimes when I come home from school and nobody's in the house." Rudy's face reflected the surprise of hearing this strange admission, and Vinnie retorted, "You'd do it too if you had an older sister!"

"Yeah," Rudy owned up, "maybe I would."

"I'm real careful how I take out her bras and put them back. She wears a 32A. That's good for her age. But here's the best part. There are no falsies in the drawer! So –"

First one, then the other broke into snickers.

"So what *you're* hopin' to see is actually there."

Rudy almost laughed. "What?!"

"I saw you sneakin' peeks at her a couple times. Hear me out, Rudy. You see, inspecting my sister's bras is as far as I can go without... violating my Italian norms." They laughed again. Vinnie wagged his head from side to side. He took another of Rudy's cigarettes. "But for *you* to see her undressed would be O.K., see?" He lit the cigarette. "In fact, it'd be a compliment to her *even if she didn't know.*"

"Vince, this is something you think about at night, right?"

Vinnie leaned across the counter. His voice dropped. "I know her presence in the pool room incites you. Weren't you trying to pierce her clothes with your eyes? You won't be happy," he waved his finger at his listener, "unless you see her once, nothing on –to get one indelible memory of what she's got." His head, protruding now at Rudy, seemed fleshless and skeletal. Smoke dribbled from his lips.

"Vince, what the heck are you talking about? Make sense, will ya!"

Vinnie shook out his arms. "Here's my offer. If I teach you what you gotta do tomorrow night and you do what I tell you and you see my sister bare-naked, you gotta let me play for free Saturday afternoons from next Saturday till when school starts. That's six Saturdays. Deal??"

Rudy was bewildered. What Vinnie was telling him, that he could see Vinnie's sister bare, sounded impossible.

"Rudy, aren't you dying to see my sister naked? Tell the truth." Vinnie had a demanding look.

"Yeah."

"Nothin' else, just naked." He poked the counter with his index finger.

"Yes."

Vinnie pushed himself up onto the countertop with his hands and whispered into Rudy's face. "This is guaranteed. But you gotta follow the instructions. Do we have a deal?"

"First I gotta know what –"

"No. First you make the deal. Shake." Vinnie extended his hand. Rudy hesitated, and Vinnie came around the counter and behind it. "Shake!" he repeated, adding his eyes and tone to the word, turning it into an imperative.

Rudy held out his hand, and Vinnie seized it and shook it forcibly, transforming his proposition into an agreement. He remained behind the counter. "Here's the plan. Tomorrow, after church and lunch, we're going up to Lake George. The spot where we go to swim and boat has a beach and a dock but no place to change, so we wear our bathing suits up there and back. Got it?"

"Yeah," said Rudy tentatively.

"My mom and Veronica sit up front, and I have the back seat to myself. They talk girl-babble and gossip going up and back –who buys her shoes at Shoe Town, who gets spaghetti on her blouse every time she eats –stuff like that. They actually pay attention to each other!" He put on a look of distaste and continued. "Anyway, we always get back home just after 9 o'clock. It's dark out then. My mom goes up and changes in her room. Veronica gets to use the bathroom first before me. Now, pay attention." He looked at Rudy, warningly, as if his oncoming words meant victory or failure. "Veronica goes to her room, turns on the lights, gets her robe. She crosses to the bathroom, strips and hangs up her bathing suit over the bathtub, puts on her robe, goes back into her room, closes the door, and puts on her pajamas. Understand, Rudy?!" Vinnie's voice was low, but his eyes were refulgent. "That's when she's naked: when she's between the bathrobe and the pajamas! She's vulnerable!"

"Yeah, but –"

"Listen! In our back yard outside her bedroom window are two apple trees. Remember what the front of my house looks like? When you dropped me off?"

"Yes."

"The back is bigger. The two apple trees are green and jam-packed with leaves and branches. She can't see out the window beyond them, so she never closes the curtains or pulls down the shade. Get it?"

"Yeah –?"

"Anyone lurking in the tree nearest the house can see her through the uncovered window!"

Rudy drew back his head. He wondered, "How could Vinnie know all this for certain, except –"

"Here's what you do, Rudy." And Vinnie laid out his scheme. "Park your car on Sand Creek Road near Osborne at 8:30 and walk over past Brickley to Mordella Street, my street. We're number 49. You and I have about the same body build, so you'll look like one of the kids who live on Mordella. Walk up to my house and go right up the driveway to the back of the house and up the tree. Act like you live there. Don't stop to look at anything. And don't act cautious. Understand?"

"Yes."

"I gotta tell ya –the tree is not easy to climb up or down. When you get up high enough, get comfortable and wait. No smokin'!" He continued to eye Rudy. "Now –after –*don't* go back to Mordella! Go over the back fence to the neighbor's yard. I cut through there once in a while. You can jump it, but make sure you got gloves on 'cause it's a chain link fence. Run alongside their garage and don't step on their flowers, or they'll think I did it. Get on Brickley Street –"

"Hey, does the guy who lives there own a dog?"

"No. But good question. Get down to Sand Creek fast and drive away. Tell me what happened Monday."

At this point, after these stipulations, Vinnie relaxed. He returned to the front of the counter. He said to Rudy, "See, this is what's called a victimless crime, like sneakin' into a movie." He glanced around the mezzanine and back. "A lot of the stuff guys do are kinds of sports at first. For instance, dueling. Then the government passes a law against it, and it's a crime." Rudy looked curiously at the adolescent advocate in front of him. Vinnie pushed on. "My sister's just right for you! See, life is a stage, Rudy, and I'm giving you a front row seat!"

Again they laughed. Vinnie reached for Rudy's cigarette pack and slipped out the last cigarette. "You know, the worst time in the car with them was last year." He lit the cigarette. "We drove down to Brooklyn. My mom's sister was gettin' married again. We had time to look around. We rode the subway into Manhattan. I got some comics you can't find up here. Them two bought necklaces, and my mother got a fold-up map of the whole subway system –it's in color –that she showed off to the woman next door. I'm tellin' you, after that trip, my brain was mush." His mouth opened into a big smile. "You wanna know what they call girls in Brooklyn?"

"They call 'em 'girls'?"

"No, they call 'em 'frills'."

"'Frills'?"

"Yeah. My cousin told me. I'm not joking you."

"What cousin?"

"My cousin in Brooklyn, Ray. He's the one who took us on the subways. He calls people up and starts arguments with them."

"What?"

"He gets numbers from the phone book, y'know, and calls them. He showed me." Vinnie's smile became even more animated. "We went in his room, and he called a man and said, 'Where's the $300 for the Porto Rican dancers we sent over last month?' I started laughin'. Ray kept a straight face. The guy kept tryin' to tell Ray he's got the wrong number. Ray kept goin', arguing, demanding. Like for five minutes. He had the guy's address right there in the book! Then he said, 'I'm comin' over now and getting my money, one way or the other!' and hung up."

"Flagrant trickery!" Rudy laughed.

"Ray calls it 'telephone abuse'." Then Vinnie said, "Oh, hey, by the way, you're out of smokes!"

"And you're buyin' the next pack! It's a wonder you don't spontaneously combust!"

Vinnie bobbled his head merrily and sent up a triumphant cone of smoke. "Oh, yeah, and I want you to teach me some of your tricks, shootin' pool."

"Tricks?"

"You know –techniques."

Just then, Sonny and his two friends came into Merle's Billiards and up to the counter. They all greeted one another; and Rudy, with feigned exasperation, said, "Sonny, I got a complaint. Your cousin's been buggin' me like a termite and smokin' all my cigarettes!" He turned the empty pack upside down.

Vinnie threw back his head and laughed. Sonny and Rudy were his favorite older people in the pool room world. Early in June, on the first Sunday of that month, he and Sonny and Rudy had gone to Pizza Hut and devoured two large pizza pies and laughed about girls and how easily flattered they were and how they needed three times as many women's clothing shops in the mall than stores that sell men's clothing. That was one of his happiest days.

Vinnie went behind the counter and patted Rudy on the shoulder, as if consoling him. Sonny and his buddies took a tray of balls and descended the two steps to the carpeted floor and the green tables.

Rudy and Vinnie looked at each other. "All right, Vince. I get off at 5. I gotta immediately re-fill the soda machines for Julian. I gotta run across to Burger King for a hamburger and coffee. Then I'll come back, and you and me'll get a back table and I'll give you some lessons. How's that!?"

Vinnie's eyes danced in their sockets. He clapped his hands around Rudy's left arm. "Aie yah!"

"Vince! Stop that! Go buy some cigarettes!"

—

Vinnie entered by the back door and perfunctorily greeted his mother. It was 10:30, his Saturday curfew. Rudy had driven him to the house, and Vinnie, passing through the kitchen, found himself wishing he were staying over at someone else's place tonight, Alan's or Sonny's. He had stayed one night on Sonny's couch the night after his mother had had her car accident and had to remain in the hospital for twenty-four hour observation. He neither held his mother dear as a parent nor did he prize her for any specific virtues. He despised his dependence on her, which necessarily had to continue for three more years until high school was done with. She laughed, often with abandon, when she conversed with Veronica but used only simple phrases and flat tones when she talked with him. She never talked with him about his future.

As he ascended the staircase, he, for the duration of several steps, thought about the surprise Rudy was in for tomorrow evening. "He better do just what I told him. He'll get more than he bargained for."

In his mind he saw Donald standing next to his sister. Donald Drake had blue eyes and blond hair and a prepossessing smile that both revealed his upper teeth and dimpled his cheeks. His chin was spatulate, and when he wore one of his polo shirts, he always left the lapels unbuttoned. With this riant physiognomy, Donald gave the impression of a Pollyanna, one who is having great fun just standing still. Cynically, Vinnie muttered, "Donald Duck!"

He took a dollar bill from his wallet. On his dresser sat a ceramic piggy bank, a barrel-shaped object with a vacuous smile. The thing had a slot in its spine but no turn-plug at its belly. Vinnie folded the dollar five times and squeezed it into the slot. The pig was more than half full of dollars and quarters, and Vinnie had its upcoming year —which will be the

the last year of its life –all figured out. Next May, he planned to take the written test for his junior operator's permit, pass it, then persuade Rudy into giving him driving lessons in his Firebird. He knew he could pass the driver's test. Phase 2 was to crack the pig open. He would count the contents and ask Sonny to help him find a good second-hand car for whatever he had saved. At graduation, he would join the Navy and leave everything behind. Everything. That was Vinnie's strategy for his future.

He undressed, put on his pajamas, and went into the bathroom to comb his hair and brush his teeth. He called "Good night, Mom" over the banister. Back in his room, he closed the door, wound his alarm clock, pulled back the bed sheet, and took his flashlight from the windowsill and placed it on his pillow. From underneath the liner of the bottom drawer of his dresser –his socks drawer –Vinnie took last January's edition of *Playboy* and opened it to the centerfold.

Here and on the neighboring pages, was Miss January, Debra Jensen (Vinnie wondered what her real name was), displayed with all her charms and temptations. The scant text accompanying the photos of Debra reported that she "… was camera shy until she took off her clothes… " On page 142 were Vinnie's favorite pictures: one of Debra standing and facing him and another of her reclining sideways on the edge of a bed, her legs ajar. "These are the only kinds of girls who should appear in girl magazines," he murmured. He laid the *Playboy* next to the flashlight. He switched off the ceiling light, untied his pajamas, and slipped in under the sheet. He clicked on the flashlight.

———

CHAPTER 15
HOW RUDY MAKES UP HIS MIND

Sunday, July 23, 1978

The next day, Rudy as usual got up late. He performed his Sunday routines; but instead of heading to his uncle's pool room, he drove to the theaters at the Northway Mall and watched *Jaws 2* and then *The Swarm*. After which, he went to a diner in Schenectady and sat in one of the booths along the side wall. He had made up his mind to climb the Vincenzas' apple tree that evening. When his sandwich arrived, he bit into it and chewed slowly and repeated to himself everything Vinnie had informed and advised him the day before. He recalled Vinnie's descriptions and instructions and tried to picture himself in the Vincenzas' driveway and back yard, in their tree, and after, going over the back fence. He figured that the only part of the mission –his word for this escapade –that depended on luck was entering the property and going up the driveway. In those few seconds a neighbor could spot him. "After the driveway, it'll be all nerve," he thought.

He imagined the fine trepidation he would feel stepping onto their driveway and the physical exertion of pulling himself up the tree, limb by limb, to the level of the house's second floor. Then waiting motionlessly among the tree's leaves and branches for who-knows-how long. He saw himself watching Veronica, finally seeing those unclothed bits of her body that all along were the occupation of his curiosity. The sight of these objects was important to Rudy, for he had never seen a girl naked, other than ones on paper. And Veronica was pretty, she was worthy of all this hardihood.

The mainspring for this evening's tryst in the tree was Vinnie's coaxing and browbeating and handshaking. Rudy took a drink of his coffee and wondered, "Does Vince have another reason for wanting to expose his sister like this? Some grudge, maybe?" He lit a cigarette to help himself think. "Ah, what more to it could there be?" He decided, "He just wants free play on Saturdays."

Rudy knew that the fun, the self-indulgence of viewing this girl for a few moments in her bedroom were outweighed by the censure he would receive if he were apprehended during this caper, say, while he was trapped up in the tree. But taking risks and proving himself were vital to Rudy. He had no intentions for a life that was cushy and unexcessive or that forestalled itself with fearful questions like, "What'll happen if I get caught?"

He drew on the cigarette and stubbed it out in the ashtray. "Enough of this cogitation," he thought. He got up to attend to the practical details. He exited the diner and drove to Sand Creek Road, looking for places where he could park near Osborne Road. He drove up Mordella Street, noting the Vincenzas' house, then around to and down Brickley Street to identify the house whose back yard abutted the Vincenzas'. Certain now of his route to and from the apple tree, Rudy returned home and to his room.

He changed into his darkest blue jeans, tightened his belt, and put on a black long-sleeve shirt. He sat down on the bed with his sneakers, replaced their worn laces, and tied them tightly on his feet. He emptied his pockets of change, matches, and his handkerchief, then removed everything from his wallet but his driver's license. "I'll take only my license and my keys," he thought.

"What else?" he asked. He went into his father's bedroom and looked at himself in the mirror on the closet door. What he saw he liked: a resolute, compact young man, eager for another episode, another test. He quirked his lips into a smile. "Time to do it."

It was after 8 PM and darkening rapidly. On his way out the house, Rudy picked up a pair of the yard gloves that he wore while running the lawn mower. At 8:30 he parked the Firebird, and just before 9, he was perched on a limb in the apple tree, balanced, breathing evenly, watchful, anxious for Veronica Vincenza to return from Lake George.

CHAPTER 16
VOYEUR IN THE APPLE TREE

Sunday evening, July 23, 1978

Like many trees, this one's trunk had forked over the years into two beams, the thicker of which bent toward the Vincenzas' house. This was the one Rudy had scaled and upon one of its protruding boughs had straddled himself. The crest of the tree was higher than the roof of the house; and like most apple trees, its branches were crooked and its bark broken and scaly. The tree was lush with flat, clustered leaves, and Rudy was very sure he could not be easily distinguished among them. The house was, just as he was, quiescent and waiting.

Veronica's window pane was ash gray in color and impermeable. He sat there, parallel with it, amusing himself with the prospect that Vinnie might have climbed up here and peeped his own sister. It was plausible, he reckoned. But in any case, he and Vinnie were now confidants and he would certainly not mention this suspicion to him.

As the light from the sky flagged and faded, the colors surrounding Rudy lost their brightness and became shades of themselves. Green became myrtle, red became plum, and anything black lost completely whatever details it had manifested earlier. He looked downward. The earth below was obscure and shadowy. It was the hour for fireflies and prowling cats. He craved a cigarette.

All of a sudden Rudy heard a car. Through the leaves he saw a light where the driveway extended into the yard. He heard the car break smoothly and its doors open, then inarticulate voices and shuffling and the back door of the house being unlocked. "This is it," he thought, his mind clear and advertent, his lips tense. The kitchen's white fluorescents came on. Someone shut a car door and in a moment closed the back door. Rudy squeezed himself against the tree, froze his muscles, and listened gingerly. He heard blurred voices from inside the kitchen. A window on the left side of the house lit up. An upstairs light on the right side went on. The occupants of the house were moving, illuminating their dwelling.

He heard what sounded like a refrigerator door slam shut. "Are they eating?" A while went by. Rudy waited, wishing he had worn his wristwatch. "Come on," he heard himself urging. He stared into Veronica's window.

All at once, light flashed and flooded from the window into his eyes, dazzling him for a second. Rudy hugged the tree; too much light shown out of the window, and he could see the color of his jeans. "Jeeze," he thought. He focused his eyes and saw her. Her back was turned to him, and she was rubbing a beach towel over her hair from front to back, drying it and pressing it back at the same time. She put the towel on her dresser, ran her fingers through her hair twice, and turned in the direction of the window –which stunned Rudy. He gasped. This was not Veronica, it was Mrs. Vincenza in a red bathing suit! "What –?"

She walked beyond the frame of the window, and Rudy wondered why she was in Veronica's room. He waited, his heart beating. She reappeared in the window with, it looked to him like, a bathrobe draped over her left arm. She went to the dresser, picked up the damp towel, and exited the room. "Am I in front of the wrong window?"

It was then he saw the mirror over the dresser facing him. The ceiling light glared on the mirror's glass, and Rudy could not see exactly what the glass was reflecting. "Am I being reflected?" He pulled himself even tighter against the tree and wrapped his legs around and under the bough and waited with the patient interest that only burglars and spies can demonstrate. From the kitchen came a boy's laughter, then a girl's. "Now what?" He could see the kitchen window but not into it; and he looked at it quizzically, trying to divine which of the two, he or Mrs. Vincenza, was in the wrong place.

Several long minutes went by.

At length, Mrs. Vincenza re-entered the room, the white bathrobe belted tightly about her. She closed the door and turned to the dresser and its mirror. With her back to the window –and to Rudy –she picked up a comb and combed back her hair, then leaned forward and checked the suntanned skin of her nose and cheeks by pressing it and spreading it with her fingertips. Pleased, she straightened. She unbelted her robe, letting it hang loose, and stood there, running her fingers again from front to back through her black, thick hair. As she thus shifted her arms to and fro for this grooming, her robe furled and swayed about her outer sides; and its pendulous movement further captivated Rudy.

Then, remaining erect, Mrs. Vincenza lifted her forearms so that her elbows pointed backward. She cupped her hands and brought them in front of her and leaned once more into the mirror, assessing herself. She parted the robe by its lapels and shrugged it off her person and flung it onto a chair. She stepped back from the dresser, put her hands on her hips –the immemorial female stance –and appraised what she saw in the mirror.

Rudy knew he dare not shift himself in any way. Mrs. Vincenza might not discern his jeans or his white sneakers in the mirror, but she might catch a simple movement.

She then raised up her arms and recommenced combing her fingers through her hair, this time shaping it toward the back into a short ponytail. These grooming motions of her uplifted arms stretched her back and leg muscles so that there was no slack in her flesh. She was, seeing her as he did from the backside, lean, sleek, and curvaceous. Rudy was marveled by this woman. His skin prickled and he sucked in his breath.

She ceased her combing motions and held her fingers in her hair, her chin elevated as if posturing to her image in the mirror. Like this, she turned about-face and stared out the window like a mannequin: abstracted, mute, exposed. There she was! Rudy's blood rushed to his groin. The ceiling light beat on her, and Rudy's nervousness left him. Rather, he bulged his eyes voraciously at this Italian, trying to ingest and imprint every facet of her in his brain, praying she would not move until he had captured and locked her body forever in his memory.

But she dropped her arms, and, retaining her carriage and attitude, she walked out of the window frame.

Rudy continued to stare into the room. "Oh, my stars! My lucky stars." He mouthed the words with deep gratitude. He felt lust and gladness exciting him, slicing and flooding through him like a heat wave. He felt like laughing and exulting for pure joy. Mrs. Vincenza was a Roman goddess. There was no one part of her that he would prize more than any other part. To Rudy, she was perfect.

A minute later, she was once again in the window, but now dressed in her pajamas. For Rudy, the evening's voyeuring was finished. He watched her, waiting for her to leave the room or turn off the light so he could descend the tree in the safety of the darkness. He decided that Mrs. Vincenza was

Edward Grosek

thirty-seven or thirty-eight years old, an inch taller than he was, and that she wore –comparing what he had just seen to Veronica's presumably correct measurements –a size 36C.

He also decided that this substitution of Mrs. Vincenza for Miss Vincenza was no accident. "Wait'll I see Vince tomorrow!"

–

The next afternoon, Monday, Rudy entered Merle's Billiards and said 'Hi' to Lloyd. Vinnie was already there, sitting among the tables and watching a one-pocket game. Rudy went to the cigarette machine, inserted seventy cents, and pulled the plunger as noisily as he could. He unlocked the store room, went in, but left the door minutely open. Very shortly, Vinnie –suntanned, grinning, exuberant, and in a red and white short-sleeve pullover –slipped in and pressed shut the door behind him. They eyed each other as two friends often do, each heartened to see the other.

"Did you do what I told you?" demanded Vinnie. "What d'you see?"

"I saw your *mother!*" Rudy said the last word fortissimo, and Vinnie laughed and giggled and snickered. "Your mom's a masterpiece, Vince!"

This avowal could mean only that the plot had succeeded –triumphantly, and Vinnie did not restrain himself. He ran to Rudy and wrapped his arms about him in a bear hug. He lifted Rudy off the floor and plunked him back down.

They laughed and sat down on two worn chairs, and Rudy began recounting the perfectly-concealed vice of last evening. He depicted Mrs. Vincenza body, part by part, with the salacious nouns and piquant adjectives that boys use when they talk indecorously about girls and women. His whole spirit enrapt, Vinnie listened, laughing, sliding himself to the edge of his seat and back, and interjecting remarks like 'Yeah!' and 'Good!'

"I wanted to, like, *worship* her, you know, when I was in the tree."

Vinnie bounced on the chair. He was overjoyed that his mom had been seen unknowingly, as if she had been stripped by some magical power while she was off guard. He clapped his hands together. "Too bad you weren't able to see up between her legs, you know!" And he thought, "That's the important part."

"That's exactly what hit me when I got back to the car. Vince, I could *not* keep my mind on driving. She kept appearing on the windshield all the way home!"

"You got more than you bargained for, man, don't say you didn't!" He laughed at his own assertion.

"Actually, she's more desirable than Veronica."

"Yeah?"

"I couldn't help comparing them when I got home." He looked seriously at Vinnie. "Everything I could say about your mother I could say about Veronica: they're both pretty. But your mother's voluptuous. I think your mother would give me a sadistic delight that I doubt I could feel if I got your sister instead." He shrugged. "That's the best I can explain it, Vince."

Here was an unexpected idea, and Vinnie furrowed his forehead. "I would have thought it… the other way around for you. I'll think more about… that tonight."

———

THE OLD MAN

CHAPTER 17
MICKEY RUNS INTO WAYNE

Friday, July 28, 1978

One of Mickey's high school teachers had advised him after class once that most any predicament he tumbles into can be remedied if he simply goes off by himself and considers and pictures in his mind everything pertinent to what he did and what he needs to do. "Better yet," added the teacher, "write down what you know about it on paper."

This somehow impressed Mickey. Late the next Friday afternoon, he drove his van to The Courtside and went inside and sat at the last stool at the end of the bar. He ordered a glass of beer and hunched himself over it, then began sipping and considering. "Let's see. I owe Montgomery Wards over $200 for the shoes I bought in April and the tires and mattress I got a week and a half ago." Mickey knew he ought to pay this amount off because every month Wards adds interest to what it terms the "unpaid balance," which grows into a bigger unpaid balance the next month. He pictured the last statement he had gotten from Wards that showed the amount due, which totaled now to a dollar and a half more than the original price of the shoes. But then, the stolen money appeared in his mind, and he thought, "I'll have thousands of dollars in October. So, I'll pay Wards a little bit now and the rest in October." He gave his beer another sip.

He had to give forty dollars each week to his father or move out of the house, but this rent included food and the telephone. "So, that's not a bad deal," he decided. His van insurance was $721 and due in mid-August. This was another necessity, and the only way Mickey could make this payment was in installments. Each insurance installment was to be sixty-six dollars. He took a napkin, wrote down '66' and multiplied it by '12.' His mouth dropped in awe. Making installments monthly will cost him seventy-one extra dollars! "Yeah, plus postage!" He crumbled up the napkin. On top of these pay-outs, the bank required him to retain fifty dollars at all times in his checking account, which he needed in order to cash his weekly paychecks.

"So, I have three regular bills hangin' on me. And I need spending money too. Damn it!" For some reason, he remembered his van's registration. But that was not due until the end of the year. "So, I won't worry about that."

Then in his mind appeared the apartment. Mickey had decided earlier in the week that when he finally gets his cut of the money, he will rent his own apartment. "It should be small, like Angela's." And then he thought, "The money I'm paying to my old man will probably cover most of the rent on the apartment." He took a mouthful of beer. "Oh, wait, I'll have to pay for a telephone too."

"I might even splurge on a better van –or a new car! A four-door. Huh!" He finished his beer. "A four-door."

This obstacle –the money –money that verily belonged to him but for the time being was out of his grasp, was also the solution. He called for a refill. "How can I get some more money to live on?"

Mickey glanced around the large room that was the core of The Courtside and looked off to the sides where the booths were. The place was still quiet and would be for another couple hours. Even so, Mickey could smell spilt beer and cigarette smoke. He leaned into the bar and began tasting his second beer. "Let's see... " But Mickey rejected each of the expedients that occurred to him. He could stay home on his nights off and watch television. "No good." He could work somewhere part-time. "That's out." Was there anything in the Columbiana Hotel that he could sell? "Uh, I'd need to drive off with half the liquor closet!"

Someone sat down next to him. He turned to see Wayne. Wayne Bloom was tall and broad-chested but not muscular. He wore black rimmed glasses, but was otherwise ordinary in his appearance. If anything he looked "college." Which was to his advantage, for last April, late in his senior year at Albany High School, Wayne had turned eighteen and that same month was accepted at Albany University. For the summer, he was working part-time as a movie projectionist on Tuesday, Wednesday, and Thursday evenings at the Delaware Theater.

Mickey owed Wayne five dollars from July 16, and instantly he knew that Wayne had caught up with him here and was looking for his money. "He probably spotted my van outside." But Mickey was five years older than Wayne, more of a veteran in the pool room and in this bar, more practiced in some of the persuasions that guys used on each other. He himself would bring up the five dollars first. He smiled invitingly to Wayne and asked eagerly, "Hey, when do you start college, Wayne?" What're you gonna study there?"

Wayne regarded Mickey. The lenses of his glasses for a moment reflected the interior lighting of The Courtside. He replied, "I'm majoring in business." Wayne characteristically spoke from the front of his mouth, and his voice, because of this habit, emerged with a weakened timbre.

Mickey motioned to the bartender for a beer for Wayne and without pausing, asked him several more questions, like, "Suppose a professor wants to make a date with one of the college girls. Can he do that?" and "Do the professors have to wear those long professor-gowns in class?" He transfixed Wayne's eyes with his, trying to seem as if he wanted to be acquainted now more intimately with this college-man-to-be. Wayne gave each question a quick thought but had to admit he did not know the answers.

The bartender set a beer in front of Wayne, and Mickey said, "Never trust a man in a bar who isn't holding a drink!" He had heard that somewhere, he could not remember where. Then he said to Wayne, "Here's what's happening with me," and he enumerated to him his debts and his plans. "I'm gonna get my own apartment in October!" Wayne had propped his right elbow on the bar, and with his hand –his fingers were tapered –he was holding his chin. Normally, Mickey enjoyed receiving attention, but here in the nearly vacant Courtside he was doling it out. He pointed to Wayne for emphasis and lied, "The rest of my mother's life insurance money is due in October."

Mickey loosed sentence after sentence. "Here's the thing, Wayne. Right now, I'm a little short. I know I owe you five dollars, and I need to borrow another ten dollars just for another, like, week. Seven days." It was here, while proposing this to Wayne, that the notion came over Mickey that he could borrow an even larger amount from Angela. "I'm in the pool room almost every day. I have a few hundred in the bank that I'm not touching," he lied again, the mendacity flowing as if it were engendering itself somehow in his mouth. "I'm scraping together what I need for my van insurance. Collision and liability. Oh, and medical coverage too. I'll have to pay it monthly. See, last year, my father paid it, but he told me he won't this year."

"Mickey," said Wayne, trying to rationalize what he had just heard, "why don't you go to Household Finance Corporation or that other one... Beneficial Finance and get a short-term loan? They won't turn you down."

"Oh, Wayne!" He flashed a cautionary smile, as if Wayne's suggestion could amount only to a monetary trap. He shook his head 'no.' "They charge almost a hundred dollars in fees and interest for a loan. I couldn't go for that." Mickey took a sip from his beer. "I checked that out."

He returned his smile to its former, friendlier shape and leaned his head close to Wayne's. "You'll let me take ten dollars, O.K., Wayne, for seven days?" He nodded hopefully.

Wayne had not known Mickey Gonzag for long. He knew where Mickey worked and reckoned him one of the pool room regulars who had never treated anyone snobbishly or derisively. He sensed that Mickey was hustling him; but he thought to himself that even so, he would be protecting his five dollars with a second loan, which Mickey would surely repay. He reached into his pants pocket for his wallet and extracted from it a ten-dollar bill.

Mickey was glad Wayne had run into him. It was just what he needed. He decided he would phone Angela early the next afternoon, for he knew exactly what to say to her. He would get the money from her! "Of course!" he thought.

But now he knew it was time to rid himself of Wayne. He changed the subject by asking Wayne several questions about his job at the Delaware Theater. "What happens if you shake the projector while it's running?" and "Don't you ever fall asleep after seeing the same movie three or four times?"

Mickey listened to Wayne's answers as attentively as he could. But this was boring, and after a couple minutes, Wayne's words were pouring over him meaninglessly. He glanced at his wristwatch, distended his eyes as if he had just realized what time it was, and exclaimed, "Whoa!" He gulped his beer. "Wayne, I should've been out of here five minutes ago!" He quickly set two one-dollar bills on the counter. He stood and patted Wayne on the shoulder. "Listen, stay and finish your beer." He moved apart and said, "I'll see you at the pool room, Wayne," and hurriedly left The Courtside.

———

CHAPTER 18
ANGELA REFUSES

July 28 and 29, 1978

So thanks to Wayne Bloom and his gullible nature, Mickey left The Courtside Friday, confident that with sweet beguilement and flatteries –the love mechanisms that every young man puts into play to persuade a girl –he could cajole Angela into opening her wallet, or better yet, her checkbook.

He stopped at Romans and drank another beer. But Romans was empty too, and he could not stop thinking about visiting Angela the next day. "I wonder how much she makes," he thought. "I'll call her after noon."

In his room that night, Mickey recalled everything he knew Angela to like. On the couch, she loved to kiss. He thought about her mouth and how mellow her lips tasted. She liked being tickled behind her ears and having her chin nuzzled. "Yeah. That's the ticket!"

He began putting into order his moves and maneuverings as if he were scheduling them: undressing himself in the living room, kissing and cuddling on the couch until she was dripping wet, carrying her to her bed, paying attention, riding her for longer than usual. "That's what she needs!"

Afterward would come the inevitable exhaustion, then compliments, maybe some goo-goo eyes while he got dressed. All these should add up to, he estimated, about thirty-five or forty minutes. "That's good enough." A grin slashed across Mickey's face. He decided to ask her for $200. Seconds later, he upped his wish to a more gainful $500.

—

Mickey slept long and slid out of bed at noon. He gave his arms and legs a good stretching, ate breakfast, shaved, showered, and readied himself for the day. After which, he telephoned Angela and told her that he very much wanted to see her that afternoon before he went to work.

Ten minutes later, Mickey was on route to Angela's apartment, seeing lucidly in his mind the money she was sure to loan to him. He drove slightly above the city speed limit from Central Avenue to Clinton Avenue, past Bleecker Stadium, and to Ontario Street, where the apartment building in which she lived was located. The van's celerity and its minute vibrations crept up Mickey's calves and thighs, and he laughed in simple anticipation of what was soon to happen.

The apartment building had been constructed in the shape of a giant L, three floors in height with an open parking lot surrounding it on three sides. Mickey parked his van and locked it and ran to the outer door of the front entry, where were listed the tenants' names and corresponding apartment room numbers. As soon as he had pushed the button to ring number 203, Angela buzzed him through the entrance. Which meant, he at once knew, that she was waiting at her door for him.

He mounted the stairs; and when he tapped at her door, sure enough, it sprang open, and there she was in her robe, smiling welcomely. Mickey stepped inside and kissed her as she closed and locked the door. He kissed her all the way to the couch, whereon he sat her, then stood impendently before her and undressed.

"Perfect so far," he said to himself.

On that afternoon, Mickey made his supreme endeavors with Angela. And for Angela, Mickey's assiduous toil and her responses to it were more than short-term satisfactions or recreational diversions, they were, she sensed that afternoon, essential ingredients of a healthy life. No matter how obliviously she immersed herself in work at the library, how much the thought of her birthmark weighed at times upon her peace of mind, how often she watched others on television doing what she was missing out on, the future was worth living for. Angela moaned enigmatically. On that afternoon, she was truly in bliss.

—

They lay there side by side for that long, pleasant minute between depletion and refreshment. He kissed her lightly, and she indulged herself with the notion that this twenty-three year old was turning out to be what she wanted –and was paying for.

Mickey held up the palm of his hand to her as if to say, 'Hold on.' He rolled off the bed, went to the living room, and returned with his clothes and her robe. He dressed himself lazily for her, smiling affectionately and watching for reciprocal looks from her. As he was stepping into his pants, Angela felt tempted to tell him that he could go to the vase and get the twenty-five dollars by himself. But she remembered that, anyway after he leaves, she must see that the door is locked. Wordlessly, she slipped from the bed and into her robe. Like all of Mickey's visits, this one was terminating at the table stand near the door.

There, Mickey looked at his watch. "I have to go to work. You were great." He put his hands on Angela's forearms and kissed her lightly on the lips. "Twenty-five dollars plus $500," he made up his mind. He asked, "Angela, uh, could you lend me –besides what you're giving me for today –$500? I really need it."

The question disconcerted Angela. She could not have intuited it after the superior servicing that Mickey had that afternoon rendered to her. "Mickey," she stammered, "I don't... want to loan you money." She might have phrased her refusal, "I *can't* loan you money," but the truth was that she *could* make the loan and chose not to.

"But I need the money for my insurance. It's $721. And I have a bill at Wards too. I *have* the money, but I can't get my hands on it till October."

His fluency and his locution sounded to Angela truthful and devoid of trickery, but the content of his last sentence seemed senseless to her. She knew that if she were to let him borrow money today, he will certainly come to her for another loan in the future.

"Come on," he asked her a second time, his hand extended, palm up. "O.K.? It's not a lot of money."

"I won't loan you money, Mickey." And again she offered no excuse for her refusal.

"Why not?" He shuffled his feet.

"You'll never have enough money," Angela thought.

"You don't know this, but me and two other guys, Sonny and Rudy, we robbed a store three weeks ago. At night. We got thousands of dollars in cash. The owner was keepin' it in the cellar under his store. I –. Anyway we took it and hid it the next day in a storage unit until October, until it's safe to spend it –when no one'll catch on. See?" Angela was listening to this, dumbfounded. "It's all in cash. The money's all tied up in small bundles. All in ten dollar bills. I'll repay you in October. I promise. Guaranteed."

Angela's mouth opened slowly. "You really robbed a store…? Who are Sonny and Rudy?"

"You don't know them."

"I know I don't know them! Are they crooks?"

"Nooo," he prolonged the word and tilted his head. "We all work for a living. Sonny works where you do, at the University."

"What?" she said softly. "How do you know him?" And she thought, "Does he know about me? Is Mickey talking to people about me?"

"We all hang out at Merle's –the pool room. Rudy works there."

"You get together in the pool room and plan robberies?"

"Yeah –no! It's not like that. Look, we have thousands of dollars that we –"

"Mickey, I believe you, but no!" "You're a gigolo," she thought.

Mickey did not want to understand that she was declining him, and repudiating him. "You'll get the money back in October." There was longing on his face, as if he believed that he still had a chance for the loan –if only she, out of compassion, changed her mind. "O.K.?" he pressed her a third time.

Angela was now holding the robe tightly around her body. "Mickey, please don't beg me any further." She was glad she had not told him all about herself. She believed him, and she did not want to meet his two friends, who, she assumed, were two older criminals who had talked him into… who knows what. She slowly shook her head back and forth to him, unconditionally, assertively, yet ready for any act or words of frustration he might make.

But Mickey made none. All he could do in reaction was wave his hand to her in a small, dismissive motion that said, "Forget you." It was the gesture of one who was at fault for his own foundering. He pivoted his head to the side, he knew that all the sex with which he had plied her that afternoon had been for nothing.

Passively he watched her move to the table and take the twenty-five dollars –his allowance –from the vase and thrust it to him. He took the bills and turned to the door. He let her reach and unlatch the lock and draw the door open for him. "See you," he uttered.

"Um," she answered.

He stepped out of the apartment and heard the door close quietly behind him and the lock click into place. He looked up and down the vacant hall. He walked to the stairs, still laden with the problem he had brought with him, once more wishing he knew more people who were well-off and from whom he could borrow.

"Damn," he whispered. He looked at his wristwatch. This simple act, checking the time, which was done no more than out of habit, jogged loose something Arnie had mentioned to him. Two days before, Arnie asked him what happened to his old tires, the ones he had replaced. "I don't know," he answered. Then Arnie told him that there was a new waitress working on weekends at Dewey's Diner. He swung down the stairs. "I can stop at that diner," he thought, "for something to eat. I could see what she looks like. Leave her a tip –a small one. Then I'll head to work and tell Arnie about her."

———

CHAPTER 19
MICKEY TELLS TOO MUCH

Sunday, July 30, 1978

The following day Mickey again slept until noon. Eating his breakfast cereal, he remembered how Angela had not wanted to understand the fact that his appeals were urgent. He had asked her with civil language and she had dismissed him arbitrarily. He sighed and began to realize that he could have been more forward and imperative. "I let her tell me 'no'."

Sonny, he knew, ought to be at Merle's Billiards that afternoon. He resolved not to make the same mistake with Sonny that he had made with Angela. He would tell Sonny with authority that he has to have $1,000 of the money they took from the Cue and Cushion's cellar. And, he will bring the Studebaker's key with him!

By 2 o'clock, he was in his van and on his way to Merle's. "One thousand dollars is only one-fortieth of what I'm entitled to. Who cares who *used* to own that dough. They don't own it anymore!" He said this out loud and immediately liked the manliness and power he heard in his voice. "Yeah. That's it. The right attitude is to sound like a priest, preachin' in his pulpit," he soliloquized, " –as if there's no alternative!"

Another thought came to him. "And if Sonny's not there yet, I'll wait. Tonight's my night off."

But Sonny was at Merle's. Again, as he had ten days
earlier, Mickey entered the pool room and went straightway
to Sonny, brought him out to the parking lot, and there, next
to his van, said, "Sonny, I have to get $1,000 of the money.
That's a reasonable amount. It's for my bills, and I have," he
chopped the air with his hand for emphasis, "to have it."

Mickey had preceded Sonny out of the building and into
the parking lot and therefore had not seen the latter's lips
tightening and his eyes tapering. But when Mickey made his
play, when he so forcibly voiced his demand, he saw Sonny's
features pause and then relax, as if he were relenting.

Directly and expressionlessly for several more seconds,
Sonny looked at Mickey. He said, "I'll tell you what. Let's
drive to Brassey's. Just you and me. D'you got your key to
the Studebaker?" Mickey nodded 'yes.' He felt his own face
reposing and smiling, as if weight were falling from it. "You
take your van and I'll drive my car, 'cause we'll probably
separate afterward."

What Sonny proposed made good sense to Mickey. He
smiled. He could take the money to Montgomery Wards and
pay some of his bill and take the rest home. His eyes brightened
as if he were in front of a Christmas tree. He and Sonny got in
their vehicles, and each turned on his ignition.

The trip from Merle's pool room to Brassey's Storage was
uneventful. Mickey was jubilant, almost flighty –almost able
to see the ten-dollar bills. "I did it! I convinced him! Watch:
I bet Sonny'll take a thousand too." He felt like beeping the
van's horn in celebration and speeding up and slowing down.
But he did neither. He wanted the money, and he knew that
such an outburst of show-offiness might irk Sonny and make
him change his mind.

Driving up Osborne Road, Mickey spotted Vinnie Vincenza on foot, going in the direction toward Central Avenue. He could not recall the boy's name, all he could think of was "that black-haired kid in Merle's who won some money off me two weeks ago."

–

Anxiously, Mickey stood in the sunshine in front of the storage unit while Sonny squatted to unlock the padlock and unclasp it from the two metal loops. Sonny stood, pocketed the lock, and gripped the handle of the overhead door. He pulled up on it. Inside, the wheels on the door panels ground noisily in the rails that ran from the concrete floor up to and along the ceiling, and Mickey saw the cream-hued Studebaker, just as they had left it three weeks ago.

Before the door reached its acme, Sonny ducked under it and into the garage; and Mickey followed. And as Mickey reached into his pocket for the Studebaker's trunk key, Sonny clicked on the light and quickly pulled the door all the way back down. Smiling, Mickey leaned over the trunk with the key and tried to remember, "Did Rudy leave the suitcase standing up or lying down?"

At the same instant that Mickey leaned over the trunk to insert the key in the lock, Sonny rolled the fingers of his right hand into a fist and flexed it, making sure that the bones of his fist, wrist, and forearm were in alignment and that the muscles throughout were tight and hard. With his other hand, he took Mickey's shoulder and turned him around. And fluently and with no warning, he swung his right arm and as hard as he could, drove his fist into Mickey's solar plexus.

Mickey buckled both at the waist and at the knees, for the blow had forced the breath out of his lungs. He grabbed his

Edward Grosek

stomach and tried to gasp. The key dropped from his fingers. Sonny unfolded his fist so that the middle knuckles of his fingers –the knuckles you knock on a hardwood door with – protruded, and with them he rapped hard on the top and sides of Mickey's skull and then on the areas behind his ears. After striking Mickey like this many times, he punched his shoulders and upper back over and over, further enervating him.

With both hands he pulled Mickey up by the hair and yanked his head back and forth. Mickey was defenseless. He coughed and panted and looked at Sonny stupefied, and Sonny slapped his face. Mickey covered his eyes with his hands, and Sonny pressed his fingertips into the cavity of his throat where the larynx meets the trachea. Mickey wheezed and tried to say something.

Sonny was aiming for those targets on Mickey's body that he knew were hurting Mickey acutely or causing him fright. He grasped Mickey's shirt in his left hand. Mickey croaked out the words, "I give up! I give up!" But Sonny punched his chest and sternum, rotated him ninety degrees, and scraped his knuckles viciously over the rib cage area under his armpit. Mickey tried to scream, and Sonny punched his groin.

Sonny drew back his hand. But he was sweating and breathing hard, and he let his arm drop. He let go of Mickey, who now was limp. The onslaught was finished. Mickey, as if deflating, collapsed; and as he slipped to the floor, his head struck the fender of Mr. Merle's Studebaker.

He lay on the cement next to the car's rear tire, dazed and humiliated, groaning, blubbering, and gulping. He remained there for some minutes. Sonny looked down angrily at him. Mickey breathed in and out, sat up, and pushed off the floor. This was more strenuous than it should have been, and he held on to the car, hoisting himself and propping himself upright against its side.

Cowed and bewildered, he looked at Sonny. For more than a minute neither spoke. Mickey pushed away from the Studebaker. "We're friends," he choked the words. He leaned and picked up the key.

"I'm out of patience, Mickey." Sonny paused to let his words take effect. "If you ask for any of the money again before October 9th, Rudy and I are going to kill you."

Again he paused, this time scrutinizing Mickey for any telltale indicator that would let him know whether or not Mickey was at last resigning himself to their agreement. He said, articulating each word, "We're not gonna let ourselves get caught because *you* need money." His lips were parted and his eyes narrowed, as if he was ready, if necessary, to resume beating Mickey.

Mickey took his shirt by the hem and brought it up to his face to wipe off the tears and spittle. He sniffled and inhaled and said, "What would you do, Sonny, if you needed money like me!" Instead of responding, Sonny stared at him, accusingly. "I even asked Angela for $500. I told her I have money and that I can pay her back, but she wouldn't loan me anything."

Sonny waxed very attentive at these words; these were words that must be explained. "When did you ask her?"

"Yesterday. I went to her –"

"She's that librarian who lives in the Bleecker Stadium Apartments?"

"Yeah."

"Why did she turn you down?" He was probing.

He sighed. "I told her I have money. I told her I have thousands of dollars."

"What?" The word came out soft and crisp.

"I told her we robbed a store. But I didn't say what store, just that we robbed it."

"You didn't... tell our names... to this girl –?"

"I just used your first name and Rudy's first –?"

Sonny's eyes flared. "*Just* our first names?! What's the matter with you!" Yet he stood there, containing himself.

"I didn't tell her how much money, just that I'll get several thousand for –"

"Mickey," again he spoke each of his words distinctly, "if she squeals on us, Rudy and I'll kill you." He was glaring at Mickey.

"I had to tell her something, I couldn't just ask for $500 out of the clear sky!" His voice and face were appealing and yet apologetic: he wanted Sonny to know he was sorry that he had had to tell any of this to Angela.

"Mickey," Sonny rotated his head in disbelief to one side and back, "I'm too stunned to be angry. She *could* blackmail you."

"She won't do that. She has a birthmark on –"

"She could, Mickey. Most librarians are self-absorbed and afraid of criminals and risky behavior."

"Ah, man, she's not like that."

"Mickey, I want you to go home and think about how you can solve your problems by yourself until October 9th. On October 9th, you can have some of the money." Sonny exhaled in disgust. "I gotta talk with Rudy. He's not gonna like how this Angela knows our names and knows about the money."

"I just wanted her to know I can pay her back whatever she loans –"

"You wouldn't pay her back anything!" He was contradicting Mickey and at once telling him the truth. "You'd never call her again." He was angry now. "You know it!"

"All she knows is that I have –"

"Let's hope she doesn't believe you! You fool! Mickey, did you tell anyone else?"

"No." There was fear showing on his mouth, and he scratched his neck.

"I have to tell all this to Rudy. He's gonna get mad." He shook his head. "Mickey, go home and stay out of Merle's for a couple days, at least."

"I –"

Sonny swore. "Mickey, do us a favor, go home. Stay there." Sonny had been standing against the side wall of the unit. He stepped away from the wall. "Maybe you better stay away from that girl." He moved to the overhead door and to its handle. The back of his head was exposed, and right then, Mickey was seized by a wish to pick one of the boards stacked against the wall next to him and bash Sonny with it. He could take his share of the money from the suitcase and drive away in his van. "What could Sonny do when he wakes up?" he thought. "Nothing." This did not seem to Mickey as something very wrong to do, but he stood there, inert and passive.

Sonny turned back and looked at him, not in anger but almost in dread, as one looks at a brother who is emigrating and who might never be seen again. "I'm not going to tell you any of this again, Mickey."

–

They exited the storage unit. Sonny knelt and re-padlocked the door. They pronounced short, dampened good-byes to each other and then parted, Mickey with a sullen, miserable, almost haggard look on his face. One might speculate that Sonny, after setting off in his Cutlass and with no one else in the car to curb his thoughts and passions, would become, as he drove, more and more infuriated. But no. Sonny needed no one to restrain him. He began listing and considering what he wanted to tell to Rudy, for he trusted Rudy and he needed his full collusion.

First, he would admit to Rudy that he –Rudy –had been right about Mickey, that Mickey was, all along, unreliable and feckless. He would repeat Mickey's ultimatum to him for $1,000 and tell how he had not rebuffed Mickey this time but instead lured him to the storage unit and there battered and pounded him into helplessness. He knew Rudy would relish this part and laugh with delight while he listened to the specifics of the beating.

Then he would recount to Rudy what Mickey had volunteered to him: that he had attempted to convince that girl friend of his to loan him $500 until he could get his hands on money he had coming, and that he had told her the money –several thousand dollars –was his share of a robbery he and two pals had pulled. "The good news," he would stress, "is that it looks like she didn't believe him 'cause she wouldn't give him the $500. The bad news is she knows our first names." He knew that at hearing this part, Rudy would almost froth at the mouth.

He would add that he warned Mickey explicitly and emphatically what would result if this Angela were to inform on them.

He would ask Rudy whether they should try to learn things about Angela. "Like what kind of car she drives, how important she is in her library, what she looks like… –or maybe not," he demurred. "Trailing her and spying on her where she works might wind up frightening her. She might go to the library director or the police. How'll Rudy want to deal with her?"

This querying and deliberating brought Sonny to more practical questions. "Should we trust Mickey until October 9th? What would he have to do further to make me mad enough to... kill him? How could I do that... without being caught?" Sonny asked these to himself, but all he was able to think of, turning from Osborne Road onto Central Avenue, was to bring Mickey to a spot where he never ordinarily went, like the Port of Albany or a farmer's barn. "And then smash him with the pry-bar?"

He and Rudy would divide the money, and they would swear never, for the rest of their lives, to speak of this affair.

"Or will I lose my nerve when the time comes?"

More questions about this girl cropped up in Sonny's mind. What if Rudy wants us to accost her and warn her away from Mickey? Was this worth doing? Was this Angela a real threat to them? Punching and pummeling Mickey was self-protection. "So whatever we do to him is O.K. What should we do about the girl?"

He reached the pool room's parking lot. As he pulled up to the building, he looked through the enormous panes of Merle's edifice and saw Rudy and Vinnie inside, lighting cigarettes together and laughing about something.

———

CHAPTER 20
MICKEY MAKES UP HIS MIND

Thursday and Friday, August 3 and 4, 1978

In 1976, Mickey's mother died, and from her life insurance policy benefits he and his sister were allotted $2,000 apiece. To Mickey, this sum of money was a prodigious boon. Unrestricted by any provisos in the insurance policy, he immediately purchased a brown 1968 Chevrolet van.

The van had a small V-8 engine, an automatic transmission, and side view mirrors mounted on metal expanders. The odometer showed 89,000 miles of wear, but the engine purred evenly, and the van's interior was clean and its seats newly upholstered. And equivalently attractive to Mickey was the van's bed of almost nine feet by five and one half feet in surface, which was accessible from both the driver's area and the rear doors.

Mickey's sister, who was older than he was, took her $2,000 and with her boyfriend moved to Syracuse.

—

Four days later, on Thursday, Mickey was on Sand Creek Road, driving the van toward Wolf Road and the Columbiana Hotel. Mickey worked a "split week" at the Columbiana: Monday through Thursday and Saturday, each day from

6 PM to 2:30 AM. In return for the inconvenience inherent in such a schedule, he received a twenty-five cent per hour night premium and –better yet –he had, after 8 PM, only one supervisor, the night manager, who was only about thirty years old.

That mid-afternoon had been hot and muggy; and now at 5:30, the heavens were dark and dingy, and from them rain was coming down in large drops. Mickey had turned on the windshield wipers. The asphalt of the road glistened black, and a silvery downpour was dancing off the car in front of him. Then lightning streaked overhead and for an instant lit up the scenery in Mickey's vision with a hoary whiteness. Mickey was insensitive to the wonder of this flash of illumination, except that it occurred to him that white must be an odd color. "Eggs are white too." This latter appraisal in turn made him think of the mattress behind him in the van, for it too was a shade of white. He thought, "I haven't used that mattress yet."

The thunder that followed –the bone-breaking sound of it –made Mickey remember the bill from the Prussian Mutual Insurance Company. "I could pay it in installments." Then he considered, "What if I just let my insurance run out?" He bit his fingernail. "No."

He turned onto Wolf Road and found himself in the right lane alongside a faded yellow delivery van. On the van's side was an aluminum frame for advertisement posters, and the one in the frame that day had the words "MILLBROOK BUTTERTOP BREAD" on it in blue letters. Since it was evening, the van was probably empty and on its way back to its bakery. Mickey glanced at the driver. The latter was about fifty years old and smiling wanly to himself, as a working-class man at the end of his day often does. This man, Mickey noted, had a beard, one that was shaved from his cheeks and throat and sculpted so that the hair ran evenly along his jawline from ear to ear.

"Hey, a chin beard!" Mickey exclaimed happily. He beeped his horn, and the driver turned for a second toward him. Seeing this man brought back to Mickey's mind the story of the retiree from Albany University, the old guy whom Sonny and Rudy one month ago had proposed robbing.

–

Hours later, Mickey was in the Columbiana's laundry room, washing the fitted bedsheets, the ones with elastic banding on their edges and corners so that the sheeting girded the mattresses and needed no under-tucking. He was brooding over his bills and feeling on his chest and shoulders the sore spots where Sonny had punched him over and over on Sunday.

"Sonny!" he said to himself cynically. "I'll get out of this pickle by myself." He decided that he had to have the money for his insurance bill and his Montgomery Wards bill. He reset washer no. 1 to recycle the load of sheets already sloshing in it so that he could have more time to deliberate on this problem.

"You know, I *should* rob that old man on Northbrick Street!" He took his lower lip with his thumb and index finger and twisted it in thought. "I'll figure this out. Forget Sonny. And Rudy too! I can keep all the money I get for the watch." To Mickey, taking objects he did not own was simply a short-cut to possessing them, just as to certain others of the same proportion of honesty, cheating on an exam was nothing more than a substitute for studying in their free time.

Tomorrow was one of Mickey's nights off from work; and it hit him that therefore, he could rob the old man tomorrow! "If anyone else can do it, so can I!"

Ideas and images jumped into and out of his head, and very quickly he was envisioning himself, carrying off the burglary tomorrow night. "It's my turn," he decided. He clenched his teeth. "I don't have to tell Sonny either. Yeah! No, wait, I'll tell him in October! Ha!" Something else occurred to him. "It's stupid to take a bus to New York. I'll sell that Rolex watch up here! In Albany!"

Mickey had the laundry room to himself, and he traipsed about it, "thinking on his feet," which was how he had once heard a contestant praised by a television game show host. "I'll wear my black shirt. I'll bring a box cutter to slice open the old man's screen door. And I'll go directly to the back door of his house as if I belonged there." He pounded his right fist onto his left palm, for yet another thought struck him. "I don't know the old geezer and he doesn't know me! So the cops can't suspect me afterward!" He laughed.

Washer no. 2 dinged. He pulled out the damp bedsheets from it and slung them into the big dryer.

—

Very late the next night, Mickey was on his way to the Cumberland Farms convenience store on Oakwood Road. All day he had thought about the "job" he was about to do. He had pictured and re-pictured himself finding the wristwatch, probably in the man's bedroom, and putting it on while he surveyed the old fool in his bed asleep. "I'll wear it to work once or twice, make Arnie's eyes stick out o' their sockets." Now, in the van, he was furnishing the apartment he would soon be renting and moving into. "It'll have three rooms, like Sonny's and Angela's, and two closets and a couch as well as a bed. And some pictures on the walls," he added, "like my old man's house. And I'll have to keep the place clean. I'll need to buy a vacuum cleaner too."

Mickey steered into the store's parking lot and drove to the side of the lot that was farthest from the store's front. The fuel gauge, he noted, showed nearly empty. He would have to remember to fill the tank on his way back. "I'll be wearing the watch on the way back!"

He parked the van and turned off its lights and motor. He looked out the windows. The night was shadowy and quiet, and Cumberland Farms was now closed. He got out, looked warily about, and shut and locked the driver's door. By himself, Mickey had never broken into a house or even into a garage, and he felt not nervousness but trepidation, as would any lone plunderer who has no one with whom to share the risk or the penalty. He admitted, "O.K., I'm scared. But I want that watch!" As he walked over the lot and toward the road, he hummed a tune. A minute later, he was across Oakwood Road and entering the woody area.

The woody area turned out to be a large tract of uneven vegetation –oak and maple trees, patches of coarse grass and weeds, prickly bushes still damp from yesterday's rain, thickets of stunted trees and scrub bushes, and a ruddy-brown dirt trail. And there was a humid, floral smell from decaying leaves and bark. Most of the trees had not grown densely together, so that much of the sky's faint light was able to come down among them. Which benefited Mickey, for he had forgotten the flashlight he had brought from home but left in the van. He noticed that his sneakers were getting wet, and he wondered, "Who made this path anyway?"

Toward the end of the trail and on one of its sides, he saw a dozen or more piles of broken bricks, as if they had been wheel-barrowed out there and dumped. "Maybe some construction workers made the path," he surmised. Fifty feet after the brick piles, the trail faded. There were a stretch of black dirt, then two rolling mounds on either side of a cleft in the earth, and then a lawn.

As Mickey reached the first mound and ascended upon it, the clouds floating overhead drifted off, and moon's light played down so that he was able to see across the pale green and lavender lawn to the old man's house. "That's the house!" The house, from where he stood, had the figure and impression of an upright pentagon; its windows, he noted, were dark and lifeless. He checked his wristwatch: it was 11:30. "Perfect," he told himself. "Old timers go to bed early." He heard a cricket chirping somewhere but nothing else.

He traversed the trough and then the second mound, wondering why no one had ever leveled them. At this point, Mickey remembered how carefully he and Sonny and Rudy had moved in Curto's pool hall; and he proceeded deliberately over the dormant expanse of lawn, glancing up at the house in case a light in one of the windows were to come on, and glancing down at the ground to make sure there was nothing on which to trip.

As he came nearer and nearer the house and nothing –no sign or warning sound in the quietude –materialized to disrupt or dissuade his progress, he felt even more bold and assured. In fact, the house seemed to be peacefully waiting for him! He drew in his breath sharply and quickened his pace. "This is the real stuff!" A few feet from the back door, he reached into his pants pocket for the box cutter. With his other hand he took hold of the small handle on the screen door –and to his astonishment found that this outer gate, inadequate as it was, was unfastened! He had not needed to bring the box cutter!

This unsecured entrance was more than a morsel of lucky pregnability, it was a bona fide promise. At once, Mickey knew the watch was as good as on his arm. He slipped into the old man's kitchen, breathing shallowly and jerking his head and flicking his eyes in all directions. There was no light here, and he paused for a moment. He felt a tremble in his hand, and he flexed and shook it. He smelled cigarette ashes and stale milk. "Old man's smell," he smirked.

This tidbit of humor on his part calmed him, and he made a bet with himself. "I'll find that watch in five minutes. Ten minutes at the most." Then he thought, "I ought to let the old man know I was here before I leave. I'll put his T.V. upside down."

———

CHAPTER 21
THE ENUCLEATION

11:30 PM Friday night, August 4, 1978

It was 11:30 that Friday night. The old University retiree whose house and yard were located at the far end of Northbrick Street was sitting at his kitchen table, smoking a cigarette in the dark. He was in his chair slouched with his legs stretched in front of him. He had slung his left arm over the back of the chair, and his right hand, in which he held the cigarette, rested on the tabletop.

This man had not, for all his years of living on this same street, made acquaintances among his neighborhood's residents; for most of them, he knew neither their full names nor their occupations and habits. Such individuals who segregate their existence –like near-hermits –from that of others claim to be amenable to friendships, if they only, so they claim, could find companions with interests consonant or at least not incompatible with their own. But in truth, these men find flaws and deficits with virtually everyone they meet and talk with. Such reclusiveness and its accompanying cerebral ferment necessarily eventuate into righteous intolerance, in his case for his colleagues at the University. Men like him are more seldom than often harmless to others but also better left alone by others. That is to say, others should neither suspect them of transgressions without good reason, nor should they presume with less than good reason to intrude in any way upon them.

Righteous and uncompromising were the two best words to designate this man's attitude and responses to what he had for years witnessed in several departments at the University. They were the very themes for the goal that he now had the time and industry to work at. He would write a novel to expose the deferential, sycophantic behavior of those who taught the so-called humanities at state universities.

Tonight, he was contemplating and imagining the scenes necessary for his fictitious characters, who will undertake a chain of actions leading to the entrapment and ruination of one of them.

As yet, he lacked a full plot development for his story but not a central character or a climax. Of these, he had a full conception. The culmination of the career and the fate of the main personage of his novel, a professor in the political science department, will be an ignominious firing from his faculty position! The task and the purpose the old man was setting for himself was to vivify with concrete examples the manifold pretense and deficiencies of this professor. He would portray him in the novel as the stereotypical state university academic who ascends in his department's hierarchy through favors, mendacity, and feigned adulation of his superiors.

This fictional professor, then, through his own attempts to assert himself over his peers, will be deceived and tripped up by the latter into a humiliating dismissal, which he will show himself to deserve. Demolishing the character whose personality dominates the book, the old man believed, was daring and original and would shock his readers.

The problem of entrapping this character with an intrigue devised and laid by his own colleagues was what the old man was turning over and over in his head when he caught sight through his screen door of a young fellow coming out from among the trees that grew behind his property. The clouds had spread apart, and white moonlight illuminated the boy, who looked to have the slimness and casual gait of someone who works in a gas station. He was hunching over and bending at the waist, making his way with quick, uncertain steps over the first and then the second hillock that were on the back perimeter of the man's yard. "Oh. Who is that?" the old man asked himself.

Whoever it was, was not taking an angular path that would bring him to the street, he was on a track directly to the man's house! In fact, he was glancing at the ground and at the house, back and forth. "Where does he think *he's* going?" The old man screwed up his eyes. "Do I know him from somewhere?" he asked himself.

"No," he answered. Without taking his eyes from this unexpected newcomer, he stubbed out his half-consumed cigarette and rose from the table. Nothing of what happened next, of what the man did next, was premeditated, yet it all flowed coherently and imperatively from his precepts.

He darted to the doorway and unfastened the screen door's latch. The boy continued to advance. The man took his broom from its spot by the refrigerator, and as the boy came closer and closer, he retreated, walking backward, out of the kitchen and into the darkness of his living room. He watched the boy take something from his pocket, try the screen door, find it unhooked, and stealthily slip into the house.

The boy closed the screen door soundlessly and stood there, letting his eyes adapt to the dimness of the unlit room. He began moving about the kitchen, passing his hand over the countertop, squinting into the shelves over the sink. He went to the refrigerator. "What's in here?" he said under his breath and opened it. Light from inside blared at him. "The hell with this!" He quickly pressed the door back in place. Again he needed to re-accustom his sight.

The man waited.

The house was still.

The boy turned and walked erectly, casually, unsuspectingly into the living room. The man tightened his two hands around the wooden shaft of the broom. He pulled back his arms, ground his teeth and stepped forward. He grunted and thrust the blunt end of the broom as forcefully as he could at the intruder's face.

Throughout his skull Mickey saw a terrible flash of white and red light and for a second thought he must have walked into a cabinet door someone had left open. Whatever it was staggered him. He tottered back, then forward. His knees folded, and he felt himself caving downward, as if he were dropping through a crater. The old man had speared the broom handle into Mickey's left eye, crushing the cornea, the pupil, and the lens and bursting the central cavity. The gel-liquid – the vitreous humor in the orb –was squashed; it flushed onto Mickey's clothes and the throw-rug on the living room floor.

Mickey pitched forward helplessly and hit the rug with his chest and head. He opened his mouth to gasp for breath and tasted a slippery liquid that was not there a minute ago. He spit. He raised his right hand to his face and felt pulpy skin. Someone took him by the other hand. "Help me," Mickey groaned.

He knew he should get up from the floor. He coughed, and this made his head hurt. He felt someone helping him, taking his hands, bringing his hands behind him. He felt string being tied around his wrists and wondered why. "Help me," he repeated. Then he felt string being tied about his ankles and knees. "No, help me up." He could not move from his prone position, someone was pressing or kneeling on him. "What kind of a place is this?" he wondered.

He felt his body being rolled or rolled into something, and this confused him further. A pain pulsed now in his head. He opened his mouth to tell whoever was helping him to lift him on his feet, but there was more of that gooey stuff between his lips. Mickey breathed in hard and tried to yell, but only burbling and sticky saliva came out. Then everything turned black.

———

CHAPTER 22
THE FATAL PAYOFF

After Midnight, August 4, 1978

Mickey woke under a cover that felt fuzzy and stiff. In fact, he could not recall this particular bedcover. He tried to move his arms, but they were pinned in back of him. He seemed to be underneath or within something. "Am I in a sleeping bag?" he wondered.

The inside of his mouth was sticky, and he tasted flashlight batteries. " –No, blood! Did I bite my tongue?" He blinked his eyes, but they felt as if they were smeared with Vaseline. He blinked more. One eye was not opening, or it was not working. "Where am I?" he tried to say. He was becoming frightened.

He heard intervals of scraping, as if someone were scooping up pebbles with a tin cup. And he heard humming. So, someone was there! Mickey forced open his mouth. His left cheek felt numb. He struggled and called out, "Help me. Help me out of here. I can't move." But his mouth was swollen, and his voice sounded feeble and encumbered, as it had after the dentist had given him Novocain a couple years ago. Somewhere in his head was a palpable ache. He tried again. "I don't know where I am!"

"You're at your funeral."

The voice had come from above. Mickey leaned back his head and tried to see out the opening of whatever was enveloping him, a tube or a carpet maybe.

"In fact, you're in your coffin. I'm digging your pit."

This did not make sense to Mickey. Through his blurry sight he made out a man who was leaning over the opening. The image Mickey saw of the man slipped downward, as a frame in a filmstrip sometimes does. He sensed that his eyes were not focusing. He blinked them several times; still, he could not see properly. "Huh?" he said, "Why?"

"So you don't try to rob me again." He was speaking softly and in a factual manner.

Mickey felt like crying. He heard a cricket chirping. "I won't try to rob you again."

"I'm seeing to that." The old man went on with his shoveling, the cricket stopped chirping, and if Mickey could have viewed the man's face, he would have beheld the unperturbed countenance of a man absorbed in work in his back yard.

"Listen... I won't do it again." Mickey's voice was slightly stronger, more resolved.

"You're right," agreed the man.

This old man was trying to kill him! Mickey felt desperate. "I have to get out of here," he thought. He said, "Call the police. You can have them arrest me."

The carpet was muffling Mickey's words, but the man understood his appeal. He halted his shoveling to respond. "The police'll only put you in jail for a while. That's all."

Mickey heard the shoveling resume. "Someone'll find out—"

"Oh, no, no one will! I saw you come all by yourself. There's a little gully in the ground here, a declivity just off my property where a creek used to run. –You crossed over it thirty minutes ago! I saw you from the kitchen door. That's where I'm diggin'! I'll drop you where I'm making it deeper –rug and all –and bury you. Tomorrow I'll buy a dozen bags of that good dirt that has manure in it from one of those home improvement stores. I'll smooth it over your grave. I'll plant grass seed on it and water it. In a couple weeks, no one'll tell the difference!"

Mickey felt horror spread over him. The old man was not finished. He said, "You and I don't know each other. If your body's discovered years from now, the cops'll suspect those Italians who own that construction company. They'll get the blame! They own the land with all the trees on it that you came through from Oakwood Road." He paused and chuckled. "So, don't you worry. Everything'll work out just fine."

Mickey was chafing from the constraint of the carpet –he was bound wrists and legs and could barely fidget –as well as from the menacing replies to his every plea. He called out, "I think my face is bleeding. I can't see straight."

"I knocked one of your eyes out," the man articulated, "with a broom handle. It's called enucleation. The blood is from your empty eye socket. *You got it all over my rug!*"

"I'm blind??" Mickey was now fully alert. He understood what had happened. "Awh! Awh!"

"Only in one eye. But you never looked at how people in the world worked for what they wanted, did you?" Then, "You chose to steal. I know your type. I'll bet somebody's helping you to live. Am I right? Your life is a farce!" He pointed down at his captive. "I'll bet you have no principles!"

The man recommenced shoveling. Mickey groaned. He strained at his bonds again, but he was nauseous and cramped within the rug. He was trapped, unless he could… what? He began sobbing. Long minutes went by.

The old man stood his shovel on its blade and leaned on the handle, tired. "Did you know that I was a professor at the University? I hated my colleagues! They were all phonies – left-wingers and back-stabbers pretending to be very busy! All they cared about were pay increments and pompous conversations! Prestige and serving on committees!" He paused. "They made me angry!"

Mickey stopped sobbing. The old man was reminiscing, and maybe there was a chance he could reason with him. "Uh, you're taking the law into your own hands!"

"You're darn right I am! I'm ridding the city of one of its thieves! Every man ought to do this sometime in his life. Decent men can't afford people like you!"

Mickey remembered a question he had heard someone ask in a television program. "Doesn't this mean you're playing God?"

"No. There's no such thing as 'playing God.' I'm just getting rid of you, that's all. Nothing more. It's not wrong to eliminate a thief!"

"I don't wanna die."

"Of course you don't. But I'll be able to live through your suffering."

Mickey remembered something else he had heard on television. "Doesn't this make you just as bad as I am?"

The old man bent down to the opening of the rolled-up carpet so that his head and Mickey's eye were only feet apart. Mickey saw his full aspect for the first time: the bristle-bearded face of a hawk-nosed, sunken-cheeked chess player who, at the tail-end of his life, had finally checkmated his opponent.

Mickey watched the mouth above him open. "How do you like meeting someone just as bad as you?!"

Mickey shuttered at the stymieing answers to his questions. The recollection of all his past pains and fears and misadventures swam up into his memory. "Let me have one more chance! I'll do anything for one more chance!" But this had no effect on the man. Then Mickey remembered the break-in and all the money he and Sonny and Rudy had taken from Curto. "Listen, me and my friends have a lot of money hidden. We stole it from one of the pool halls on Central Avenue. A month ago. It's all in a storage garage. I'll share my half with you. I swear. Come on!"

"Yeah, you're a moron!"

"No!" Mickey felt the old man dragging the rolled carpet –with him inside, powerless –toward the grave. He shrieked, "Wait!"

"Wait for what?" To one side of the man's face floated the spectral-white moon, as if it were watching Mickey over his captor's shoulder.

"Wait –"

"The sooner I get done with you the sooner I can get to bed. I'm worn out from this damn digging! You were sleeping for the last half hour!"

"Nah! Come on! Please don't kill me! I don't want to die!"

"You just be happy I'm not torturing you before I dump you in the hole!"

This was no consolation for Mickey. He was in the rug rolling downward, then thudding into his destination: he came to rest facing sideways.

"Now… I want you to listen to me. Premature burial is also called zoothapsis. There's a new word for your vocabulary! Here's what'll happen next. You'll hear me shoveling the dirt on you, and you will even smell the dirt. You'll think of the sky and the house you grew up in and your friends. They'd save you if they could. Soon, all will be black and silent. Since the soil about you will be loose, you'll have air, and you should persist for an hour, or less. Then you'll become insensible... and lose consciousness."

The executioner looked upon his subject and smiled. He shook his finger. "No impunity for you, whoever you are!"

"You don't even know my name!"

"Useless information!" Earth dropped and pattered on the carpet. "And now, your halcyon days are over, and we're going our separate ways, you to your doom."

Mickey looked up and saw dirt falling on him. He was terrified and began yelping and screaming, flailing his head side to side, thrashing his body and his legs. "I don't want to die!" he begged.

"You should have thought of this at the same time you decided to *rob my house!*" He leaned over the carpet. "Better still, think of all the things you've taken from others. Some person worked for each of those things. You didn't. How long do you think others should work for you? How long should we go on working for you crooks before we eradicate you?"

Those were the last words Mickey Gonzag heard. He began crying profusely and despairingly.

The old man tossed down shovelful after shovelful of dirt, this time without stopping, until the thief-in-the-carpet and his inglorious tomb were covered. "Crude," he thought. He stood still over the site for a long moment, feeling guilt, qualm, and fear for what he had done. He was convinced that the moral idea of killing a robber on his own property was irrefutably sound. Yet, he knew that the punishment he would receive, if the police were to dig up the evidence, would outweigh his conceit that he had done something extraordinary to reduce stealing.

"Ironic." He wanted a cigarette. He placed his shovel quietly in his wheelbarrow and began wheeling it back to the house.

–

Before daylight, what the man had prescribed for Mickey came to pass. The interment, the enclosed space, the gradual depletion of oxygen and accumulation of carbon dioxide in mickey's blood, his coughing and jerking around in the carpet –ended in exhaustion, semi-awareness, and suffocation. And the next day, after the old man had finished filling the entrenchment with the bags of new dirt, everything in his back yard looked pretty much as it had earlier in the week.

———

SONNY

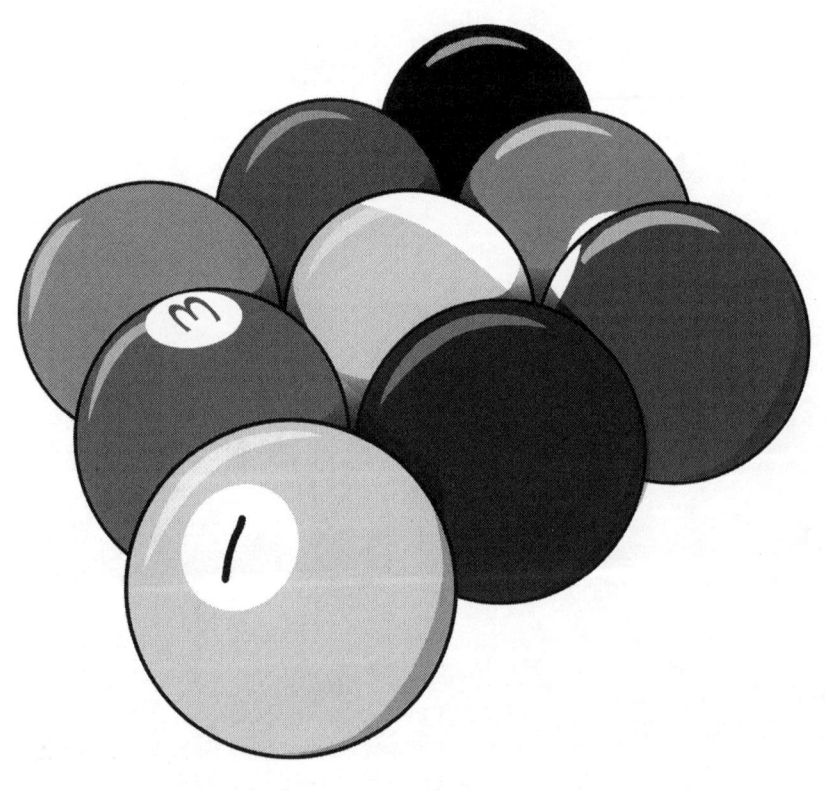

CHAPTER 23
VANISHED!

August 19 to August 20, 1978

It was Saturday, two weeks later. That afternoon the sun was unobstructed by any clouds in the sky, and it was steadily suffusing the city with its rays and heat.

Sonny pushed open the front door of Merle's Billiards. Merle's was air conditioned, and immediately he felt himself refreshed. He stopped to glance about –what every guy does when he enters his hang-out –and saw his two friends from work among the twenty-five or so players on the carpeted floor. Vinnie too was there. Vinnie had on a tee shirt with a print of a hysterical guitarist on its front. He was smiling and talking to a young fellow who looked like a college student. "Probably hustling him," thought Sonny.

"Hey. Sonny." He turned and saw Rudy behind the front counter. Rudy jerked his head tersely to one side, the common gesture for "C'm 'ere! I want to talk to you."

Sonny moved to the counter, and Rudy said to him, "Listen to this. Dan Socola came in yesterday, about seven."

"Socola?"

"He used to hang out here. About your size. After high school, he got in the plumbers' union. He hangs out at the Cue and Cushion now. He went right to the middle of the mezzanine and started talking point-blank to everyone. He said the Cue and Cushion was robbed of a lot of money last month. Everyone stopped watchin' the games and listened to him. Socola said Curto's put out a $10,000 reward for anyone who gives him the name of the guy who broke in and robbed the place."

Sonny leaned his forearms on the counter. "So, Curto went to the police, and now he's going public?"

"No. Socola said Curto has two cops he knows workin' on this, but they're workin' off the record."

"What?"

"Yeah. Someone said, 'Why didn't Curto file a report?' Socola said he didn't know why."

"Two cops are working on this off duty?"

"Yeah. Someone asked Socola how much money was stolen, but Socola said, 'Curto didn't say'."

"He doesn't dare say how much."

"I don't think a cop can accept a reward for solving a crime if he's assigned to work on the case." Rudy took out a cigarette. "So, these two cops are workin' on this off the clock." He lit up. "They'll split the ten grand if *they* figure out who did it. Unless someone squeals to Curto first."

It was ironic that Rudy and Sonny should be discussing their own jeopardy. Neither was smiling; they both knew who "someone" referred to.

Rudy exhaled downward over his lower lip. "Oh, yeah, Socola said Curto *will* find who did it. And he repeated '$10,000' several times."

"Sounds like Socola was sent here to tell our room about the reward."

"That's what I think too. It made me remember Brighelli's comin' in that afternoon with Shannahan and lookin' at everyone in the place. I think that was part of this whole business."

Rudy looked around the room. Vinnie was now playing straight pool with the college boy. Rudy took the card for the latter's table and pushed it into the front opening of the time clock. The clock made a clunking sound and printed a new time on the card. Rudy re-marked it for two players beginning at the new time and slipped it back into its wall slot.

"Maybe… "

"What?"

"Maybe Curto has no clues! Maybe he's eliminated all the suspects in his own place."

"So he's startin' to fish here, huh?"

"Then we're safe! As long as we stay smart. We gottta just act ordinary, what we were doing all along!"

Three men came in the front door, expiring and smiling as they felt Merle's cool air. They asked for table 3 by the windows, and Rudy smiled knowingly and handed them a tray of balls. He turned to Sonny and said, "You know, Curto might have, like, a friend in our room. Someone who keeps him informed about what's going on here." The three men reached table 3. Rudy took a new card, clocked them in, and slipped the card into wall slot 3.

Sonny said, "That's O.K." His mouth widened into a smile. "We're not in trouble unless we talk too much. We'll keep to what we planned –"

"Yeah." Rudy was nodding.

"We won't change anything."

Then Rudy said, "Socola didn't stay long. But after that, Wayne came in. He started askin' everybody about Gonzag."

"Everybody?" Sonny's smile flattened. "What for?"

"Gonzag owes him fifteen dollars. I guess Wayne's more mad at himself than Gonzag for giving over that money."

"What did'ya tell him?"

"Well, Wayne made me realize I hadn't seen Gonzag for nearly three weeks. That's all I could tell him." He shrugged. "We got his address from the phone book. Wayne said he was goin' to Gonzag's house. Then he left."

"You know, we gotta find Mickey. There's too much going on. We can't leave him alone, he'll mess up somehow. I'll tell you what. I'll go over to the hotel now and see if he's there and set up a meeting for us three."

But at 6:15, Sonny phoned Merle's and told Rudy that Mickey had not shown up at the Columbiana for the last two weeks, and that Monday he will be terminated. Then Sonny said, "I'll go to his house tomorrow during the day and see if his old man's at home. Maybe Mickey's been sick all this while."

"I doubt it," thought Rudy.

—

The following afternoon, Sunday afternoon, Sonny came into Merle's. Lloyd was on duty at the front counter, and Rudy was sitting in the mezzanine, waiting, watching the room fill slowly with players. He and Sonny went into the work room, and Rudy closed the door.

They sat and Sonny told what he had learned. "I talked to Mr. Gonzag just now. Mickey hasn't been home for two weeks. He said he phoned the hotel, the police, and the local hospitals. Nothing."

"What did the police say?"

"He said he had to go downtown to police headquarters for that. A detective told him Mickey was not in custody, but that most missing twenty-three year olds turn out to be just runaways."

"They wouldn't actually do anything?"

"No. Then Mr. Gonzag said he got a call this week from a towing company. Guess which one."

"Which one?"

"Brassey's."

"What!?"

"The full name is Brassey's Storage, Towing and Recovery. Mickey's van was parked for several days in the Cumberland Farms' parking lot."

"Oh, Jeeze! What was it doin' there?"

"No one knows. The manager had it towed. Brassey's told Mr. Gonzag it charges tows by the day. So he went back with this news to police headquarters. The detective told him the same thing: a vanished twenty-three year old isn't a priority, even if his vehicle isn't missing!"

Rudy pursed his lips. "Funny the police won't look for Gonzag." He lit a cigarette. "Well, that's good for us. We don't want him talkin' to the police." Then he exclaimed, "Cumberland Farms?! Hey, is there any chance he tried to get into that man's house on Northbrick?"

This took Sonny by surprise. "Even if he did, he wouldn't have abandoned his van."

Rudy paused. "He *must* have gone out of state somehow."

"Maybe."

"Now we're just guessin'. No matter what, we can't explain the van! Except that he can't afford it."

"Think about this. We're looking for Mickey. So's Wayne. So's Curto, even though he doesn't know it." Sonny lowered his voice. "If those two cops knew all this stuff, they'd want to talk to Mickey!"

"That's right! They'd see the coincidences. They'd start lookin' for him."

"We're safe," Sonny said as if making a conclusion to their suppositions, " –unless Mickey gets caught somehow."

"Let's go out," said Rudy.

They came out of the work room and found the pool room now at near capacity. Rudy closed the door and stepped to the mezzanine's railing. He looked out at the pageant of players orbiting the green tablebeds. To Rudy, pool was the finest of indoor sports. To him, there could be no equivalent to the firmament of action that he was seeing and hearing: the wooden shafts waving over the tables, the jets of cigarette smoke and occasional glimpses of money, the cacophony of laughs and groans from the shooters themselves. Even the calico-colored carpet lying under everything was part of this arena.

And the pool business was lucrative. Multiplying the number of customers he counted among the tables by the table rate Julian charged, Rudy estimated that by closing time, his uncle should take in close to $300. "More than $300, when we count in the take from the cigarette and soda machines."

–

Later in the evening while Rudy was in the middle of a straight pool game, he remembered his father's Studebaker. For several seconds, the thought disrupted his concentration.

"Jeeze! What if Gonzag broke into the storage unit! What if he cut open the lock with a bolt cutter, took all the money, and ran off. That *is* possible!" he thought. "Gonzag could leave town and live off the $120,000 until it's all gone. He could come back in a year and make like he doesn't know a thing!"

———

CHAPTER 24
THE STUDEBAKER

Monday, August 21, 1978

On Monday, Rudy and Sonny met at Brassey's Storage. The dispatcher in the office told them in no uncertain terms that Mickey's van was and will be confined in Brassey's impound lot until its towing charge was paid in full. They drove to the storage units. Sonny unpadlocked the door, and Rudy opened the Studebaker's trunk with his father's spare key and then the suitcase with his suitcase key. They lifted the lid: the money was there, intact, as they had left it.

Sonny stabbed the air with his finger. "That means he wasn't here!"

"Could he be doin' this to try to trick us into doing something, like taking some of the money out for ourselves?"

"No." Sonny's lips were turned downward. "I don't think so. But, now what?"

"Just what you said. We stick to our agreement. We adhere to it. We don't change anything till October 9th." Rudy's voice was firm, unwavering. "But then, we'll have to move the money. By the way, my old man asked about the car a couple days ago. He trusts me, but sooner or later he might wanna talk with Logano."

"Well, then… we'll have to bring the car back. We'll just leave the money here inside. What if we split up the cash, say in six months, and Mickey pops up next summer?"

"He'll scream his head off if he thinks we're cutting him out of his share!"

For the first time since the last time he saw Mickey, Sonny's face showed anger. "I'm fed up! I'm not going to jail for Mickey." He shook his head. "If he opens his mouth, he's finished!"

"I'm with you, whatever we decide on. We stick together. No backtracking." Rudy felt himself speak the words from his throat.

They were silent for a moment. Sonny said, "All right. Let's put everything back."

They relocked the suitcase, the trunk, and the overhead door. As they were about to part, Rudy said, "You gotta be at work at six. I'm going to Romans and The Courtside and see if I can get anything from the bartenders. But I'm *not*," he stressed, "going to phone Wayne. We *don't* want him to know anyone else is lookin' for Gonzag."

"Right."

—

Five days later the thought hit Sonny. That Friday night at work, some impalpable stimulus stirred up his memory, and he remembered what Mickey had said to him about Angela, the librarian. He decided he would go and meet her the next day.

———

ANGELA

CHAPTER 25
ANGELA AND SONNY

Saturday, August 26, 1978

Angela set her pen down on the kitchen table. It was Saturday afternoon, well past 2 o'clock. She had finished writing another book review for *Catholic Library World*. Like most magazines, this one did not remunerate its reviewers for their "donations," but at the end of the year, Angela could list hers in her annual personnel report under "Academic Contributions."

She looked at the draft of the review lying in front of her. She had concluded it with a comment that was favorable to the author and his book; but, she admitted to herself, reading through the book had been unstimulating, and in some spots tiresome. Monday in her office in the library, she would type a finished version and mail it to *Catholic Library World*'s editor.

Angela sighed. She sat at the table in cut-offs and a tee shirt, listening for a few moments to the quiet in her kitchen. She looked up at the walls. These she had, over time, ornamented with pictures she had scissored from art magazines and set in wooden frames. She liked the way they looked, both the depictions themselves and the sequence in which she had arranged them.

It was the weekend. Mickey had not phoned her for a full month. She could tidy up the apartment and go to an early movie. *The Buddy Holly Story* and *Eyes of Laura Mars* were still playing in the Albany area. Her eyes lifted to the clock. It was approaching three. She got up from the table; she undressed, went into the bathroom and into the shower.

She dried herself and put on her robe. Again she looked at the clock. Her eyes descended to the carpet. She rubbed her chin, then decided to go to a restaurant for an early supper and afterward to the movies to see *Eyes of Laura Mars*.

Someone rapped with his knuckles on her apartment door. The rapping was crisp and abrupt, and it startled her. "Mickey!" she thought in that instant, and a tremor coursed down her spine. But it could not be Mickey, his knock was more subdued. And he had not phoned ahead. Angela gripped the collars of her robe and went to the door. She unlatched the dead bolt and pulled open the door as far as the chain lock would let her. A young fellow with thick black hair and curvaceous Italian lips smiled deferentially to her, and she thought, "He has the wrong apartment."

"Hi. My name is Sonny Peggaluso." He was looking into Angela's eyes. "I'm a friend of Mickey Gonzag. Is he with you? Do you know where he is?"

Angela, of course, had not expected this. Sonny went on. "No one's seen Mickey in three weeks. I talked with his father a few days ago, and he doesn't know where Mickey is."

She knew by this that here was one of Mickey's friends –accomplices –and that his coming to her apartment meant that he knew about her and Mickey and that he probably knew where she worked. "You're the only person we haven't asked... Angela, right?"

Angela scanned over this friend of Mickey's. He had a winning appearance. He had on a short sleeve shirt that had a pocket on the front and a button at the collar, denim jeans that were not bleached or faded, and low-cut construction shoes, the kind that you could wear casually. He did not, Angela noted, fidget with his hands when he was speaking; and more so than his apparel and self-constraint, he seemed oblivious to her birthmark.

She tested him. "Where do you work?"

"At the University. On night sanitation."

"Are you alone?"

Sonny nodded. "It's just me."

She sensed he was speaking candidly. She released the chain and opened the door. "Come in... Sonny... Peggaluso?"

"Yes."

She re-bolted the door, and as the two made their way to the couch, Sonny began. "Mr. Gonzag told me that he got a call from a towing outfit about a week after Mickey stopped coming home. Mickey's van was parked in a convenience store's lot for several days. The store manager had it towed."

Angela and Sonny seated themselves on the couch, each on one of its end cushions. "Mr. Gonzag said he went to the police, but they said Mickey wasn't in Albany County jail. They said he was probably a runaway." Sonny's arms drew Angela's attention; they were smooth and muscular. He continued. "Mickey owes people some money, but I don't think he'd run away because of that."

"Probably not. He told me he owes Montgomery Wards money." Angela was holding the robe together with her right hand. She exuded the fresh sweetness of a girl who had just showered.

"When's the last time you saw him?"

"The end of July. Four weeks ago. He tried to borrow $500, but I said no."

"You don't dare loan money to Mickey!" He dipped his head and smiled knowingly.

"I know that. But then he said he had the money, except he can't get his hands on it." She was watching Sonny carefully. "He told me you and he and somebody named Rudy –he works at the pool room? –broke into a store at night and took thousands of dollars. He said you put it all in a storage unit?" She raised her eyebrows as if asking for confirmation of this last bit of information.

Sonny's face slackened. This last sentence changed the subject matter and the ambiance completely. Where the money was hidden was too much for this girl, this outsider, to know. "What all do you... What all did Mickey tell you?" He asked this soberly, concernedly, as one who was lost might respectfully ask for directions.

Angela smiled. She and this Italian each knew something mysterious about the other. "Not much more, Sonny. You three are afraid to divide up the loot and spend it. That's all." She gazed at him unflinchingly. "I'm not a squealer, Sonny." Then, "Mickey told me the three of you hang out at Merle's pool room. I've never been there." She leaned toward him, engrossed, for here was a young man... with secrets. "What else is there? You can tell me."

Before he answered, Sonny thought. Or rather, the question forced him to assess what he knew of Angela: she was rational, reasonably intrusive, not pretentious. Nor was she disloyal to Mickey, for it was he who had told her too much. There could be no use in lying to her. He regarded her birthmark. It was not too flagrant.

"All right. I won't tell you the name of the place we hit, but the owner didn't go to the police. Well, not officially. He called in a couple of cops he knows and offered them a reward for the name of the robber. Then he opened up the reward to everybody. Cash, under the table, to whoever points out the robber. Then, the he'll do the rest. But there's no evidence – nothing –for the cops to go on!"

"How do you know all this?"

"The owner 'put out the word'." Sonny smiled at the gangster expression.

"So, Mickey's on the loose. You two are worried."

"There's one more thing. Rudy thinks Mickey could be in jail out of state. Maybe. But even so, he wouldn't have just forgotten about his van. That's about it."

Angela reclined herself against the back of the couch and looked with curiosity at her unexpected guest. Her lips were parted. She was breathing shallowly. She was alert and languorous at the same time.

———

Edward Grosek

CHAPTER 26
ANGELA TAKES A CHANCE

Saturday, August 26, 1978

Seeing her repose against the couch's back and the hints of arousal in her mien, Sonny sensed that Angela's thoughts were drifting from the course of their conversation. "Maybe...," he thought to himself. He slid onto the middle cushion, which had been separating them, and said, "Correct me if I'm wrong. Angela, Mickey didn't appreciate you."

Surprised by this, she said nothing. He took her by the elbows, drew himself up, and said, "Stand up." They both rose to their feet, and Angela felt her throat constrict. Sonny gently took from her hands the collars of her bathrobe. Her eyes widened, her skin tingled. Submissively, she lowered her arms. Sonny drew apart the robe, narrowly at first, then fully. He released his grip, and the garment dropped limply to the floor. Sonny's head jerked back an inch, and he studied her as a man would appraise a statue of a nude in a museum: incrementally, organ by organ, the contours, the symmetry, the proportions.

Sonny's youthful allurements were inches away, and Angela looked at him bravely, resigned to whatever was to happen. Sonny, thrilled with this girl –she did not reach for her fallen cloak! –blushed with lust. He cried softly, "You're beautiful!" The words wafted into her brain like sunshine.

196

Sonny clasped her, pulled her close to him and began kissing her. After a minute, he stopped and declared, "You're stunning!" With his left hand, he took the back of her neck. This time as he kissed her, he squeezed her breasts with his free hand.

Angela's skin was "tight." It was the kind of skin that did not just stretch protectively over a body but that wreathed around it elastically like the leather wrapping on a steering wheel.

Sonny ran his hands to her waist, and there pressed his fingers into the soft skin above her pelvis. Involuntarily, she pushed back from him, and he motioned with his chin to the couch. "Lie down and stay down."

Angela knew what her lying down on the couch meant. She told herself, "This is what you wanted, isn't it –one of Mickey's friends?" She sat down. "Turn off the lights," she said softly and resonantly. She turned herself and reclined upon the cushions. She was dripping –was it from the newness of this seducer and his virility or was it from the risk she was taking?

Sonny clicked off the lights and in the dimness began stripping off his clothes, letting them drop upon the carpet. Angela watched him. She wondered whether she was a nymphomaniac, a girl living with a continual sexual prurience, but with no intention of retaining her partners as boyfriends. "God, I hope so," she thought.

He finished and sprang to the couch, grinning. His grin was sheepish but also purposeful and avaricious. Shamelessly, he climbed between her legs and lowered himself. Angela had let herself become overcome by Sonny's flatteries and encroachments, and now she felt him encircling her with his arms. She whispered, "Aren't you going to –"

"No, sweetheart, this way is more pleasurable. Trust me." Then… she heard Sonny breathe the words, "I am *so* lucky," and she laughed in triumph.

—

It *was* more pleasurable, so much more instantly delightful and gratifying that, for both of them, the act was over within moments. But what else could two people on the very day they meet expect but the most divine and swift of conjunctions! Sonny rolled off Angela, off the couch and onto the floor with a thud. Underneath his back was her robe. He closed his eyes and "crashed" for thirty seconds.

Angela too let herself relax. They looked at each other, and Angela laughed, this time in celebration.

"That was…," Sonny remembered a superlative he had heard recently, "Herculean!"

"Ummm. Mine was… interstellar."

Sonny looked about the room, gathering the energy he needed to stand upright. He pulled the robe from beneath him and handed it to Angela.

He got up. She swung her legs off the couch. "Wow," she said to herself, "I needed that!"

"I'll get you a towel."

Angela motioned with her head. "Linen closet." She smiled at his nakedness.

Seconds later, she was back inside her robe, and he was on his feet, toweling himself. Both were still feeling the pleasant palpitations from their exertions. He wrapped the towel about his waist and returned to the couch, and they sat side by side.

Sonny's eyes panned across the living room. They stopped at Angela's television. "Mickey gave me the T.V. that I have in my apartment." They were looking at each other leisurely, yet attentively. "He walked off with it from where he works. Nobody would buy it from him, so he gave it to me. So, I owed him. I talked Rudy into letting him go with us on the break-in. Rudy says Mickey's a world-class half-wit." He chuckled.

She too chuckled. "Why did you rob the store?"

"Besides the money? We thought we could pull it off!" He shrugged. "That was it. Getting away with it."

"You risked your job for that!?"

"Yeah. For the sport of it. For that."

Sonny's answer was direct, unevasive, the kind of frank reply a working man was unafraid to give. Angela wanted to be able to do that. "The next time you and Rudy go out on a job, let me in on it and take me with you."

The very proposition dumbfounded Sonny. His mouth opened. "What –?" Again Angela raised her eyebrows and looked back at him levelly. "Aren't you afraid of getting caught?" He was smiling.

"Well –yes!" Then she asked, "Do you and Rudy have something lined up that I could get in on? I really want –"

He shook his head 'no' slowly. "Rudy doesn't want to do anything more till next year… probably till next spring."

There had been a momentum up to this point, and Angela wanted to sustain it. She lifted her chin. "Well, Sonny, since I know so much, don't you think Rudy ought to meet me? I assume he's… about your age –?" She could not suppress her grin.

He shrugged. "Yeah. You wanna meet him?"

"Yes."

"Lemme use your phone. What time is it? Rudy's working. He gets off at five. Maybe we could all go to The Courtside for sandwiches and beer. –You ever been there?"

"No." Angela felt a tremble in her breast, and again she said to herself, "This is what you wanted, isn't it?!"

The phone sat on an end table adjacent to the couch. Sonny reached, picked up the receiver, and dialed Merle's Billiards. They heard the brittle click of someone picking up at the other end.

"Rudy? Hey, it's me. Listen, I'm at Angela's." Angela could hear Rudy's voice but could not make out his exact words. "Yeah, *that* Angela. She doesn't know where Mickey is, but he told her a lot about... " Rudy said something. "Well, not everything, but... " Again Rudy spoke. "She's known about it for a full month! Look, let's all go out to The Courtside and talk. You'll like her. She's reasonable. She's good-looking. We'll take my car." He turned to Angela. "I'll drive you back, after."

The words "What luck!" went through Angela's mind. Light-headed, she threaded a stray lock of hair behind her ear. Was everything really changing for her?

She wanted to be fresh when she meets Rudy. She said to Sonny, "I need to rinse off in the shower."

"You need to douche in the shower," he thought to himself and laughed.

Angela laughed reciprocally. She went into her bedroom, tossed her robe on the bed, and strode into her bathroom. After rinsing herself hurriedly, she shut off the shower. Sonny was still talking on the phone, and she thought, "I'll bet he's bragging to Rudy. What's he telling him –everything?" On the bathroom door was a full-length mirror. Angela threw back her shoulders and checked her reflection. She put her hands on her hips. Vitality swept through her; her eyes widened, and she laughed happily.

Minutes later, she stepped from her bedroom and stood in its door frame. She had on stretch jeans, sneakers with dark red shoelaces, and a yellow rayon pullover that fit her snugly and that had a wide neck-opening and sleeves that descended to her elbows. Underneath, she wore a bra that had conically-shaped cups that she had bought but never worn outside of her apartment. She was beaming. Her mind was clear as a bell, and her complexion was radiant, except perhaps for that patch of skin above her lip, which was somehow losing its old importance.

Sonny liked what he saw, and the word "wow" formed on his lips. He put his mouth to the phone's receiver and said, "We're gonna leave in a couple minutes."

"I'm ready," she said stately, enunciating the words so that Rudy could hear. "You better get your stuff back on." She was grinning.

"Wait'll you see her, she looks great!" Rudy asked Sonny something, to which he replied, "Yeah, uh… we're leavin' now. See ya."

He hung up the phone, and Angela moved into the living room and watched him dress. When he had finished, when he pushed himself off the couch, she took her keys from the vase and two cards from the drawer of the small table. She opened the apartment door. After they passed into the hallway, she closed the door behind them and tugged at the knob to make sure it had locked.

She raised her head. Her neck was erect and her lips were smiling blandly, but to no one in particular. Perhaps she was hoping to be caught by some of the building's other tenants, emerging from her apartment with this Italian.

It was 4:30 PM.

———

Chapter 27
Angela in the Cutlass

Saturday, August 26, 1978

Sonny drove the Cutlass onto Merle's front parking lot and shut off the motor. It was ten minutes to five. The car faced Merle's windows, and through them Angela saw for the first time a real pool room with its tables and players. She peered curiously at this view of men and boys making lever-like strokes with pointed wooden sticks and then strutting around and around the big tables. These movements, she could tell, were peculiar to this sport. They fascinated her. "Let's watch," she said softly. Her eyes began shuttling from table to table.

Minutes went by. An older man unobtrusively sitting on one of the chairs in the mezzanine rose and came to the front counter. He and the young man who had been behind the cash register exchanged words and then places. The young man walked past the vending machines to a door near the rest rooms, unlocked it, and went inside.

"That's Rudy. He's probably washing up now."

"Oh." Angela was trying to make sense of what she was observing. "How do they all keep score?" she asked herself. She turned her head to Sonny. "You know, Sonny, this doesn't seem like a game girls can get themselves interested in, does it?"

"You're right. It's one of *our* games."

She smiled at his remark. Rudy came out the front entrance; and as he headed toward Sonny's car, her face expanded in recognition. "Sonny, I know *him!*"

Rudy opened the driver's door and leaned down to better see this girl who had provided herself to both Mickey and Sonny. She turned her face unashamedly to him, he saw the birthmark, and she said, "I know *you*, Rudy." Her voice was spiraling in simple joy. "You came in to use the *Thomas Registers* to look up some companies!"

"Oh... yeah, in the library."

Sonny shifted himself against the steering wheel. Rudy tilted forward the driver's seat and squeezed onto the back seat. Angela twisted with her waist so that she could face Rudy between the bucket seats. She inhaled, her chest protruded, and Rudy's eyes dilated. Here was –he sensed it! –an approachable girl, and the inevitable interrogatives entered his mind: "Is she Sonny's girlfriend? Does he want her just for himself?"

The two grinned at each other. The hair on the sides of Rudy's head was combed back "old style," and on the front of his shirt were smudges of blue chalk. He took out his cigarettes. "Want one?" His eyes were aimed at Angela's.

"I don't smoke."

"Not yet," said Sonny. "I bet she starts smoking... in a couple weeks."

Angela let herself laugh gaily. She thought, "Sonny's probably told him everything. They were talking on the phone for ten minutes."

Rudy rolled down one of the back windows and lit up. Angela liked the simple masculine motion that Rudy's hand made, striking the match toward himself on the folded pack and touching it to the cigarette to bring it to life. He inhaled, and she said, "Rudy, tell me something about the pool business."

"It's not complex." He looked absently at his cigarette for a moment. "I think the bottom line is that the owner has to run it himself. That's my uncle Julian behind the counter." Rudy pointed to Julian with his cigarette. "He owns the business. He's here every night. You can't," he shook his head, "set up a room and hire a manager to run it. You can do that for... maybe a chain store, like a shoe store, but not for a business that has to, like, cultivate steady customers."

This sounded logical to Angela. "Does the pool room make money?"

"We take in $200 or more every day –just from the tables. But remember, we pay $1,000 a month rent on the building plus electricity, insurance, and so on. We re-cloth two or three tables every year. That costs money. We put on two small tournaments. But we advertise 'em in the papers. I'm full time. We have a part-timer. Julian has to set aside money for his old age. So, yeah, it's been makin' money all along." He paused and twiddled the cigarette between his second and third fingers. "We compete with bowling, golf in the summer... skating rinks in the winter... –"

"The race tracks," interjected Sonny.

"Yeh, the race tracks. But we're not comparable to any of these." Then he confessed, "I'd like to buy into the room someday... and put on a big tournament."

Again Angela looked through Merle's plate glass windows. She liked the way the shooters focused intensely on the colored balls, oblivious to the others in the room, and then swung their pool sticks. She turned back to Rudy. "No girls allowed on the tables?"

"Yeah, they're allowed. But this is where guys learn... like, guys' logic –to smoke, swear, beat other guys out of their money, talk about broads... "

They all laughed. To Angela, today was her turn; she was one of these "broads."

It was then that Rudy decided that Angela was not Sonny's girlfriend. He slid forward and rested his forearms on the tops of the two bucket seats, a move that gathered the three into a proximity, a familiarity that Angela could feel immediately. Even more now, she wanted to be like these two pool-hallers, who infracted laws and conversed with insolent freedom. And, most essentially for her, they both continued to disregard as if it were nonexistent the mottle lying upon her face.

"Let's go," said Sonny. Rudy was quietly lusting over Angela, who had pivoted her head a degree to show him her left profile, her "good side." Sonny reached to turn the ignition key.

But Angela straightened. "Wait. I know *that* man."

Sonny stopped. "Which one?"

"The one with the necktie... in the powder blue shirt... leaning over the table right now." She motioned with her finger to a man playing pool on a table in the second row from the windows. This man had thick lips, a bulbous nose, and creases under his eyes from squinting. There was little or no humor in his expression, and he seemed to be making comments continuously, whether he was shooting or not.

"That's George Libby," said Rudy, his voice suddenly antagonistic and his lips now in a straight line. "He cheats."

This accusation seemed odd to Angela. She looked again at George Libby. Libby was playing with a young man about Sonny's age who had lush black hair piled upon his head and combed in front into a pompadour. As he moved about the table, his hair undulated and floated, but without losing its shape. "How could Libby cheat? He's out in the open."

"I'll tell you how." Rudy pulled himself closer to the front seats. "He talks while you're shooting. He hides the chalks –he drops them in his pocket. When you win a game, he puts off paying you till you're into the next game, then he claims he paid you!"

Sonny asked, "How do you know him, Angela?"

"He uses my library. He's a CPA accountant... a certified public accountant bookkeeper. He uses the accounting standards booklets in the business reference area. And the IRS *Bulletins* in the government documents department. A couple times, he asked me for Tax Court *Reporter* volumes. The government publishes those too." She went on. "He comes in with a satchel-case that's full of papers. It's bigger than a briefcase. It has, like, accordion pleats at both ends. He takes over a whole table in the back and spreads his stuff all over it." She paused. "Then, after, he goes to the Xerox machine and makes copies of whatever he was working on."

She added, "I got nosy, and once, when he was in the men's room, I peeked... at the papers lying on his table. I saw his letterhead. He has an office –I forget exactly where –downtown on North Pearl Street, I think."

"Wait a minute," said Rudy, sparked by Angela's intrusiveness upon this –to him –unsavory man. "You know, I heard Libby helped a business in Albany... or Schenectady to go out of business –or maybe it was to go bankrupt." Clearly, he wanted to know more about George Libby.

"I don't know anything about Libby. But I know that businesses hire CPAs to certify their bookkeeping, you know, to validate it." She paused. "To hide gaps in their bookkeeping. Especially to hide money or inventory."

"Huh!" muttered Sonny.

She said, "Here's something I read once. Let's say two businessmen who trust each other –two dentists or two men who own jewelry shops –exchange checks for $1,500. They come out even. But each can show his canceled check to his accountant and claim he bought $1,500 worth of merchandise or supplies from the other businessman. Of course, he cashes the check he received for $1,500 –in dollars, and sets that amount aside. He has to set it aside in cash. When he files his taxes or files for bankruptcy, he lists the $1,500 of the canceled check as an expenditure. Get it?"

"You can do that?"

Angela nodded. "All you need are receipts. You can paint your office yourself and then write out a receipt for the paint job from a guy who doesn't exist for, say, seventy-five dollars cash. You replace the seventy-five dollars in your cash register with the receipt. Now," she thrust out her index finger, "if you do these things over time, you can sock away, probably, thousands of dollars."

Rudy and Sonny looked at each other. "So…, " Rudy began.

"So, your accountant friend signs off on your records, and you keep the cash out of sight."

"How do you know all this?" Sonny asked.

Angela smiled. "I read." A shade of apology showed on her countenance. "I read too much, I guess."

But even this new knowledge, that Libby was not unskilled in his profession, could balance out Rudy's aversion for him. He pulled on what was left of his cigarette and thrust it out the car window. "You know," he blew smoke through his nose and said to Sonny, "I'd really like to punish this guy somehow!" He looked at Angela. "He comes in on weekends and sits in the mezzanine, like, for a long time, watchin', lookin' for an easy game. I told Vince not to play 'im." Then Rudy said, "It's too bad we can't set him up to take the rap for our job!"

To Angela, Rudy's invective was an outburst of male envy. But also to her, Libby meant nothing. She peered carefully at the man's face. His face was wider than its length, a sign, she had once read, of a dishonest man; and his lower lip drooped sloppily and formed a small "V." She took up Rudy's thread. "We… " she was including herself, "could plant some of the money on him –in his satchel. Then –" she raised her eyebrows to Sonny and Rudy, "we wait till he goes in a store or in the mall, we phone the police anonymously and warn them that we just spotted a man carrying a gun entering the store. I can make the call," she said resolutely. "The cops'll rush to the store if they hear a female's voice. They'll take Libby by the arms and search him and his satchel."

"What happens when the cops don't find a gun on him?" Sonny asked.

Angela leaned closer to him. "All the cops need to find is the money! Libby'll say the money wasn't his. The cops won't arrest him, but they'll tell other cops!"

"All right, but how do we get the money into his case?" asked Sonny. "We'd have to tail him to see where his office is and who hires him and where his car is so we can tip the cops where to catch him."

"I bet we can find his office by looking him up in the yellow pages," said Rudy.

"Mickey told me the money is tied up into lots of bundles. Right?" Angela paused, but neither of the two nodded in acknowledgement. This was what Angela had been waiting for –action. She saw it now excitedly, clearly, as one sees the road ahead after a rainstorm has cleansed the air. "Give me two or three of the bundles, and I'll take them to the library and slip them into one of the pockets in his satchel –it has side pockets that zip up. I'll watch for him to go into the men's room and do it then. I'll press the money 'way down deep. Then I'll phone you two immediately."

The plan was simple and linear, and Rudy liked its intent, namely to frame Libby and leave him to wonder why someone had hidden wads of money on him that he had never before seen. There was humor in this, and he smiled.

Angela shifted herself toward the center of the car. "Planting the money'll be risky, but I'll pull it off, and if he doesn't notice the money right away, he'll be walking around with the evidence." She shuttled her head from Sonny to Rudy and back. "Well, I'll do this after you two decide you want this to happen… and after you," she raised her lip, baiting them with a half-smile, "decide to trust me with the money." She was entreating these two, whom she had met only today, to let her in with them, after the fact, but no less than up to her neck!

"I think," began Rudy, "if this works… " He almost said, "we'll have gotten away with everything." But he did not complete his sentence.

Sonny raised his chin. It was clean-shaven and masculine, and he preened it thoughtfully with his fingertips. He had to know how strong Angela was. He asked her, "Angela, did you ever do anything like… this where you needed cold-blooded self-control?"

It was a business question and yet, an opportunity for Angela. "No, but let me tell you something." Again she looked from Sonny to Rudy and back. "I've been starving at the University. I work with 'colleagues,' not people. They're all sedate. Static. They're all afraid to say what's on their minds. They say 'college women' instead of 'college girls.' They 'abhor' fighting. They 'adore' opera. All of them!

One of them in the library thinks the librarians ought to call ourselves 'information scientists'!" She turned to Rudy. "I need something once in a while that'll make my heart pump –I mean like an oil rig!" She said to him, "I can do what you want." She turned to Sonny. "I can make an agreement and carry out my part and not get caught!"

"Am I over-selling myself?" she thought. She stopped talking.

Sonny made a slight movement backward with his neck. "O.K.," he said tentatively. He wanted to hear what Rudy might have to say.

"We cased out a guy before. Remember?" Rudy meant the old man whose house was on Northbrick Street. "We gotta be more thorough this time."

Sonny said, "What if Libby figures out that the money *must* have been planted *in* the library?"

Angela rotated her wrist so that her palm was right side up. "That's all he'll figure out. What more can he figure out?" She made an exaggerated shrug. "*Whom,*" she stressed the word, "can he point the finger at?"

"Yeah," Sonny said. He sounded very nearly convinced. "This shouldn't be too hard... or take too long. And one thing I like is Libby has no connections to any of us. It'll work –"

" –if we make it work and stick to our plan!"

Sonny motioned with his head to Rudy, then to Angela. "He's talked with both of you. He doesn't really know me, so I'll have to find his office building and shadow him and find out when he goes to his clients' stores or... " he flicked out his hand, "whatever Libby does... his comings and goings. All right," he said to Angela, "we'll put you on probation... make you prove yourself." With these words, their scheme to ascribe suspicion to George Libby was approved. Angela's smile widened with delight.

The three laughed in unanimity; three chums and now a coterie of plotters precipitant for adventure. Yet, each had singular thoughts. Sonny knew that on October 9ᵗʰ, he and Rudy would have to begin removing the money from its hideout in the storage unit, whether or not Mickey reappeared. Angela made up her mind that if Mickey should materialize after today, she would never again pay him money for coming to her apartment. "I'm pulling up the drawbridge," she laughed silently.

And Rudy was certain –was already fantasying –that whether or not George Libby is set up and pinned with the blame, he could, with some luck, talk his way into Angela's apartment. "She's available! She's get-able!" he told himself. "I just need to get her phone number tonight."

"Let's go to The Courtside!"

"One last thing," said Rudy. "Gonzag's not involved in this at all. Agreed?!"

"Right." Sonny shook his head back and forth. "We don't tell any of this to him. He's gone off the face of the earth."

"Except for his van on Oakwood Road!" Again Rudy distended his lips downward. He spread out his hands to Angela. "The last thing I want is to learn that he's in a coma in a hospital somewhere." He pointed at Angela. "But that's still on my list! I'm simply hopin' somebody picked him up and drugged him and is holdin' him in a cellar somewhere." Sonny coughed out a laugh. "The only worry is –"

" –is that someday he'll let the whole thing slip out." Angela finished the sentence. "Right?"

"If he lets it slip out, then he'll disappear one more time." The words brought a hush for several seconds to the car. From

Edward Grosek

Central Avenue, they heard the street's random traffic noises. Sonny smiled. "Let's go to The Courtside and get better acquainted."

Angela grinned. "As if we don't know each other!" she said to herself.

Sonny turned the key in the ignition. The car's engine revved alive and quickened. "Oh, hey!" Rudy spoke out. "I promised Vince I'd be back here by 10 and give him a ride home." He checked his wristwatch. It was just after 6 o'clock. His eyes moved from his watch to Angela's yellow pullover.

Angela turned once again to Merle's Billiards' windows. "Who's Vince?" She meant, "Which one is Vince?"

"He's my cousin. We're second cousins," said Sonny. "We'll be back before 10."

Angela scanned among the many young men and teenagers inside, looking for another good-looking Italian.

———

CHAPTER 28
CAUGHT

August 26 to September 4, 1978

Sonny, Angela, and Rudy made their way inside The Courtside to one of the cushioned booths and sat down. Pennants of various football teams were tacked to the wall in back of them, and on an adjacent wall hung framed photographs of basketball players. On another wall a television set was mounted. Its screen showed a baseball game already several innings along; and faintly, Angela could hear the sportscaster commenting.

Their sandwiches and the mugs and pitcher of beer arrived. They talked about their cars, their favorite popular songs, funny things that had happened to them. Rudy brought up Mickey Gonzag. "Turns out, Gonzag lost his job at the hotel. He was workin' there as a lackey!" It took a moment for Angela to realize that Rudy's remark was facetious, as well as it was disparaging. They laughed.

The sandwiches, the closeness, the prandial chatter further predisposed the three to one another. Angela was glad she had let Sonny into her apartment and met him and now Rudy. These two lived for themselves. They took little for granted, and they were self-confident and resourceful. It was their thinking, their mentalities, she knew, with which she must renovate her own; and before that, it was their esteem and their trust she

213

would have to merit. She decided that she would stop writing book reviews. "That was a waste of time. A rut I got into," she thought. "I'm like a flower that needs new soil. How can I get into that pool room?"

The pitcher dropped below half full. Rudy lit a cigarette and inhaled. He looked at Angela. It was time to resume the plot-making that would shine the Albany police's searchlight on George Libby. He began questioning her, at first as if he were mildly curious. He wanted to hear how well she could put into words and thereby prove to him what he and Sonny expected of her.

"Does Libby know your name? Where in the library does he sit ordinarily? Who sits nearby? Where do you sit? How many minutes does Libby normally spend in the men's room? Does he leave his satchel zipped or unzipped? What're the chances a student'll walk in and see you put the money in Libby's satchel? What'll you do as soon as you plant the bills?"

The last question was very important. Angela replied, "I'll walk away. I won't look back."

Sonny had cleaned the library, its carpeting and stairwells and rest rooms, many times and so knew the building. He was satisfied with Angela's answers and rose from the booth. "I'm going to run to the men's room."

He walked off. Rudy too was pleased. He thought Angela had responded as if she wanted to do her part and will do it. He extinguished his cigarette and relaxed. He wanted to ask her, "Can I have your phone number?" Instead, his eyes once more dropped blatantly onto her breasts. Before today, no one had ever gaped at her so crudely. She thought back to that bazaar of males she had observed earlier through the front windows of Merle's building. "That's what *all* those pool hall guys have in the backs of their minds!" she said to herself.

"What's her cup size?" Rudy wondered, again preoccupied with his carnal thoughts.

Angela took from her pocket a card and on it with her neatest handwriting put her phone number. "Rudy, can you call me Tuesday, say around 6 o'clock?" She slid the card to him. "I should be home from the library by then." She looked at him, wittingly.

Again, Rudy's blood temperature rose in anticipation, for he knew what this gesture probably meant. "I'll bet she's like a flower whose petals open easily!" he thought. He slipped the card into his wallet and grinned.

–

And so it was that Angela acquired, by her good fortune and impulsiveness, another consort. After that Tuesday, Rudy's "lucky day," she saw him and Sonny in the safety of her apartment, one of them at a time, on alternating weekends. At first, neither liked these biweekly intermissions, but, Angela explained to them, "I don't dare let either of you get too much of me."

As for George Libby, The three conspirators carried out what they had devised that Saturday afternoon in the car and later at The Courtside. The next day Sonny and Rudy removed three bundles of money from the Studebaker and gave them to Angela, who got her chance on Friday to secrete them inside Libby's satchel. The concealment was less of an intricacy than one might imagine. At the right moment, the moment Angela was watching for –when Libby rose and entered the men's room –she strode to the table Libby was using, removed the packets of bills from the envelope she was carrying them in, and stuffed them into one of his satchel's zippered pockets.

She walked away into the stacks and back to the reference desk.

The next step demand less audacity than persistence. On Monday morning, that is on September 4th, Sonny drove to Libby's downtown office, parked there on Pearl Street, and began his surveillance. He sat in his car, holding his eyes fast on his quarry's storefront, ignoring the pedestrians and cars passing by and, as best as he could, willfully keeping his mind from wandering. After an hour, he wished he had thought to bring his thermos bottle of coffee. He lowered the window and breathed in and out deeply. A police car went by, and Sonny took out from his glove compartment a road map, opened it and pretended to study it. For a long while this was about all that happened.

Finally, Libby left the building and drove uptown to an antique shop on Ontario Street. Sonny followed. He circled the block and parked on the other side of the street. This particular antique business was an emporium of well-crafted old furniture, restored and polished and tagged with extravagantly high prices. The exterior of the shop was of varnished woodwork, and over the door was an unembellished sign that stated, "Scarlett's." The interior was brightly lit; and through Scarlett's windows Sonny could see such antiquated appointments as a book case with glass doors, desks, a silvery umbrella stand with ivory-handled canes in it, a painting displayed on an easel, an all-white piano with a vase on it, and old fashioned ornate floor lamps, all plugged in and lit.

Libby had entered the shop with his swollen satchel case. This was Sonny's chance. He ran to a telephone booth, phoned Angela at her office, and gave to her the antique shop's location and a short description of Libby's attire. He ran back to his car, got in, slouched down, and waited.

An Albany police car rushed up to the antique shop and braked. Two uniformed officers moved quickly from the vehicle and inside the building. In front of Mr. Scarlett, the owner of the business and one of his best clients, George Libby was apprehended. The more thickset and surly of the policemen seized Libby's satchel. Imperiously, arrogantly, he yanked open all the zippers, began thrusting his big hand into its compartments and pockets –and lifted out the three rubber-banded bunches of bills. Like this, with the money in his fingers, he froze for a second.

Libby and Mr. Scarlett were dumbfounded by this onrush of drama. "What're you –? That's not my money," Libby blurted defensively. He was watching the policeman carefully, yet tremulously. Most policemen in Albany were overbearing men, and this one began insolently fanning through the cash, counting the ten dollar bills.

At this point in the confusion, Sonny, who had got out of his car and crossed the street, strolled innocently past Scarlett's windows. He turned his head and saw the tell-tale money in the officer's hands. "Good," he grunted between his teeth: that was the proof that Angela had played her part as she had promised.

"What do you mean, it's not *your* money?" said the second policeman. This man also was large, not in girth but in height, and he too exuded vulgarity. He and his partner had found no handgun on Libby nor could they see one in plain view. Libby shifted his eyes to this other man and hesitated, trying to think, trying to pull his mind from its paralysis. He swallowed.

"There's about three grand here," announced the first policeman. He glared at Libby, accusingly. Was someone playing a prank on the police department?

Three thousand dollars was a large sum. "Who put it there?" Libby wondered. He shook his head to clear his mind. His mouth flopped open. "It belongs to one of my other clients," he replied, salvaging both himself and the mystery money from the two policemen; for if he had disavowed the money, whatever its provenance, the policemen would surely have confiscated it.

"Officers, Mr. Libby has been my accountant for more than ten years," said Mr. Scarlett. He was shaking his head and rubbing his hands together, as if washing them. "Why are you here?" They all looked at each other. The second policeman walked quickly about the store, looking in the aisles and behind the counters. He returned and regarded the first policeman, who nodded to him knowingly, and then plunked the bundles of ten dollar bills he was holding down on the lid of the white piano. Without a word of explanation or apology, the two looked about the shop one last time and left. Mr. Scarlett exhaled loudly.

Two nights later, George Libby's office on Pearl Street was broken into, and its contents –the desk, the file cabinets, the carpeting, the potted plant –were torn apart and splintered into pieces. Apparently, someone had used carpenters' tools to pry and wrench open every enclosure in the office where Libby might have concealed whatever the rifler was searching for. Even the picture frames displaying Libby's diplomas were smashed. What remained in the room was left scattered over the floor and against the walls. The entire office space looked like the shambles of an abandoned house.

Bewildered, shocked, wondering whom he should suspect for this damage, Libby wept openly in the presence of the police detectives who were investigating. These latter men acted as if this particular crime were inconsequential, as if they knew already that nothing fruitful from their inspection would transpire. Nothing did, except a superficial report of it in the *Albany Times Union*.

The following month, Libby moved his practice to Schenectady.

———

Edward Grosek

CHAPTER 29
MERLE'S BILLIARDS

September 24, 1978

During Sonny's second visit to her apartment, Angela discovered that the most effective tactic for inducing a loverboy to return again and again was the massage: gripping, twisting, kneading, squeezing the flesh of his shoulders and back. Angela labored with her hands and fingers like this for several minutes. Then, rolling whichever it was –Sonny or Rudy, on top of her, she compelled him into his role in their intimacy.

It was on Rudy's third trip to "the apartment" –the abridged term they used to refer to Angela's residence plus the enjoyments gotten therein –that Angela learned more from him about Julian Merle's business. They had finished and were in the living room, putting back on their clothes, and Rudy brought up Mr. Tarantelli.

"He's the man who puts new cloth on the tables when it gets worn. There's a lot to a pool table." Rudy was aglow, smiling amicably and pulling on his socks. "He does two or three tables every spring. Everybody knows him. He strips a table, levels it, re-cloths it. It takes him all day. The table comes out brand-new."

"So," Angela thought, "you don't need to be a player to be an insider."

They sat on the couch, and Rudy told her about Mr. Finkle. "Harry Finkle owns the building we're in. And he owns the car wash down the avenue and... other property in Albany. That's where his office is, the car wash. Once last winter he was getting ready to go out just as I came in with the rent check. I handed it over." Rudy was setting up the punch line. "He took it. Picture him –tall and thin, always wears a suit. He took his hat from a coat rack. It was a derby hat. He looked at me as if he were demonstrating how a hat works. He, like, fitted it on to his head with mechanical precision." Rudy imitated the motion Finkle made, screwing the hat down onto his skull. Angela chuckled. "Finkle wants to renegotiate the rent lease with Julian."

"What –he wants to raise the rent?"

Rudy nodded. "He wants Julian to sign a more favorable rent contract in case, he said, he decides to sell the building."

"Could Julian buy it? Does he want Julian to buy it?"

"Julian doesn't have enough to buy the property. He'd have to get a bank loan. See, then he couldn't retire! He'd have to use up all his savings."

"Wait." She held up her hand. "It sounds like Finkle's giving Julian first chance to buy it."

"Maybe."

"Just the building?"

"The building and the front and back parking lots... and the side driveway."

"What's the contract like?"

"Julian has a twenty year lease. He started up in 1963. So he has another five years."

Angela let herself flop against the couch's back. "He's asking Julian to raise his own rent voluntarily for five years?"

"That's about it, yeah."

"This Finkle's a nervy guy!"

"He wants to jack up the rent starting January to $1,200 a month." Rudy looked uncertain about all this. "Julian'd have to increase the table rates."

Angela put her fingertips up to her forehead. "But can't Julian say 'no'?"

"Well, yeah. But then Finkle can put it on the market... with a realtor –and you don't know who might buy it! Julian said this is what he was hinting. But –"

"A new owner can't raise Julian's rent arbitrarily."

"No, but he could refuse to make any repairs on the building, if they were needed. He could retaliate like that. Right now –I'll give you an example –the back parking lot area needs resurfacing." Rudy was fully dressed now. "Some of the asphalt is broken up badly."

"Gee," said Angela sympathetically.

"We got a perfect location too." Rudy's brow was wrinkled. "Julian said Finkle wants to buy into another investment in Albany. He thinks it's a new apartment construction, a big one. That's where there's money –in middle class rents. And that's why he needs money."

This was intriguing. Angela brought herself back up and leaned toward Rudy. "Can't Finkle borrow the money from a bank?"

"He'd... yeah, probably want *not* to borrow any money if possible, doesn't it figure?" Rudy wanted a cigarette, but he restrained the desire. "See, back in June or July, Finkle was about to sell a big plot of land out Western Avenue to a couple guys, developers. He told that to Julian last spring. But then, the guys couldn't pay up, they lost the money somehow. So –no dice, nothin' happened."

"It *is* a perfect location," Angela agreed abstractedly. She was picturing what she had seen of the outside of Merle's Billiards. The single-story building, standing by itself, spaciously separated from Central Avenue by its front parking lot.

"Julian says Finkle's been hopin' the developers'll come up with the money."

"What does Finkle want for the property?"

"Julian said a hundred thousand."

"A hundred thousand dollars," she repeated to herself.

———

Edward Grosek

CHAPTER 30
THE FINAL PLAN

September 27 to September 30, 1978

All at once the plan came to Angela! After finishing her time that Wednesday afternoon at the main reference desk, she was on her way, walking back to her office. She was wishing she had someone in the library, a friend she could confide in, to tell about her double life. "Well, it's not a double life, I didn't use an alias with those guys."

Ahead in the hallway she saw Sue Maher closing and locking the office supplies storeroom. Sue was one of the library's catalogers. Unlike referencing library information, cataloging library books is performed in a sector of the building that is segregated from the public. Most catalogers, therefore, come to work, if not well-clad, comfortably frocked. Today Sue had on violet dress coveralls over an embroidered blouse. The upper part of the coveralls, the vest, had pockets. The sleeves of the blouse Sue had rolled up, and on her feet she was wearing what looked to Angela like bedroom slippers.

As they approached each other, the two librarians exchanged 'hellos.' Sue affected a brief courtesy smile. The latter she exercised by tensing upward the small muscles above the ends of her lips. Angela's smile was more extensive and wide-eyed, the sort of girlish facial expression that one obtains from a sense of joyous living.

They passed each other by.

It was then, just after this path-crossing, that the strategy for resolving Sonny and Rudy's predicament and for remedying her own insularity conjured itself up. In that moment, the perfect resolution displayed itself, scene by scene, in Angela's mind. More than an expedient, it was a full disposition for the two implausible problems: how to bring out into the open and employ safely the loot and, simultaneously, how to enter the fellowship of pool-hallers who hung out at Merle's Billiards.

Stimulated, Angela quickened her pace. She entered her office and closed its door and sat down at her desk. On a sheet of paper she began outlining –or rather, sequencing –the ideas that had shown themselves so visually to her moments ago. She studied them, and on another sheet she listed her assets.

She rubbed her forehead with her fingertips. "This is a big risk. I'll lose everything if it falls through." She licked her tongue over her lips. "I'll have to convince Rudy first." She pursed her lips. "First comes Rudy. Can I convince him? He'll have more questions than the other two."

She dialed Merle's Billiards.

—

"Rudy, let's buy the building!"

Rudy was stirring cream into his coffee when he heard these words. His hand stopped, and his expression waxed, descending from amiably passive to blank. "What building?"

"Let's you and me and Sonny buy the building and the parking lot!" He knew now what building: his face showed it. "Look, if we're the landlords, then we won't raise Julian's rent!" And by her tone and the flush of urgency in her face, Rudy knew Angela meant exactly what she was asking.

It was after 5:30 that same day. Angela and Rudy were at a small table next to a window in Dewey's, one of the diners on Fuller Road. The waitress had brought their coffees and gone back behind the counter to make up the sandwiches they had ordered.

"I can put up one-third of the hundred thousand. I totaled up my savings this afternoon. I've been on the payroll savings plan for almost eight years, and I have a certificate of deposit my aunt gave me for graduation. Are you willing to buy a third?" She leaned her forearms on the table. "What about Sonny?"

She saw on Rudy's face comprehension of her proposal. But, she sensed a hesitation to answer and thereby admit implicitly to the size of the stolen money. "Rudy," she lowered her voice, "I'm telling you my secrets. Mickey told me you three were afraid you'd call attention to the money if your friends saw you spending it. But here's the perfect way to use it without anybody's learning that you have it!"

Not only was Angela's proposition unexpected, her vigorous advancement of it was forcing Rudy to discuss the robbery money outside of Sonny's presence! Again he felt conflicted. But her argument for buying the building made sense. And buying it with Curto's money was… ironic? Ingenious?

He held himself there, not drinking his coffee, trying to look indifferent, and yet with his mind poised, alert, as a pool player would remain near his table, inertly waiting for his opponent to miss his next shot. He needed more inducement. He said softly, "What else?" and reached in his shirt pocket for his cigarettes.

The waitress came with their sandwiches, each one on a plain white platter. Rudy lit his cigarette and smiled to her, courteously but not dallyingly; she was pretty and it figured that she had a boyfriend. She smiled back and checked his clothing, trying to estimate what amount he might leave for a tip. His shirt was fully unbuttoned, and underneath he had on a dark blue tee shirt. "Seventy-five cents," she thought, hoping for more. She turned back to the lunch counter.

"There's more to this," Angela resumed. "I can be the front-man. I can shield your money, and Sonny's." But she wanted to persuade, not exhort. She slowed herself. "We can tell the customers that I and a couple professors from the University formed a company to buy the property as a business investment. No one's going to check into it." She picked up her sandwich. Seeing this, Rudy picked up his.

She bit shallowly into the sandwich. "If you still like the idea by Friday, we'll tell it to Sonny. It's no good unless all three of us like it. If he likes it, we'll sell it to Julian on Sunday." She regarded Rudy, piercing his eyes with hers, wanting him to say nothing until she has finished. "If he likes it, we can all pitch it to Harry Finkle next week." She inhaled, as if drawing strength to continue. She took another small bite of the sandwich. "I think Finkle'll go for it. It'll be a cash sale. He wants cash as soon as possible, no?" She paused, and Rudy nodded. "If he likes it, you and I and Sonny'll dress up and go hire a corporate lawyer so we can form a company."

"A lawyer?"

She puffed out her cheeks and exhaled. "He'll do the legal work for us. There're lots of lawyers in the phone book." She took a third bite. "The lawyer'll apply for incorporation with New York State –or maybe just partnership, we'll see. As soon as he does that, we can set up, you know, a business bank account. We'll put our thirds into it. After the sale, Julian will pay our corporation the thousand dollars rent just as he pays

Finkle now. Rudy, after a couple months, we should have enough to repair the parking lot!"

Rudy continued to listen. A wraith of cigarette smoke above his head was gently dissipating. "At the end of next year, there'll be some money unspent. We'll pay ourselves a dividend from it. It won't be much, the first year, but... " She left the sentence unfinished.

"Who's gonna write the checks?"

"Well, if we do form the company, I'll have to be the president. You'll be the treasurer. We'll draw up a short constitution, and we'll all sign it. It'll be up to you and me to go to a bank —whatever bank Julian uses —and set up our account. We can keep the company records in a file cabinet. Sonny can keep the keys to the cabinet. How's that?"

"Sounds O.K. So far," Rudy admitted. He liked the way Angela was laying out the plan, but he knew he should not commit himself immediately. "We each own a third?"

"Julian comes in for one percent. That makes a hundred percent. There's one more advantage." She thrust out her index finger. "Get this. We'll go to the same insurance company, say Liberty, for both Julian's business and our building. And, we'll switch all our car insurances, even Julian's, to Liberty. Liberty'll give us breaks on our car premiums."

"They'll do that?"

"Sure. I'm getting a small break now 'cause I work for the University."

"I didn't know they did that. —Hey, won't we have to pay property taxes to the city?"

"To the county. The county'll send us a bill, and the treasurer," Angela grinned at Rudy, "will write a check from our rent money." She felt satisfied, as she so often did at the library's reference desk after furnishing a piece of needed information to a student. "Now... if we do this and it gets off the ground the way we want, I'll take a couple night classes in business at Albany Business College."

"Hmmm." Rudy smiled. "This is getting adventurous."

Angela began actually eating her sandwich, pausing to chew then to drink. Impulsively she asked, "Let me try one of your cigarettes."

"Sure." Rudy took his pack and shucked it to dislodge a couple cigarettes part-way out. Angela took one and put the filter end between her lips. She watched Rudy's lambent image in the window as he struck the match and put its small yellow flame to the tobacco end. She inhaled –and coughed. Clinching the cigarette in the cleft between her index and middle fingers, she withdrew it. Her lips protruded into a sour figuration, and Rudy laughed.

"It's our chance –" She shook her head. "Rudy, it's our chance to make our own luck." She set the cigarette in the ashtray. "Yughh!"

Rudy brought his napkin to his mouth and wiped away his smile. "What about Gonzag?" He was testing Angela.

"When he shows up, I'll tell him the cover story: me and some University professors bought the property as an experimental investment."

"Sonny'll want to know what's in it for you."

She inhaled. "I'll tell Sonny the truth. I'm fed up being a librarian every day of the week! I just want to work there for the pay." She picked up her cigarette.

–

Rudy thought that Angela's idea, or rather her enterprise, made better sense than the alternative: trickling the money out of its hideaway and hoping that no one catches him or Sonny or Gonzag spending it. By late Friday afternoon, he was as enthusiastic for the plan as Angela, its author. They explained it to Sonny. "Sooner or later," Rudy said to him, "we'll have to do something... with the money."

"What about Mickey?"

"I don't know. It depends on how he acts –and what he wants when he shows up in town."

To Sonny, Rudy was the strategist. "If you like it, I'm with you."

—

The next afternoon, Rudy toured Angela through the building. She had on a skirt that reached to her knees and flared a little, a patterned blouse with a fitted bodice, and white Nike dress shoes, no socks. Her head was erect, and she showed off, even through this casual ensemble, a feline grace to her body. In Rudy's eyes she looked today, if not provocative, pretty.

He took her into the office, then told her how he filled the soda and cigarette machines and cleaned the mezzanine and the carpet. He took her into his work room. He explained how the cue stick lockers were used and showed how players can keep score by dialing points on the tables' counters. And he demonstrated how the house charged players with the time clock.

Angela marveled at all this. As they moved through Merle's Billiards, Rudy felt growing in him pride, both for his job and in having Angela alongside him as his audience.

But the room began to fill with customers, and Rudy had to assume his station behind the front counter. Imperturbably, Angela walked across the mezzanine to one of the small tables near the railing. On her face could be seen felicity and expectation, as if she were entering a circus arena. She sat and began watching and listening.

Now and then one of the players on the floor noticed her, and she smiled to him, parting her lips minutely, just as she smiled out of habit in the library to a student with whom she happened to make eye contact. Soon she thought, "Some of these guys are good-looking. I better not stare."

Eventually, she found herself watching those players who seemed to make most of their shots, who looked absorbed and yet calculating, as they orbited their tables and stroked their pool sticks. "This is a beautiful game," she said to herself. "I wonder who the best player in the room is."

Vinnie and two of his friends came in. All three were lithe boys, wearing trim-fitting jeans and black tee shirts with gaudy rock-band images on the fronts. One of the boys had long hair that was pony-tailed back to his neck. The other was a blond. His hair was parted in the middle and layered and blow-dried along the sides of his head. School was in full session, and Vinnie was bringing in new customers. "Hey! Rudy! Let us have," he looked across the room, "table 24." He noticed Angela. "Who's that?" he asked with a motion of his head.

"Her name's Angela. She's a friend of me and Sonny."

"Oh, yeah?" Vinnie clucked his tongue and stretched his mouth into an enormous smile, trying to ruffle Rudy. He looked to his friends and back.

"Yeah!" retorted Rudy, the ends of his lips upturned. "A real good friend!"

Vinnie regarded Angela a second time, then turned back. "No one's seen Gonzag yet, huh?" Rudy shook his head. "Still out of town, then?"

"Find another pigeon!"

"Still owes Wayne fifteen dollars?"

"Yep."

"Gimme a ride home after 10 o'clock?"

"Maybe." Rudy made another petite smile. Now he had the upper hand. "You gotta empty the ashtrays twice. Before I get off and before we leave."

"O.K." Vinnie straightened his face. "How 'bout a smoke?"

Rudy started. His eyes shot out. He clenched his teeth and through them said, "You got a pack right now in your shirt pocket! I can see it!"

"Oh, yeah. Yeah, force of habit!" Vinnie grinned broadly. His two friends laughed.

———

CHAPTER 31
THE NEGOTIATORS

October 1 to October 6, 1978

The next day was Sunday, the first of October. At 4 o'clock that afternoon, an hour before Lloyd's time at the counter ended, Julian Merle entered the pool room, saw Rudy, and waved him into the office. He wondered what his nephew wanted to talk about. "That key duplicator was certainly a waste!" he thought. Rudy had already carried chairs from the mezzanine into the office. He, Sonny, and Angela filed in, he closed the door, and they sat in front of Julian's desk, he in back of it on a high-backed chair. Rudy introduced Angela to his uncle. Angela looked at him, smiling assertively; and he looked back at her calmly, thinking, "Is she pregnant? What is this?"

Rudy opened the meeting by recapping what all four of them knew, that Harry Finkle needed money and badly enough to want to sell the building that housed Merle's Billiards. "This is our chance to get the building from Finkle!"

Angela talked next. She had prepared herself for her part by rehearsing the sentences and ideas she wanted to put across to Julian and by practicing looks of sureness of purpose in her bathroom mirror. Speaking deferentially, she outlined the company she and her two partners wanted to form and assured Julian that its purpose will be to buy the property from Finkle

233

and after, to maintain it. "Each of us will own equally thirty-three percent of the company. And, Julian," she addressed him familiarly, "we want you to own the remaining one percent. Please remember," she told him, "we're talking about the property. You will continue to own and run the business." She paused, then covered by memory the points and matters to which she and Rudy and Sonny had agreed.

Julian listened. Of course, he was surprised, but his was the surprise of an older man whose routines were being disrupted by these three young people who wanted, it seemed, to become investors.

Angela finished by promising, "We won't raise your rent, and we will resurface the parking areas."

Julian was silent for a full minute. The three friends waited. He asked Angela who she was, and she slid a sheet of paper over his desktop to him. On it she had written her name, job title, address, and phone number. "I've been working at the University for eight years. That's where I met Sonny. Before that, I worked at Schenectady Community College's library."

He said, "I'll think about this," but then immediately asked, "Where did you 'capitalists' get all your money? Finkle will want to know."

But they were ready for such a scrutiny. Their answers tumbled out.

"Playing cards."

"Hustling pool."

"I inherited a lot of mine."

"Me too. Some of mine. Some is my old college money."

"I live at home."

"We all work."

"None of us have expensive hobbies. We don't wear expensive clothes."

Julian had been in business too long not to be hesitant —suspiciously hesitant. He looked at Rudy. On Rudy's face were the patience and mild expectation of someone waiting in line to buy movie tickets. "Where did Rudy get such money?" Julian wondered. "From his father?" His eyes moved to Sonny. Sonny had said little so far, for he liked the way the negotiations were flowing. He smiled to Julian the way he smiled to his barber.

Julian asked each of them what he –and she –wanted to get out of this new company. Their responses were simple. Sonny said he wanted a start toward becoming a businessman. "It's either this or go back and take classes."

"I think our room can be a leader in the pool business someday," Rudy contended. "I told you a couple times I want us to put on the New York State straight pool championship next year. This is how we can make money to pay for it."

Angela raised her head and confronted Julian squarely, brandishing her face. He could not help seeing the firm lips, the whites of her teeth, her birthmark. She said, "I'm secure in my library job. Now I want a sideline in the real world." He nodded his understanding. At this point, Angela sensed that they might be overwhelming the man with their explanations and answers. She leaned forward. "Julian, we'll leave now, and you decide whether this is a good idea for you or not."

Again Julian replied that he will "mull it over." He liked the way Angela had carried off her part in the meeting, and he had no doubt it was she who had conceived and engineered the performance. Most appealing to him was the elemental idea of not paying rent out of his profits to Finkle. But none of the three had given more than glib, easy answers to his most important questions: Where had they gotten all that money? Why really were the three of them pooling it together?

He was convinced they had not stolen or embezzled it. He read the newspapers every day, and there was no mention recently of such a large theft. "Maybe they know more about acquiring money than I do," he thought. "But what about Finkle? Will he want proof that their money is good?"

The next day Julian paid the month's rent to Harry Finkle at his office in the car wash. He had not, this far, made up his mind and so, said nothing else to his landlord. On Wednesday, he telephoned Finkle and asked to meet with him on Friday. He told Finkle only that he thought he has a buyer for the property. He specified, "A cash buyer."

–

On Thursday, Sonny came to Angela's office in the library. Without knocking, he entered and closed the door behind him. It was past 4 o'clock, and Angela was at her desk. Sonny pulled a chair up to the desk, and with no preface to the matter that had brought him here, he asked her, "What if –just suppose – Finkle suspects that the money we're offering him is the same money that the guy we took it from was going to pay him for that land out Western Avenue?"

It was an awkward sentence, the sort of amalgam of hasty words that someone who had suddenly become alarmed would make. "Is he losing his nerve?" Angela wondered. "Is he afraid of putting up his money?" She narrowed her face and held up the palm of her hand and considered the content of what she had just heard. She leaned forward and cocked her head. "Sonny, I take it that the guy –or guys you stole from want the land Finkle owns."

"Yeah. It's possible."

"That's what this guy does, he buys land and builds on it?"

"Yes."

"How would Finkle make the connection?"

"He couldn't, for sure. But he could figure. Lots of people know about the missing money."

"So, this guy who wants the land is the one you're really hiding the money from?"

"Right."

"And Finkle still possesses the land?"

"Yes."

She looked at Sonny, and the ends of her lips curled up. "Finkle still has the land. He wants to sell the building –to liquidate it –that's what he told Julian, right?" Sonny bit his fingernail. "We're giving him the cash he wants for his next investment! He's not gonna squeal on us, he's gonna protect us! He's gonna cover up the entire sale so no one sees the details or finds out our names. Sonny, I almost hope he suspects us!"

"No!"

"We've got to be careful not to drop any hints, but either way, whether he suspects or not, we're safe!"

"You think so?"

"Definitely. Finkle has to have this money, right?" She waited for him to nod. "Our company buys the property, he gets the cash and he still has that land on Western Avenue. He can sell it next year!"

"So… " Sonny felt his initial concern ebbing.

"So I'll bet he expedites the sale! I'll bet he helps us walk through it so we take all the right steps!"

–

On Friday morning, Lloyd opened up the room. Rudy and Sonny had put on white shirts and colored neckties, and

Julian wore his brown sport jacket. Angela had on the kind of dressy blouse, skirt and shoes a librarian would wear for a job interview. They gathered on the car wash's lot and in another minute were in Harry Finkle's office, seated in front of the man's desk.

Julian introduced his partners to Finkle, then straightaway he said, "Harry, we want to form a company and buy the property from you. We scraped together the amount you named two months ago."

Finkle was as tall as Sonny. His hair was brushed straight back, and he wore a custom-made suit, the well-tailored kind that made him look stylishly lean. He raised his black eyebrows, then, through a small smile, showed his teeth. "In cash?"

"Of course."

"Do I understand that each of you will be a cash participant in this venture?"

They all said, "Yes," and nodded.

"Are any of you borrowing money to be involved in it?"

"No," they replied.

Again, Finkle lingered deliberately. "I know Rudy. Tell me about yourself." He indicated Sonny.

"I had two years of college. I got divorced. I got a job in maintenance at the University. I've been there for four years. I have my own apartment, and I hang out at Merle's. I inherited some money. I want to use it, to invest it to see what kind of businessman I can be."

Finkle gazed for several seconds at Sonny. "Businessman," he said, as if the word amused him. There was no way for anyone in the office to divine whether he approved or not of Sonny or what Sonny had just told him. He pivoted his head to Angela; his face said, "You're next."

Angela opened the manila folder she had brought with her and took from it a sheet of paper. "I've been at the University for eight years, Mr. Finkle. This is my résumé. I enjoy my job, and now I want a sideline. I don't have expensive tastes. I too saved up my share of the money."

Finkle studied the résumé line by line, as a scientist might peruse the lab notes of a fellow scientist. "Admirable," he said laconically. He slipped the sheet into the top drawer of his desk. He cupped his jaw with his left palm and caressed it in thought. His hand moved to his throat and massaged it. "How much are each of you putting in?"

"Harry, we're going to keep that our company secret."

"You're right, Julian. O.K., Sonny, spell your last name for me." Sonny spelled 'Peggaluso,' and Finkle copied it onto a slip of paper. "Now," he slowed his sentences, as if he were issuing a formal notice to the prospective buyers. "I have to turn over your offer to my attorney. He'll check each of you for any criminal records and for your credit status. I believe everything you told me. But I need verification. In the meantime, you… can check up on me if you like." Finkle made a self-satisfied smile, as if his permission could lead only to an obvious conclusion. "When my attorney gives me his results, I'll phone Julian. I have both your numbers," he said to Julian.

He cast his eyes to Rudy. "By the way," he drawled, "did Julian tell you… my two sons and I built your building with our own hands in 1963! We saved a pretty penny by doing the work ourselves." And with that bit of condescending recollection, Finkle, by a simple torsion of his face, indicated to his four auditors that the meeting with him was at its end.

–

Before phoning his attorney, though, Harry Finkle remained seated at his desk, in thought. "Julian and his nephew will probably own most of this company. They probably talked the other two into buying in."

"Maybe not," he countered himself. "How did Julian find those two other backers? Especially the girl? How did he open up to them the idea of sinking money into my rental property?" His face became hawkish and concentrated. He said softly, "Maybe there's someone else, some link from the pool room to that librarian." Then, as he did routinely with all his business dealings, he asked himself, "What else don't I know about this? We'll see what Marty comes up with."

But Martin Marko, Finkle's attorney, found nothing inauspicious or suspicious or even doubtful about any of the four. Rudy Merle, it seemed, never borrowed money or owned a credit card. Years ago, Sonny Peggaluso was caught speeding in Albany County and got a ticket. Angela Lubelski proved to be a steady, if not boring, librarian. "Harry, I even went into the library and watched her. She stayed on the public desk till 3, then went to her office. She left at 5."

Marko was not finished. "So they look clean, Harry. What I can't figure is how the money can total up to a hund'rt grand."

"What do you think?"

"Well, the two young guys can't be good for more than a couple thousand apiece. The old man, you told me, can't come close to a hund'rt thou." Marko spread out his hands. "Now, the Lubelski girl," his hands remained spread apart, "she comes out of nowhere, out of the dusty book stacks in a library, and presto, Julian has the hund'rt K! See my point, Harry?"

"Spell it out, Marty."

"The big quantum of that money, Harry, is out of *her* pocketbook!" Marko smiled by thrusting out his lower lip. "They're taking that young dame for a ride!" He nodded up and down knowingly.

Finkle frowned. "Could that be true?" he wondered. "Marty, how do you suppose she went from a book-worm to an investor? There's gap. D'you see it?"

"Peggaluso seduced her? They work at the University."

Finkle paused and thought. "Why her?"

"She told Peggaluso she's flush? Here's a long shot, Harry. Last month I was talkin' to my brother's kid. He tends bar nights at Romans."

"Romans?"

"It's off Central Avenue. The place makes money, but it's never crowded. He mentioned to me that he once bought an expensive necklace from a guy who said it was a gift from his girlfriend, a librarian. Marky —"

"Marky?"

"That's his nickname. He said the guy sold it to him for a sawbuck, and he resold it for thirty dollars to another customer."

"Could this guy be the missing link?" thought Finkle. "What kind —is this Romans a pick-up bar?"

"No. I don't think so. I think it's a watering hole." Marko chuckled.

"So this guy picked her up somehow, squeezed her purse, and passed her on to Peggaluso?"

"Could be. This is a pretty fluid city."

Finkle toyed with his earlobe. He was considering whether this lead was worth pursuing. Maybe it was. He eyed his lawyer and smiled. "Marty, get hold of Marky and see what you can find on this 'guy'."

Marko returned in less than two hours. He read from his note pad. "Harry, the kid's name is Mickey Gonzag."

"Gonzag?"

"Yeah. In his twenties. Works nights at a hotel. Never has much money. Used to come in for a beer or two. Stopped coming in about three months ago. And get this, he told Marky he plays pool!"

"That's gotta be it, Marty! That's the linkup!" He glowed pink at the lawyer. "Gonzag, Lubelski, Peggaluso, Merle! You were right –Julian Merle chanced on her. He hustled her! But what's in it for her? Is there something she doesn't want known?"

"Harry, let me tail her for a week, and –"

Finkle shook his head. "We don't have to dig any deeper." He made his decision. "The money's good, Marty. And I want to move," he raised his brows eagerly to the lawyer, "before she changes her mind!" "I want that hundred thousand," he said to himself.

———

CHAPTER 32
PHONE CALLS

October 9 to October 23, 1978

The busy season for pool-playing begins in the fall. By the second week of October, Merle's was, in the evenings, lively and often crowded. Its customers were coming in wearing light jackets, and the window sign that all summer had advertised "AIR CONDITIONED" was now propped against one of the walls in Rudy's work room.

On October 9th, the date they had chosen back in July to begin paying themselves small amounts of the stolen money, Sonny and Rudy decided to wait another two weeks –at the most –for Mickey. "I don't like it," Sonny told Rudy. "In fact, this is aggravating me."

The next day, Angela started working behind the front counter. For four hours, from 6 to 10 PM on Tuesday and Thursday evenings, she punched time cards, charged customers, refilled the soda machines, emptied ashtrays, and whenever she could, referred to Merle's as a "billiard lounge." At first, Julian watched her from one of the chairs in the mezzanine. When he became convinced that Angela could adequately control the counter and the room, he went into his office and read one of his books.

That month, Gene Groat switched from the Cue and Cushion to Merle's Billiards. Merle's was Gene's "home" room now, and he and Rudy played long straight pool games of 100 points for five and then ten dollars a game. Indecisively, the money went back and forth. These games –or rather these duels –pleased Julian, for they drew and held onlookers, who in turn wanted to play more and better pool. Rudy was not the best player at Merle's –several of the older men were able to beat him routinely. But he was young and tenacious, and conspicuous. Rudy was playing almost every evening, developing his own distinct mannerisms and flourishes in stance and stroke. At times, other players, having watched him on the tables, asked him for advice on basic elements of pool-playing, like forming bridges or using english or playing position. Rudy, unafraid of possible new competitors, taught them what he knew. "He has iron in him," Julian thought proudly.

These games "bemazed" Angela. She invented this verb to describe seeing a shooter break from one rack to the next, seamlessly running twenty and sometimes thirty crayon-colored balls without missing. To her, pool had revealed itself to be the most captivating of competitions played on four legs. It was far more intriguing than watching two men sit and play, say, chess or poker.

Donald Drake and his high school pals –they were all juniors –came into Merle's too. But they were irregular customers, young guys who came in to play when they "felt like it" and for whom pool was an amusement. One Thursday evening, one of these occasionals, a particularly well-dressed boy with black-rimmed glasses, stepped away from the group and up to the counter and asked Angela what the "blotch" on her face was. Aloud and distinctly, he asked, "Like, what's the story on that?"

The boy held his face artlessly –he was very likely a good actor in class too; but his question was no less than an impudent attempt to make Angela feel ill at ease there at the front counter. Rudy was in the mezzanine, and hearing this, his mouth fell open.

Before he could react, Angela replied. "It's a birthmark. I was born with it on my face." This she said unapologetically. "That's the worst place for a birthmark, isn't it?" she asked, holding the boy, now speechless, with her eyes. "I used to be self-conscious about it. *Not anymore!*" And although she had raised her voice a fraction, she was experiencing no resentment for this small incident, and she smiled to him.

He smiled back feebly and moved to the rail, then to behind Donald.

"Wow," Rudy thought, "that took… guts!"

The money games fed and fattened Vinnie's imagination. Vinnie fantasied himself someday playing against Rudy head to head. He had become, now that more students from the University were coming in, an unashamed hustler. It was easy for him to meet these collegians. He simply approached their table as they were playing and said "Hi," innocently and at the same time vivaciously. He lifted his dark eyebrows, ran his fingers through his hair, and told them his name. Often, he shook hands with them. And sometimes, before walking away, Vinnie cocked his head to them coyly. He knew that the next time one of them came in, especially by himself, he would be an "acquaintance" of Vinnie's, and Vinnie could, familiarly and with the right pitch, steer him into a game for a dollar or more.

This was "small time," Vinnie knew; but, he rationalized, "It's O.K. to do this when you're about my age."

–

On the third Saturday in October, Vinnie and another boy, this one with hair parted in the middle and hanging limply over the sides of his head, walked into Merle's and up to the counter. Vinnie usually asked for a back table; but this afternoon, he announced that he wanted table 4, one of the tables along the building's front windows. Rudy, who was ready with a snappy retort for Vinnie's inevitable "Lemme have a smoke, will yuh?" pushed a tray of balls across the counter. But at the moment Vinnie was about to speak those very words, Wayne Bloom drove into the front parking lot, which drew Rudy's and the boys' attention.

"Oooh. Perfect timing," Vinnie muttered to himself. He motioned at Wayne with his head and said to his friend, "See, here comes Wayne. He's why you shouldn't go to college. Me and Alan took thirteen dollars off him in July." It was a smart-aleck remark, and the two laughed.

Wayne made his way to the entrance; and as soon as he opened the door, Vinnie called out, "Wayne!"

Wayne seemed a bit more stout now, perhaps because of the brown and copper checkered woolen sweater he was wearing. And he looked displeased somehow, as if he had had to go out of his way to come here. He ignored Vinnie's greeting and turned his back to the two boys. "Rudy, did Mickey come in yet? Did he leave something with you for me?"

Rudy gaped back at Wayne and shook his head. "Nobody's seen Gonzag for months."

"Wayne, come on, let's play three-way 9-ball! Quarter on the 9."

Wayne rotated at the hip. Vinnie was grinning like a crocodile. "No, Vincenza, I can't shoot anymore. I'm in college. You know that!" He wheeled back to Rudy.

"Wait," Vinnie said softly to his friend and again motioned at Wayne with his head. The friend smiled blankly.

"Rudy, Mickey phoned my house yesterday and said he has the money he owes me."

"You talked to him?"

"He told my mother. I was in class. He told her he's working up in Saratoga at the harness track. He said he'll be in Albany for the day and'll come in here with the money." On Wayne's face was alarm and disappointment, the look of a man who has just missed the last bus of the day.

"He hasn't come in yet, Wayne."

"Let's go," said Vinnie to his friend. They stepped down from the mezzanine to the carpet and walked toward table 4.

Wayne pulled the ends of his lips into a frown. "Call me, O.K., Rudy, when he comes in?"

"Sure. Gimme your number."

The next afternoon Rudy called Sonny into the work room and there told all of the preceding to him. Sonny immediately tried to think what it meant. But what was there to think about since none of it made sense! "Let's phone Bloom. Maybe he caught up with Mickey somehow."

They went into Julian's office, and Rudy dialed the number Wayne had given to him. Wayne was at home; but he said no, that Mickey had not called him a second time. Rudy phoned Mr. Gonzag, who gave him the same response, that he had not heard from his son since August.

"Let's phone Brassey's. Let's see, did he pick up his van." Again Rudy phoned. The man who answered checked his

papers and replied that the "vehicle was still in impound."
Rudy and Sonny looked at each other, perplexed.

The two returned to the work room and closed the door.
There was revulsion, an almost nauseous revulsion on Sonny's
face, and he cursed. "You know, it's just like him! Abandon
his own van. Call Bloom, then renege on him!"

Rudy wanted to say, "I told you so." He was glad that
Sonny was becoming as annoyed with Mickey as he had
been all along. But instead he asked, "You wanna drive up to
Saratoga? See if we can spot him?"

"Ahh! If we saw him and he saw us, he might say he moved
out of town and he wants all of his money 'cause no one knows
him in Saratoga." It was then, after this peevish reply, that
the notion to kill Mickey again welled up in Sonny's mind.
He stepped forward, as if going somewhere, then whirled to
Rudy. "We got a lot going for us, Rudy. Here's the thing –
Mickey could open his mouth and make one slip-up, and we'd
–think of all we'd lose!" He scowled.

"Yeah," Rudy agreed.

Sonny paced the floor. "Here's another thing. We can't pull
any more jobs." Rudy lit a cigarette. Sonny turned back, his
eyelids lowered now, his brows pressed closer together, his
voice stony. "What if he shows up at Angela's place!" The
muscles of his jaw began to draw themselves into knots.

"O.K. What d'ya wanna do?" He meant, "What'll we do?"

"I don't know." He pointed at Rudy. "Wait! I know what
to do. We're going to get the money out of your car's trunk."
Sonny was thinking rapidly. "I gotta get reimbursed for the
storage rent and the padlock. We'll divide what's left three
ways."

"All right with me." Rudy had wanted to retrieve the Studebaker for two weeks, since October 9th. "I gotta recharge the battery and bring the can of water and drive it back home."

"We'll each hide our own money." But then, "Where do we keep Mickey's share? He's gotta show up someday."

"I got the perfect place," said Rudy coolly. "I'll show you. Help me move the work table."

They pulled the work table several feet from the wall. Underneath was a round drain about one foot in diameter. Over it and screwed onto it with three flat-head machine screws was a grate. "We never wash the floor in here. I vacuum it. So, Julian said, 'Let's seal up the pipe so mice don't crawl into it'."

"What do you mean?"

"The drain is just a pipe that lets out through a hole out back, through the cinder blocks. Julian plugged it there with, like, a wood cork and some rags. Then he tarred it."

"So… "

"We wrap Gonzag's money in a trash bag, set it down in this drain, and screw the grate back on."

"The table covers it?"

"Yeah. So when Gonzag comes around again, we'll say it'll take us twenty-four hours to get his money. We can't tell him where it's at."

"How long do we keep it here?"

Rudy pondered this for a moment. "Let's face it." He turned on the sink faucet and drowned out his cigarette. "Indefinitely." He dropped the soggy butt in the trash. "That creature's in jail somewhere, Sonny. When he gets out, he'll want his money."

"What if Mickey stays away for five years?" Sonny meant, "Will we leave his money here that long?"

"What else? It's his money. Besides," continued Rudy philosophically, "he'll be a different Gonzag when they let him out. He might not be so… docile, if you know what I mean."

–

Sonny and Rudy opened the storage unit and then the trunk of the Studebaker. There awaited the loot. Sonny took one of the bundles and from it counted off his reimbursement. They divided the rest in thirds, tied up each third in a separate trash bag, and laid the bags in the trunk of Sonny's Cutlass. If Rudy were to get caught driving his father's unregistered car, it might be searched or even towed, but his money would be safe with Sonny.

Several minutes later, the Studebaker was once more alive and backing out of the unit. Rudy, nervous and trembling, drove it to his house and behind the garage. With his bag of money, he ran up to his room, then with Sonny, returned to Merle's and the work room, where the two buried Mickey's bag in the drain, all as they had planned.

They sighed and sat down. "That's that." Rudy lit a cigarette.

By the following afternoon, the ire and anxiety that Sonny had been feeling over Mickey's apparent truancy had dwindled. Driving to work, he tried to assess conceptually his and Rudy's problem, that Mickey Gonzag was inconstant with his money and unpredictable in his behavior and penchants.

Insight came to him. "Rudy was right all along! I gotta play this for keeps. If he starts in again, demanding too much at once…, I'll have to bring him out of town and do it. Somewhere in the country. By myself."

He turned the Cutlass onto Fuller Road. In seconds he was alongside the two diners. "It won't do any good," Sonny told himself, "to warn him again." He passed by the bakery, then over Railroad Avenue. "Can I do it?" He repeated the terrible question.

He drove under the Route 90 overpass. The sky was graying –trying to rain maybe –and against it he saw limned the University's pale white dormitory towers.

He sighed, and it was almost a sob. "He used to be my friend. If it weren't for Mickey… " He saw Mickey laughing, and his heart grew morose. "Can I do it? I don't know."

Sonny entered the west parking lot and parked the car. "I don't know." The opaque windows of the towers looked bodingly at him. He swallowed. "Maybe not… God, I hope I never see him again." He locked the car and walked, his eyes downcast, toward his job in the University complex.

———

CHAPTER 33
NEAT TRICKS

November 13 to December 24, 1978

In the final seven weeks of 1978, much transpired. The JARS Company, which Julian and the other three principals named acronymically from the first letters of their names, was formed. The Company had a lawyer, a bank account, and letterhead stationery –sheets and envelopes that Angela designed and had printed. In late November, the closing on the property at 1050 Central Avenue took place in Martin Marko's offices. When the deed and other papers were signed and the building and land no longer belonged to Harry Finkle, they all rose happily from the table. Rudy held out his hand to the ex-landlord. He said, "Good luck…, Harry." He grinned, and Finkle had to smile at the picayune audacity.

In mid-November, Sonny and Rudy made two decisions. They decided to lock away the remainder of their shares of the stolen money in bank safety deposit boxes. And they agreed never to discuss the money between themselves or with Angela again.

Rudy turned twenty-one years old that month, and shortly after his birthday, ran fifty-five balls and out in a money game against Johnny Ninas, another defector from the Cue and Cushion. Rudy, much more distinct now in his posture and bearing, again drew a small crowd of spectators.

By November's end, Julian was thinking to himself that Angela was capable of working one of his evenings. He had begun to want one day a week off from the pool room and chewed over the idea, as older men do. "Mondays," he reflected on the day, "Mondays would be good for me." Angela herself had a new gaiety in her manner and was smoking Salems. Vinnie was "acquainted" with more than a dozen college boys, one of whom had given him rides home twice. Mr. Merle lost hope finally of finding a water pump for his Studebaker and sold it to a junk yard for parts. And Wayne Bloom became so assimilated to university life, or perhaps so metamorphosed by it, that he, like Mickey Gonzag, was hereafter never seen in Merle's again.

On the last Wednesday of November, in the evening, Angela was at one of the mezzanine tables, seated there and enjoying the "romance," as she called it, of the room: the striving of the players over their tables, their banter, the wisps of their cigarette smoke, and the muted music from the public address system that tinkled across the room and to which nobody actually listened. By now, she knew all the balls by their colors, she knew what the "rake" was, and she knew what it meant when she heard a shooter plead, "Get legs!" to a slowly moving ball.

On a table in mid-room Rudy was playing with a young man, one with whom he seemed to be familiar. Angela had seen this fellow before; he was the one whose black hair was parted on the left and combed upward and over so that it swirled up into a wave above his forehead. Angela liked his hair, his face, his small mouth, and his attire –bell bottom pants encircled by a wide belt, a loose shirt with paisley designs, and shiny high-backed leather shoes. She liked the way he threw back his head when he missed and the way he braced himself, legs apart, while it was Rudy's' turn to shoot.

At the moment, it was Rudy's turn. His black-haired opponent, Ron Boucher, stood pensively, his arms folded over his upright cue stick. During all their games, Rudy kept, as the games progressed, a small number of points ahead of Ron. And when Rudy did miss, he seemed never to leave a ball in break-shot position, which prevented Ron from continuing into the next rack.

Ron was wondering whether this was somehow not accidental. Could Rudy be such a skilled hustler that he could engineer their table so that he won, but by only a close score, time after time? Ron's face was vibrant yet contemplative, and this conspicuous fusion of attitudes also attracted Angela's attention.

She thought, "These fellows don't realize how lucky they are to have a hang-out like Merle's. A place where they can be guys. Maybe I could write a story about… –no! I should write an article that tells about Merle's and try to get it in the *Times-Union*. There's a good idea! I'll need a couple nice photos to go with it."

Meanwhile at the curb in front of the building, Vinnie Vincenza was exiting his mother's car. Earlier, he had helped her with the grocery shopping, and now she was dropping him off at Merle's. Through the front windows he saw Angela. "Pecc-a-dillo!"

"What?"

He turned to his mother. "Thanks, Mom." He closed the car door and waved. They parted, she gliding into the avenue's traffic, and he –thin-faced and buoyant, a fifteen and a half year old pool room kid, smiling with anticipation –striding to the front door. He pulled it open wide. "Yes!"

Vinnie's exuberant entrance caught Angela's attention; she turned toward him. "Here comes that rapscallion," she thought. They both smiled, both showing their teeth. Jauntily, briskly, Vinnie came to her table and sat. Instead of a greeting, he produced a pack of cigarettes. "Want one?"

"Let me guess," she teased, "you smoke Turkish cigarettes, non-filtered?"

"No, Mar'bles."

"What?" She saw the red and white design of the pack. "Oh." She took one. They both lit up. "Wee-uh, these are strong!"

Vinnie gave her the same direct look he gave to the college boys. "I like to see girls smoking cigarettes. They look cool."

The ends of Angela's lips raised slightly.

"Nice shot!" Angela and Vinnie turned to the effusive outburst. It had come from the middle of the room, from the young man whom Rudy was playing.

Vinnie lowered his voice. "See the guy Rudy's shootin'?"

"Yes. They're playing straight pool, right? I don't know what they're playing for." She meant, "I don't know how much money they're playing for."

"Yeh. His name's Ron Boucher. He knows a lot, but he comes in only maybe once a week. In between, he gets out of stroke."

"He gets a little rusty?"

"Yeah. See, you gotta be in here five or six times a week, shootin'." He dragged thoughtfully on his cigarette. "I figure they'll be shootin' for another hour. Then I'm gonna ask Boucher for a game. For whatever he'll play me for. I think I can take him."

Vinnie's ambitious words took Angela aback. "Vinnie, he'll be all warmed up. Suppose he wants to play for ten dollars?"

"I got an emergency ten in my wallet."

"Isn't that a risk?"

"It's pressure. That's how you get better –shootin' better players. Wantin' their money." Then he said, "When you go up against someone like Boucher or Groat, there has to be some weight on you, some like," he was searching for the right word, "urgency, otherwise you won't be tryin' to beat the guy mercilessly. See?" He butted out his Mar'ble. "Watch me later."

Angela smiled, more at Vinnie's show of adolescent perspicuity than at his adventurism. "I will."

Abruptly then, he changed the subject. "We just came from Price Chopper. I had to help my mother with the groceries. She let me off here. You know the fresh meat section at the back end of the store?"

"Yes."

"Where they have packaged meats –ribeyes and T-bones?"

"Yes."

"Well, this butcher came out from the cutting room with a tray of meats. They were all wrapped in cellophane. They all had price stickers on top."

"O.K." She was listening.

"Anyhow, the butcher was exactly the same height as me. So you could tell what he weighed. What did he weigh?"

Angela looked down, through the table. She looked up. "He weighed –" She was stumped.

Vinnie snapped his fingers merrily. "He's a butcher." He pointed at Angela. "He weighs meat! Ah, ha, ha!"

Angela fought back a smile, then laughed with Vinnie. It was a silly trick. They turned back to Rudy's game.

Angela looked slyly at Vinnie. "Did Rudy ever show you how he can open the time clock to clean and oil it?"

"No."

"He showed me." She let a few moments go by. "That clock's a timepiece. So's an alarm clock, a wristwatch. What timepiece has the fewest number of moving parts?"

"An electric clock!"

"No, that's got buttons." She bobbled her head mockingly at him. "A sundial."

"Oh. I get it."

"Now, here's an easy one. What timepiece has the most moving parts?"

Vinnie searched his mind for the various clocks he had seen. "Yeah, I know. That big clock on the courthouse dome!"

"Nooo," she said slowly to stretch out the answer and tantalize him. "An hourglass." She grinned enormously, and they both laughed.

"Aie yah!" he said.

"Since you didn't come up with the right answer, Vinnie, you have to do me a favor."

She stood, and he asked, "What?"

"You have to help me carry in a bookcase I have in my car."

"A bookcase?"

"And a box of books. I've got a dictionary and a Spanish dictionary –you're taking Spanish this year, right? –and a book of maps."

"What the hell?" he thought.

"And Julian needs a shelf on it for his paperback novels. Come on." Angela led the way, and Vinnie, of course, tailed her.

As they carried the bookcase around the front counter and into the office, Angela looked again at Ron Boucher. He was chalking his cue. She hoped Vinnie will play him later, after he and Rudy were through. She would watch their game.

They set the case against one of the walls. Vinnie ran back to the car and brought in the box of books. He looked in it and remembered something. "Where's that map we brought back? I know what I can do!"

Two days later, a Friday evening, Angela was once again at the last table in the mezzanine. It was her first day as a co-owner of the building and parking lots, and she was excited. So were her partners. But since Sonny was working tonight, they had made plans to celebrate on Sunday afternoon at one of the big restaurants.

She sat there, scanning the players, hoping to see dollars appear and change hands, the sure signs of earnest, two-fisted pool-playing.

At one of the other mezzanine tables, one of the old-timers was talking in a gruff, croaky voice. "I saw him play straights in Ames back in the '50s. That's when you had to be there." He vented his next sentence. "There'll never be his like again, not in our time nor any other! No more Ames either."

Angela wondered what he was talking about.

The front door opened and Vinnie entered. He wore a windbreaker with one of his rocker tee shirts underneath. As he eyed and approached Angela, he smiled, letting one side of his upper lip curve up impishly, as if he had something ironic or even mischievous to reveal.

He sat down at her table, and she sensed that he had just showered, just washed his hair and put on fresh clothes. "What's he up to?" she wondered.

He looked around the room. None of the serious players had come in yet, and he pointed this out to Angela. As he took out his cigarettes –they were his catalysts of conversation – Angela took out hers, and they lit up.

He said, "You know what a series of numbers is, don'cha?"

"Yes."

"Like 3, 5, 7, 11, 13, 17 –the next is 19, right?"

"They're… called prime numbers?"

"Right. Now, I know a number series that you won't be able to figure out." Again he curled his upper lip.

"And?" She was smiling, waiting for more.

"It's a series used by the government for about seventy-five years."

"And… "

"And here it is!" Vinnie took a slip of paper from his pocket and on it wrote 4, 14, 23, 34, 42, 59. He looked up. "What's the next number, Angela?" he challenged.

Angela slid the paper nearer to her and began subtracting the numbers, one from another, looking for a pattern. She put out her cigarette. Adding or subtracting any two numbers did not produce any of the remaining numbers. "The government uses these?" She grimaced. "For what?"

Vinnie exhaled with satisfaction. "Give up?"

"I may as well."

"The next number is 125!"

Angela's face turned incredulous, confused, as if the number could not be 125. "How do you get 125?"

"Here's your proof!" From his back pocket Vinnie took a sheet that had been folded several times. He unfolded what became a map of New York City. He pointed to printing on the lower left corner. "See, it says this map was published by the New York City Transit Authority. That means New York City government."

"Yeah?"

"Yeah. Now, see the A-Train, Angela? The blue line? It stops at 4th Street, 14th Street, 23rd, 34th, 42nd, 59th, and then goes express up to 125th Street!" He imitated Angela's prodigious smile. "They built the subways about seventy-five years ago, so… Well, you get it." His joy frolicked over his face.

"I have to admit," she said, thoroughly amused now, "that was clever."

"It's jugglery. I found *that* word in your big dictionary." He put out his cigarette and recounted how he, his mother and sister had gone to New York last year and what they brought back as souvenirs. He picked up the map and refolded it, turning and plying it together, and slid it back into his pocket. He laughed, for there was more to come. "Since you didn't come up with the right number, Angela, you have to do me a favor."

He stood, and she asked, "What?"

"You have to give me a ride. Come on." He led the way to the door, and Angela followed him.

They got into Angela's car, and she started it. Vinnie rolled down his window and leisurely hung his elbow over the sill. He laid his head back and smiled indulgently. Angela maneuvered to the lip of the parking lot and stopped. "Go left?"

"No. Go right."

"Where are we going? Don't you live in Colonie?" She steered into the lane going to the right, to the business and residential part of Albany.

Lazily, Vinnie opened his eyes. "I want you to give me a ride to your apartment." The words came out smoothly, undemandingly, yet confidently, just the way he had rehearsed them over and over in his room. "

"Vinnie –"

"I'm not asking for a lot, you know."

"Vinnie –"

"You don't have to take me there. But remember, I'm an Italian, and it *is* 1978, Angela."

She turned and saw his thick eyebrows, his eager brown eyes. "You're an Italian –?" she mimicked.

He pushed in the cigarette lighter and pulled two cigarettes from his pocket. "I'll light one for you."

"Look, Vinnie –"

"I don't brag, Angela. And I'm not possessive." He lit the cigarettes.

"Do I have a natural penchant for this?" she thought. "Does it show?"

He handed her the cigarette, and she took it.

–

It was the evening before Christmas Day. Merle's had closed at 5 o'clock and would be closed all day on Christmas itself. Angela had finished readying herself. Sonny was to pick her up at 6:30, and they all were going to Pizza Hut. Not The Courtside because Vinnie was not old enough to enter a bar. This was O.K. to Angela, she preferred tall sodas to tall beers.

"I ought to start a diary," she mused. "This was a fabulous year. Four guys."

Her purse and keys were waiting on the table with the oblate vase. The thermostat was turned down to sixty-five degrees, the apartment was dusted and tidied and her hair brushed and fluffed.

As she slipped into her jacket, she looked in the mirror she had put up over the table. Impulsively, she laughed. "Next year! I'm gonna just come right out and ask Ron to dinner! That'll be my resolution."

She heard a horn outside in the parking lot.

THE END